WISHBONE

Also by Justine Pucella Winans

The Otherwoods

WISHBONE

JUSTINE PUCELLA WINANS

BLOOMSBURY
CHILDREN'S BOOKS
NEW YORK LONDON OXFORD NEW DELHI SYDNEY

BLOOMSBURY CHILDREN'S BOOKS
Bloomsbury Publishing Inc., part of Bloomsbury Publishing Plc
1385 Broadway, New York, NY 10018

BLOOMSBURY, BLOOMSBURY CHILDREN'S BOOKS, and the Diana logo
are trademarks of Bloomsbury Publishing Plc

First published in the United States of America in September 2024
by Bloomsbury Children's Books

Bloomsbury books may be purchased for business or promotional use. For information on bulk purchases
please contact Macmillan Corporate and Premium Sales Department at specialmarkets@macmillan.com

Library of Congress Cataloging-in-Publication Data
Names: Winans, Justine Pucella, author.
Title: Wishbone / by Justine Pucella Winans.
Description: New York: Bloomsbury Children's Books, 2024
Summary: A rescued cat named Wishbone grants siblings Ollie and Mia's every wish, but their desires,
which have a steep price, are threatened by a shadow man called The Mage who covets Wishbone's power.
Identifiers: LCCN 2024015797 (print) | LCCN 2024015798 (e-book)
ISBN 978-1-5476-1257-4 (hardcover) • ISBN 978-1-5476-1258-1 (e-pub)
Subjects: CYAC: Magic—Fiction. | Wishes—Fiction. | Cats—Fiction. | Siblings—Fiction. |
Family life—Fiction. | LGBTQ+ people—Fiction. | Horror stories. | LCGFT: Horror fiction. | Novels.
Classification: LCC PZ7.1.W5833 Wi 2024 (print) | LCC PZ7.1.W5833 (e-book) | DDC [Fic]—dc23
LC record available at https://lccn.loc.gov/2024015797
LC e-book record available at https://lccn.loc.gov/2024015798

Book design by John Candell
Typeset by Westchester Publishing Services
Printed and bound in the U.S.A.
2 4 6 8 10 9 7 5 3 1

To find out more about our authors and books visit www.bloomsbury.com
and sign up for our newsletters.

To all of us who need to hear
that even at your most unlikable
you are never unlovable
and even at your most uncertain
you have always been enough

WISHBONE

1

Ollie Is in Trouble

IN HIS VERY NEARLY thirteen years of life, Ollie Di Costa had a knack for learning things the hard way. Like, touching a baking sheet right out of the oven can leave a scar, and to always check that the sugar and salt are labeled correctly before adding them to your cake batter, and—most importantly and not limited to baking—it was better to do things yourself.

He almost forgot the most important lesson during that particular lunch period. He set off on a mission to find as many books with a demiboy protagonist as he could, and avoid any unwanted conversation. Which, in Ollie's case, was all conversation. But when it turned out finding books about demiboys was harder than expected, he asked the librarian for help. Thankfully, she didn't ask Ollie *why* he was looking for demiboy stories, and just kindly pointed out the nonfiction books that droned on about gender. Ugh. The last thing Ollie wanted was to feel like being queer gave him extra homework. Even trying to read those glorified textbooks made his eyes glaze over as his mind moved on to more important things, like the perfect ratio of blue and red food coloring to make an even prettier lilac frosting than the one he mixed in cooking class the period before.

No, Ollie needed to read about demiboys on adventures, or out solving mysteries, or fighting monsters—something that he could relate to that wasn't so *boring*. Thankfully, he managed to find a few (two were about demigirls, but he figured it was the same general idea) and returned to his library table.

The second part of his mission—avoiding unnecessary conversation—was going well, considering no one ate lunch in the library besides weird kids with no friends (himself included) and weird kids with lots of friends (the drama club). So Ollie could read unbothered.

Or so he thought.

"What is this?" a voice sneered, snatching up the journal where Ollie jotted a few notes down. The pages crinkled and ripped, splitting to reveal the mocking face of Jake Barney. A sigh escaped Ollie before he could stop it. He'd rather read the entire nonfiction section back-to-back than deal with Jake.

Ollie couldn't really say he got along with a lot of people in general, but there were certain types of people he absolutely *did not* get along with at all, and Jake Barney was all of them combined. He could hardly believe there had been a time he thought Jake was his friend. Of course, that was also when his next closest friend was a Puss in Boots plushie he carried everywhere, so elementary school Ollie had limited options. Jake was loud, mean, had a complete disregard for personal space, and was the last person Ollie wanted to see any day at any given time, but especially not right now.

Because at that moment, Jake was making a face at a secret so young and exciting to Ollie he hadn't even told his sister yet. He hadn't told anyone.

He certainly hadn't expected his newest coming out to start like this.

"Demiboy?" Jake asked, reading Ollie's journal. "What? You're not even a real boy anymore?"

Ollie could feel his anger simmering within him. It always started that way. A little spark on the stovetop. Not large enough to boil, not right away, but still too strong to easily extinguish. Ollie knew himself well enough to know that if he spoke, he would only say things that would get him in more trouble, so he clenched his jaw and said nothing.

That was what Mia always told him to do. Ignore people like Jake. They weren't worth it.

Jake turned to his friends, who sometimes acted more like two extra shadows that laughed and agreed with whatever he said. Their names were Kirk and Brian, but they could all essentially be summed up into Jake+. "Ollie made us go through all that trouble of calling him a boy, and now he changed his mind again."

Ollie's fingers clenched into fists. The dial on his anger slowly turned, the flames rising more. His skin pricked, and he was itching to jump, to wipe the smug look off Jake's face. Brian and Kirk gave awkward laughs/grunts, like they didn't want to disappoint Jake but also felt that the conversation was something that might get them in trouble. Ollie glanced over to the librarian's desk, but of course, adults never seemed to be around in cases of blatant transphobia. It was just Ollie's luck.

Still. It was probably better this way. He didn't really need other people to get involved and make matters worse.

"Jake, cut it out, that's not cool."

Oh no. Oh no.

Ollie didn't even want to turn toward the voice, but he recognized it immediately. It was the same voice that got Most Likely to Be Famous at their fifth-grade graduation and sang the national anthem at just about every football game and assembly Hillside Middle School had. Noah Choi. One of the most popular kids in seventh grade and definitely not the person Ollie wanted to be awkwardly outed to.

Plus, Noah's voice caused the entire rest of the drama club to turn toward them, the printed-out scripts in front of them completely forgotten.

It was bad enough Ollie got made fun of for who he was, but now Noah had made it worse by bringing in an entire audience. Not to mention, theater kids weren't exactly known for being *quiet*. Ollie thought of going to his history class after this, only for everyone to whisper about him not being enough of a boy, and his muscles tensed so tightly his nails dug into the skin of his palms.

What was it Mia always told him? Deep breaths?

"What?" Jake scoffed. "Is this nerd your little boyfriend now?"

Noah's face flushed. Normally, the styled bangs that fell over the side of his forehead gave him a confident look, but in that moment, he almost seemed to hide behind them. Ollie felt so bad that Noah had become a target that he decided to forgive him for his terrible idea of getting involved in the first place.

Besides, it was hard to hold a grudge against someone like Noah Choi.

Ollie tried to focus on counting his breaths, but every time the number rose in his head, he imagined smacking Jake in the face. It wasn't very calming and peaceful of him, but the image was satisfying.

No, Ollie reminded himself. *He isn't worth it. You'll just get in trouble again.*

Seeing that he got a reaction out of Noah only made Jake puff up more, like some kind of ridiculous frog who thought he was a crocodile. Then either Brian or Kirk made some noise that must have sounded like laughter to Jake, and it only egged him on. Ollie was still working on slowing his breathing and thinking (not-quite-so) peaceful thoughts when Jake locked his gaze on the two cupcakes Ollie saved from his cooking class the period before. Ollie had been planning on taking a photo to add to his secret baking Instagram, proud of the small flowers he'd piped over the tops of the cakes. He even cut slightly into his lunch, staying after to finish the leaves, but Mrs. Andrade called them "breathtaking" and "artistry," which caused Ollie to have to excuse himself quickly to hide his blush.

But now Ollie's cheeks flamed for a whole new reason as he watched Jake grab the cellophane around the cupcakes, crushing them both between his hands and destroying the delicate floral piping art before tossing the sugary mess of plastic at Noah's feet.

"There," Jake said. "A gift from your boyfriend or whatever he is."

Ollie could no longer count, or breathe, or any of the things Mia told him to do when his anger got out of hand. Not only did Jake destroy his cupcakes, but he was clearly making Noah uncomfortable as well. If Noah was queer, Jake would practically be outing him, and if he wasn't, it was still messed up and embarrassing. Jake had gone too far. The flames were too high, fizzing and popping, and before Ollie even really thought about what he was doing, he leapt from the table and shoved Jake onto the floor. The drama club cheered, and everyone except Noah started the ever-original chant of "fight, fight, fight!"

Ollie grabbed on to Jake's shirt with one hand and lifted the other to hit Jake right in the face, but of course the librarian was here now, pulling Ollie away and chastising him without knowing what had led him to this point.

Ollie's anger didn't quite extinguish, but it was overpowered by instant regret. Mostly for getting caught.

"Every one of you to the principal's office *now*," the librarian ordered.

He was in so much trouble. Probably more trouble than he had ever been in before. Enough to earn a ton of nagging from Mia later, and maybe even a suspension, and Ollie really didn't want to know what a few days at home in that scenario would be like.

Just another day when Ollie had to learn something the hard way.

2

When Leaving School Early Manages to Be a Bad Thing

OLLIE SAT IN THE principal's office, waiting for his parents to pick him up. The good news was that Ollie hadn't gotten a suspension since Noah Choi and the rest of the drama club stood up for him, saying Jake had started the whole thing. Noah had even given Ollie a slight smile as he left the office, telling him, "Nice tackle." The bad news was the principal still thought it was better for Ollie to go home for the rest of the day. Normally, that would seem like good news. To other kids, it probably would've been.

But they didn't have to deal with parents like Ollie's.

His dad hadn't even answered the call from the principal, and Ollie was almost surprised his mom did. Both of them had been in the middle of the workday, and even if they hadn't been, it was weird for the principal to call them since sometimes Ollie felt like Mia was actually the one responsible for him. Ollie even suggested calling Mia over at the high school instead, but the principal seemed to think Ollie was trying to get out of trouble.

As if his sister wasn't stricter about this kind of thing than his parents.

Ollie sighed, leaning back in the main office chair. The office just had to have windows on nearly every side, so he was in full view. It was already the end of fifth period, which meant everyone walking by could see Ollie being sent home.

If he was going to get in trouble either way, Ollie really should have hit Jake before the librarian pulled him away. What a missed opportunity. It only made him feel worse.

Ollie peeked at his phone, holding it level to his lap. He opened his Instagram. None of the pictures had his face, or really any identifying features other than his white hands. Instead, it was filled with his baking. His camera quality wasn't anywhere near the best, and his baking equipment was even more limited, but sheer talent, far too many failed attempts, and the occasional cut and burn eventually got him to two thousand followers.

Except he hadn't posted at all that week. Ollie bit his lip. The floral cupcakes would've been perfect. And suddenly he was angry all over again.

Maybe Mia wasn't always right. Violence may not have been the answer, but it was an option he really wished he would've taken.

"Put your phone away," the secretary, Mrs. Kozlov, snapped from her desk.

Ollie rolled his eyes. "I'm talking to my parents. Since they kind of have to come get me?" A lie, but she didn't know that.

She pursed her lips. "You kids, always on your phones." Almost immediately after the words hit the air, her own phone pinged, and she picked it up to start typing with only one pointer finger.

Ollie wasn't even surprised. Adults were all hypocrites like that. Ollie knew it better than anyone. Still, he slid his phone into his pocket.

A little tap on the window behind him made him turn around. Lauren, one of Ollie's classmates, stood on the other side of the glass, her curly red hair forced into two long pigtails as she gestured for Ollie to meet her in the hall.

"My dad's lost," Ollie said. "I'm going to step out to call him. It's like a dead zone in here, you should really get that checked or you might miss your Facebook notification or whatever ancient technology grandparents use."

Mrs. Kozlov started to say something, but Ollie waltzed into the hallway to meet Lauren. He figured the secretary would be too lazy and engrossed in her phone to follow, and it seemed like he was right.

"Heard you got in trouble for beating up Jake Barney," Lauren said as a greeting.

Ollie snorted. "I wish. I only pushed him."

"Too bad," Lauren said. "He's kind of the worst."

At least some people got it. "I'll make sure to hit him next time," Ollie joked.

Lauren wasn't exactly a *friend*. Ollie didn't have friends, not like how most people thought of them. The kind that hung out at each other's houses and went out on weekends and rode bikes or planned trips to Disneyland or whatever. Best friends were a lie sold to kids by movies to make them feel lonely if they didn't have one, and Ollie knew friendships weren't all sunshine and ugly string bracelets. They were a one-way ticket to getting hurt.

What had happened with Jake proved that.

They'd met in kindergarten and been friends all through elementary school—the kind of friends who *did* see each other outside school, meeting up in parks or playing Nintendo at Jake's house until Ollie had to go home. But when Ollie came out as trans at the start of sixth grade . . . Jake didn't take it well.

In fact, "not taking it well" was kind of an understatement. It would've been one thing if Jake had just stopped talking to Ollie—which he had—but no. He had to make Ollie's life miserable. Once, after Ollie started using the boys' locker room, Jake stole his clothes during gym class, replacing them with some ugly dress from the lost and found. Jake and his goons had stood around snickering as Ollie opened his locker, confused before realizing what was going on and, worse, that Jake was behind it. As if having to play dodgeball in a binder wasn't annoying enough, Ollie felt completely betrayed.

He wore his gym clothes for the rest of the day. And smashed a chocolate milk carton on Jake's head. It was the official end of their friendship and the start of Ollie's close relationship with getting called into the principal's office.

Now, Ollie knew better than to trust people. They find one thing about you that they don't like and it's over. Even though Lauren knew he was queer and trans already, there would be something else she wouldn't like. There always was. Ollie knew his transness shouldn't be a problem—he loved that he was trans—but he also knew there were plenty of other things about him that were reasonably unlikeable. It was easier to hide those things when people weren't so close.

So, Lauren was like . . . a school friend. Someone who Ollie liked enough that he could count on her for group projects. She liked cooking and baking almost as much as Ollie, which was why they partnered up in that class as well.

Lauren held out one of her cellophane-wrapped cupcakes. "I heard yours got messed up, so I thought I'd give you one of mine," she said. "It isn't nearly as pretty as yours were, of course, but . . . it's something."

It was something, even though Lauren was probably only doing it because she felt bad for him. Her cupcake was simply topped with a swirling mound of frosting—not exactly exciting enough for Ollie's feed. She wasn't as into the decorating aspects of baking as him. She didn't care if a dessert was post-worthy as long as it tasted good.

"Thanks," he said, taking it. He felt like his voice always came out with more attitude than intended, so he put on a smile and added a "really" to hopefully come closer to sounding grateful.

It seemed to work, since Lauren returned the smile and clasped her hands together. "Oh! I almost forgot. There's a new bakery that opened over in Glendale, and it's apparently amazing. Do you want to come with me and my mom after school tomorrow?"

Ollie's chest tightened.

School friends didn't hang out after school. That was kind of the point. Still, Ollie felt weird saying that directly. He kind of thought they had an unspoken understanding. Unless, of course, it was only a pity invite.

That made way more sense, thinking on it. Lauren's mom knew she had a partner in cooking class and probably asked her to invite him. Mrs. Young seemed like she'd be that kind of mom. If anything, Lauren was probably hoping that Ollie would decline.

"I don't think my parents will let me now," Ollie said. He pointed back to the office. "Anyway, I probably should wait in there. Mrs. Kozlov already hates me."

"Oh. Yeah." Lauren's eyes looked a little disappointed. Maybe she was underwhelmed with Ollie's response to the cupcake? He really had to work on his smile. Lauren quickly perked up again. "See you tomorrow in class, then?"

"If I don't get expelled."

She shook her head. "Well, try not to."

"No promises."

Lauren waved and walked off just as Ollie's dad walked in through the front doors. Ollie almost let out a sigh of relief. If his dad had come alone, that would make things a lot easier.

Ollie's dad frowned slightly, looking at Ollie. "Aren't you supposed to be in the office?"

"You just have to sign me out, it's not a big deal," Ollie muttered.

Thankfully, his dad did just that, and Mrs. Kozlov couldn't even say anything. It was relatively painless, until they approached his parents' shared Nissan that looked like it was made before the internet and wore every one of its years. The car itself wasn't the problem, though; it was the pretty, five-foot-four woman with the tensed forehead in the passenger seat.

Ollie loved his parents. What he didn't love was his parents *together*. That was when the problems arose. Mr. and Mrs. Di Costa weren't the kind of married couple who showed they loved each other. Ollie was rather certain they didn't. They acted more like roommates who could barely go five minutes without arguing.

Ollie started the stopwatch on his phone as he got into the car.

Along with the engine, the scolding started right away.

"You can't keep getting in trouble like this," his dad started. "We can only take so much time off work to come get you."

"That's not the point," his mom countered. "The point is that you can't go around pushing other kids. What if he hit his head on the table or something? It could've been terrible, Ollie, and you have to realize that actions have consequences."

Ollie forced himself to take a deep breath as he looked away from the stopwatch. "It's not like I'm pushing people for no reason. Jake was being homophobic and a total jerk."

Except "jerk" wasn't *quite* the word Ollie used.

"Oliver Di Costa," his dad snapped. "Watch your mouth."

Right. Because he was so good at doing that while he yelled back and forth with Mom in the middle of the night.

Still, Ollie apologized. "Sorry," he muttered, "but I was doing the right thing."

His mom turned around, holding the side of the car seat to meet his eyes with her big hazel ones. "Just because the other person is mean first doesn't mean you can act like that. You're not Batman. You can't hurt people because you think they're behaving badly. I know you don't exactly have the best role model when it comes to dealing with anger—"

Ollie's dad scoffed. With his voice already raised, he asked, "Are you saying *I'm* the one with anger problems?"

"Well, you're not exactly a good example for our son. Look at you, acting like a complete jerk already."

Ollie's mom didn't say "jerk" either.

"Oh, but you're the shining example of a parent. Why do you think he talks like that?"

Despite being the focus of the argument, Ollie was all but forgotten in the back seat. He glanced down at his phone again. Two minutes and thirteen seconds on the stopwatch. He had been a little too generous with five, apparently. His parents kept bickering and yelling the entire drive home, getting to such a point that when they pulled to a stop outside their complex, his mom slammed the car door and Ollie awkwardly had to go out after her. His dad didn't follow, and Ollie could hear the car pull away as his mom put the key into the door of their motel-style apartment. She made a beeline for the primary bedroom, muttering a weak apology about having a headache before slamming the door behind her.

Just like that, Ollie was alone.

It wasn't being alone that he minded so much. It was the anger that still buzzed in him. He wanted to yell and slam doors and run away like his parents, but he couldn't—wouldn't—do any of those things. Because then he'd be just like them, and that was the last thing he wanted. So, he'd just bake something instead.

Ollie opened the fridge. No butter. The eggs were long expired. He threw them out. His eyes started to sting with frustrated tears, but maybe he didn't have to give up entirely. He opened the cupboard where the baking ingredients were kept, but there wasn't even flour left. Only sugar, imitation vanilla of questionable age, and random spices. So much for rage baking.

He grabbed the largest bottle of spices he could find and hurled it against the wall, the container cracking and a blend of Italian seasoning scattering all over the floor. It felt nice to shatter something, although seeing it spread all over the white kitchen tile gave the satisfaction a sour note. He'd clean it up later.

Then Ollie remembered the cupcake from Lauren. He

couldn't re-bake it, but he could transform it. Ollie cleared a space on the counter by moving the stack of late bills and got the cupcake out of his backpack. He unwrapped it and scooped the icing off the top, putting it into a ziploc bag. After cutting off a tiny piece of one corner, he squeezed the frosting back onto the cake. It was far from perfect, all in the same bright pink and with only the one troublesome tip, but Ollie painstakingly piped tiny petals onto the cupcake's surface. By the end, it was passable.

He borrowed Mia's ring light and put some fake flowers from the table's centerpiece in the shot to get a somewhat decent picture.

experimenting with only using a ziploc bag—sometimes you have to improvise when the dishwasher is still running

What a liar. Their apartment didn't even have a dishwasher. He added some appropriate hashtags and posted the picture. Good enough.

Ollie scrolled through his feed, and the first post that appeared was of one of his favorite bakers, Miss Sugar N' Spice. She posted a picture of a beautiful layered cake, frosting colored like the trans pride flag, on a fancy white stand, her big, clean kitchen behind her and her smiling face right in the picture. Posted five minutes ago, it already had fifteen thousand likes.

Ollie had one like so far. From a bot. Plus a sad cupcake and a dirty kitchen.

He still liked Miss Sugar N' Spice's picture. He may have been down about his own situation, but it made him happy to see a successful trans person living the dream. Maybe that could be him someday.

But for now, Ollie did what he did best, next to baking and getting easily annoyed, and cleaned up the mess he made by himself.

3

When Things Go from Good to . . . Not

OLLIE WAS STILL BY himself when Mia came home around five o'clock. She'd had a short shift at her part-time job after school. Mia didn't even have to ask about their parents. When their car was gone and their bedroom door was shut, she knew. There wasn't any disappointment on her face as she shrugged off her backpack and let it hit the floor. Her eyes were tired and rimmed in red as she kept her car keys clenched tight.

"I got some leftovers from the deli. Want to picnic at the beach?"

Ollie couldn't say no, even if he wanted to. The Di Costa siblings had a sacred ritual. When one of them wanted to go to the beach, they went if they could. No questions asked. The beach was where they talked about the things they couldn't say at home, where they got away from the tension of it all.

The beach was always filled with people, but sometimes, it really felt like it existed only for them.

The traffic was terrible, although Los Angeles traffic was always terrible, so by the time they arrived at Manhattan Beach, the sun was beginning to set, streaking rich oranges and pinks across the sky. Mia grabbed the beach towels (a green one with a lizard in sunglasses for Ollie and a purple one with a unicorn-kitten for Mia, their clearance bin best) that were always in her trunk that only closed when you really slammed it. She bought the car off their uncle for three hundred dollars when she turned sixteen. It sometimes took begging, coaxing, crying, and a good smack to start, but it got them where they needed to go. After Ollie rolled up the window (a hand crank, like they were living in ancient times!), he carried the brown paper bag of leftovers Mia was able to get from work.

While Southern California didn't exactly have seasons, there was a bit of a chill in the November air, so it was easy to find a spot away from others.

Ollie stretched out his ankles, digging them in the sand as he pushed his feet forward, little piles growing at the end of his heels, cold against his pinkish skin. Mia unpacked mixed-up cuts of lunch meats and cheeses and put them on the towels between them before pulling down the sleeves of her USC hoodie. Strands of hair blew into her mouth as she tried to eat a piece of cheese, and she cursed. She had the same hair as Ollie—waves that couldn't decide if they wanted to be blond, brown, or red, and almost seemed to change depending on the light. In the slowly setting sun, it looked more on the brown-red end of the spectrum, as her dark hazelnut eyes sparkled in the fading light.

"Is this that good salami?" Ollie asked, grabbing a piece.

"It's all good when it's free, so just eat it."

He did. Based on how things had been going with their parents, they'd probably be on their own for dinner that night anyway.

"So you wanna tell me what happened today?" Mia asked. "Mom texted that you got in trouble."

Ollie groaned, leaning back on his elbows. "It wasn't a big deal. People are acting like I broke this guy's leg or something."

"Did you?"

Ollie rolled his eyes. "Obviously not."

"So . . . ," Mia pressed. "What did you do?"

Ollie opened his mouth to answer but stopped himself. He could've glided over the actual events, simply saying that Jake made fun of him without saying why. He could have. Mia would've let him. But he wanted to tell her. Mia was supposed to be the person he told everything to first. It didn't sit right with him that Jake and maybe half the drama kids knew something about Ollie that his big sister didn't.

"Jake was making fun of me because I think I'm a demiboy," Ollie said.

He hadn't said it aloud before, but it sounded good. Right. He liked the way it tasted. Sea salt and sharp cheddar.

Ollie was just a boy. Most of the time. But sometimes, he would shed that gender like a coat and be both all genders and no genders. Everything and nothing. Just Ollie. But it wasn't that the coat was a bad thing. When he put it back on, body yearning for cover, the coat felt like home.

He knew Mia would understand this—or at least try to—but he couldn't tell his parents.

They understood being trans as if it was a one-way bus ticket to someone's true self. They thought that once Ollie arrived in Boy, he would never leave. They wouldn't understand why he didn't want to live there forever, go all in and set his roots down. They wouldn't understand that the bus didn't only have two stops, and the ones that Ollie frequented weren't just ends, point A to point B. If being trans was a bus, it was one that flew through the clouds and dove into the deep blue and any other direction imaginable. It was one where you could come to and leave anytime. Stay in one stop for years or maybe never even stop at all.

"Jake saw me taking notes on some books I found. I tried to breathe and everything like you told me to, but he started calling me this other boy's boyfriend, and I could tell that boy was uncomfortable, so . . . I mean, I had to do something." Ollie bit his lip. "And Jake smashed my cupcakes on top of everything."

Mia nodded. "Got it. I mean, if someone's being literally transphobic, that's a valid reason to get mad."

"So I should have punched him in the face?"

Mia chuckled despite herself. "Don't push it."

Ollie stared off at the water. Mia was always so good at handling her anger and thinking of other people and their feelings. It was why Ollie always asked for her advice on how to stay calm, even if he was bad at taking it. Sometimes, he wished he was more like her, because the alternative was . . .

"You don't think I'm just like them, right?" Ollie asked. "I mean, Mom and Dad?"

Mia widened her eyes behind her glasses. "What?"

"With the Jake thing, and then I also smashed some seasoning and made a huge mess, just like Mom does, and I mean, I was the reason they started fighting today in the first place. So I have to be making it worse."

Ollie rubbed his sleeve over his face. He didn't want to cry. He felt Mia pull him in with one arm. "Hey," she said softly. "Their fighting isn't your fault. Don't ever think it is. And you're not like them. They fight because they feel bad and want to make others feel worse, but you fight because you feel bad and you want to make things better."

A few tears stuck in the corner of his eye. Shoot. Mia always knew the right thing to say.

"Thanks," he mumbled. Cheeks still hot, Ollie finished off the last piece of salami. He watched his sister slowly nibbling on a piece of cheese, remembering her red-rimmed eyes when she walked into the apartment. "What's up with you? You seem tired."

"I'm always tired."

"*More* tired. Like you were overthinking something." Mia opened her mouth, but Ollie interrupted. "Don't say you're always overthinking. What's wrong?"

Mia looked over at the other people on the beach, all far away.

"They can't hear us, you know." To prove his point, he sat up tall. "Oh no, Mia! I just pooped my pants!"

She glared at him. "Stop it."

"Oh, how I wish I could," Ollie cried out, his voice rising with each word. "But now there's poop all over the sand! Poop everywhere! All I know is poop!"

Mia was practically doubled over laughing, even though she was trying to say "shut up" when she had the breath to do it. No one even looked at them. It didn't matter how many times Ollie yelled out "poop," the wind swallowed them all, along with coming outs and confessions.

Eventually, they both quieted down.

"I'm in love with my best friend's girlfriend," Mia said finally, "and I don't know how to not be."

"Wait. Like, *David's* girlfriend? *Joanie?*"

Mia sighed. "Is it that messed up?"

David had been Mia's best friend for as long as Ollie could remember. He only started dating Joanie earlier in the year, but it instantly seemed like Mia was demoted to third wheel. Still, Ollie had no idea Mia liked her, too.

"Does he know?"

"He knew we both had a crush on her before they started dating, but he had the courage to tell her and . . . I didn't," Mia admitted. "I told him I was okay with it, and I thought I'd get over it, but I haven't. Clearly."

Ollie didn't really know what to say. He barely had a grasp on how close friendships worked, let alone *dating*. As far as he could tell, dating mostly meant having to get dropped off at places to meet up after school and holding hands in the hallway between classes, which was probably a little too middle school for Mia's problems.

He had to think of something comforting.

"That's rough," he said.

Mia rolled her eyes but regained a smile. "Yeah. Tell me about it." Mia tilted her head toward Ollie. "That's why I like that you stand up for yourself and get angry. Sometimes I feel like I'm *too* cautious. It would be nice to be able to just say how I feel and let it all out sometimes."

It was weird. Ollie would never think Mia would have any reason to want to be different. She was always calm and thoughtful and understanding, even to people who didn't deserve it. It was the exact opposite of their parents, making her like a breath of fresh air in their stuffy, tense apartment. Ollie didn't get it, and he wasn't about to be understanding to people like Jake, but he looked up to Mia for it. He really admired her. Even though she had a tendency to not throw away the box after taking the last Pop-Tart.

Ollie ate one of the cuts of hard cheese where the knife had slipped at the end and misshaped it. "I'm sorry you're dealing with that. Sometimes . . . sometimes it feels like we can't catch a break."

Mia bit her lip. Her eyes looked glassy. "It's gonna get better. I promise. Once I'm eighteen, you can stay with me and at least we won't have to worry about Mom and Dad on top of everything else."

"Right, because what you really need when you go off to college next year is your little brother around."

She gave him a playful shove. "I offer you help and these fancy snacks, and you give me *sass*." Her expression shifted to something sure. Certain. "We'll figure it out, though. We always do."

Ollie appreciated that, but he was mad that they even *had* to figure out things on their own. It wasn't fair. Why did friends have to betray their friends, and why did their parents have to hate each other more than they liked each other, and why did Ollie keep having to defend himself over and over and over again?

None of it was fair, and the whole world was annoying, and Ollie wanted to scream about it.

But before he had the chance, he heard a strange sound slip through the silencing wind. It was a soft, pained sort of sound, like the sad moans of a small, wounded animal.

"Do you hear that?" Ollie asked.

Mia gave him a look. "What?"

Ollie shushed her to listen. The sound continued, but it seemed to come from *under* the sand. Ollie put his ear close to the ground, and the cries grew louder. Was something buried *alive*?

Ollie immediately started digging, tossing sand away and not caring if it went onto his towel or even close to the few pieces of food they had left. Mia cursed next to him, but he hardly listened.

"Ollie, what are you doing?!"

The sound was so close. Ollie just had to keep digging, grains of sand stuck under his nails and numbing his hands.

"Something is under here! I think it's an animal, it sounds hu—"

Then something looped around Ollie's wrist, closing on it tight. Ollie yelped and stopped digging. A strange black vine only about the width of a charger cable tightened around his arm. Ollie could only stare at it. Mia's eyes were wide. "Uh . . . Ollie?" She squeaked, reaching for the vine as if to pull it off him. "What is that?"

Ollie didn't have a chance to answer. Suddenly, another one wrapped around his right ankle and dragged him down into the sand. Mia screamed his name and reached for his hand. She grabbed tightly, trying to pull Ollie back up and out, but another vine curled around his wrist and yanked. He screamed, the sand moving around him, his body slipping through. He tried to kick and twist out of the vine's grasp, but it didn't budge, just kept pulling him down, down, down.

The sand was up to his chest, and he kept falling, the towel and picnic remains getting buried with him.

More vines wrapped around him, pulling across his face until he was neck-deep and sand coated his tongue. Mia clawed at the vines, trying everything to get him out, but nothing was helping. He was stuck, he was panicked. It hurt, and he couldn't breathe, and he needed to get free.

But he couldn't.

With the sounds of that pained animal and his own sister's screams, Ollie's vision went black as he disappeared beneath the surface of the beach.

4

The Very Creepy Backward Beach

THE NEXT THING OLLIE knew, his body smacked against the ground, the wind knocked right out of him. His lungs gasped for air. Finally, they were able to claim it and his breathing returned as his vision focused. He stared up at an angry orange sky, gray smoke swirling around in it. Was there a wildfire nearby he hadn't heard about? But no. This didn't look like any smoke Ollie had seen before, and since he'd lived in California his whole life, he'd seen plenty.

Ollie dug his hands into the sand to sit up. He took in the area around him. It looked like Manhattan Beach, the exact same spot they had been.

But it was also completely different.

Birds still flew overhead, but in the wrong direction. Their beaks pointed forward, but it was like they were being pulled the opposite way.

The sand was filled with those thin black vines, coating the beach like a spider's web. They'd thankfully let go of Ollie's legs, but they seemed to slither and squirm when Ollie looked at them too long, to the point where he wasn't sure if they were moving or if his eyes were playing tricks on him.

"Mia?" Ollie called. His voice was higher in his desperation. He hated it. "Mia?"

She was gone. Everyone who had been on the beach was gone.

Or, rather, most of them were gone. There was someone, standing close to one of the lifeguard towers, which was broken and splintered from the vines.

Ollie hurried to his feet, trying to avoid the vines as much as possible as he stepped toward the lifeguard tower.

"Hello?" Ollie called out. "Um . . . what happened? Is this like a solar eclipse or something?"

He approached the person but slowed as he got closer. He could see now that their skin was a sickly gray. And they weren't moving at all.

Ollie winced. "Are you all right?"

The person's head turned. Ollie felt like he was watching in slow motion as their face swiveled toward him, revealing a wide smile and rising gray smoke coming from their eye sockets.

Ollie jumped but tried to hide his reaction. "Uh, sorry, never mind, I think I'll figure it out myself . . . way over there. 'Bye."

He ran in the opposite direction, making sure the strange person didn't follow. It looked like there were more people farther down the beach, but Ollie wasn't going to make that mistake again. He really should've known better than to try to ask for help.

He could figure out where he was himself. Right? He had to. First, he just had to find out if he really fell through the sand and, if he did, if he was somehow underneath the beach. Although Ollie didn't pay much attention in science class, he was pretty sure there wasn't an entirely different world under the dirt. There definitely weren't people. Not living ones, anyway. He glanced back toward the lifeguard stand. What in the world happened to that person? And would it happen to him?

He couldn't think like that. Ollie just had to get back. Maybe he could call for help?

Ollie pulled his phone from his pocket. No service. He watched as the time changed from 6:17 to 6:16. Ollie blinked. That definitely had to be his mind playing tricks on him. He stared at the clock until it flicked again–6:15.

It was moving backward, just like the birds.

Ollie took a cautious step forward, back toward where he first found himself on the strange beach. His towel was there, only the image of the lizard seemed to be facing the opposite direction. He picked it up, wanting some kind of comfort, and took the wrapped piece of prosciutto that had apparently made the trip with it. Yes, Ollie was freaked out, but even a freaked-out Ollie couldn't justify wasting a perfectly good piece of food.

But the most important thing was figuring out where he was and how he could get out of there. Ollie didn't like the feeling he got from this beach. The air was heavier, denser, and something sinister seemed to lurk in the distance, just out of sight. Something worse than the creepy person by the lifeguard tower. He could feel it deep in his bones, he needed to *go*.

Ollie threw the towel over his shoulder and put his phone and the paper-wrapped meat in his pocket to free up his hands. He didn't know if he was going to have to fight someone to get away, but it seemed like he needed to be ready for anything.

He saw another beach setup, similar to the one the people nearest to them had. He remembered the girl had a bag that said "Los Angeles," and the guy had a surfboard. The couple was nowhere in sight, and while the surfboard was covered in black vines, the bag looked relatively similar. Except it said "Selegna Sol" in the same bright blue font.

Was everything on the beach backward?

Then Ollie heard it again. The sad, desperate noise he'd started digging for. He turned toward it but couldn't see anything. Still, he didn't have many other options, so Ollie followed the sound. When he got closer, he noticed small drops of blood staining the sand.

Ollie rushed his pace and came up to a hole in the ground. Inside it, there was a cat with brilliant white fur. Only its front paw was coated in red and it had a tag on its ear. Ollie also spotted a second tail and thought for a moment maybe two cats were in there, but as he looked closer, he realized the tails were connected, both sprouting from the same spot but splitting into a V.

"What the . . . ?"

The cat looked up at Ollie, and its fur rose, ears bending back as it revealed its sharp teeth with a loud hiss.

Ollie laughed. "Smart cat. You shouldn't trust anyone." His eyes moved from the cat's tails back to its bleeding paw. Ollie couldn't tell how bad the injury was, but based on the yowling he'd heard earlier, it didn't seem great. He took the piece of lunch meat and held it out in front of him, kneeling on the ground. The cat hissed again. "I'm only trying to help, I swear. I'm not going to hurt you." Ollie lowered his voice. "I'd only hurt someone who deserved it, and something tells me you didn't do anything to deserve that, huh?"

Cautiously, the cat lifted its injured paw and stepped closer on the other three legs, nose twitching as it sniffed the prosciutto and Ollie's fingers. While it looked like the cat didn't quite trust Ollie, its want for the snack outweighed that fear, and it began licking at the salted meat.

Ollie dropped the meat next to him to rip a piece of fabric off the bottom of his shirt. It wasn't exactly the best quality, so it tore pretty easily. "You're gonna be mad, I know," Ollie said. "But we need to stop the bleeding until we can get help."

At least, he was pretty sure they did. Ollie didn't really know how to take care of human injuries, let alone animal ones.

The cat hissed again when Ollie reached for its paw, so he had to use the towel to trap the cat a little and lift it out of the hole. It was enough to tie the shirt fabric on the injury. Offended, the cat hissed at Ollie once more before returning to the discarded meat, awkwardly twitching its wrapped leg. Its two tails even looked sassy, moving around as it chewed on small pieces of meat.

Ollie found himself laughing. "You're lucky you're cute," he told the cat. "Because your personality's terrible."

The cat looked back at him. Ollie reached out his fingers toward the cat once more.

"I don't mind, though," Ollie said. He gave a little smile. "To tell you the truth, I've heard that my personality's terrible, too."

He didn't know why he was talking to the cat; he knew it didn't understand him. But still, it got his mind off the strange place he was currently in. Feeling less alone made it seem like things were okay.

Or okay enough. Ollie never really felt totally okay.

Maybe something about the sound of his voice made a difference, because the cat sniffed Ollie's fingers and then bumped its head against Ollie's hand. Ollie scratched it behind the ears, and the cat weaved around Ollie's legs.

"And there's your butthole. Didn't ask to see that, but thanks," Ollie said as the cat paused in front of him, tails up in the air. "And it looks like you're a boy. Didn't need to see that either, but good to know. Do you have a name?"

There wasn't a collar or anything around the cat's neck. Ollie touched the clip on his ear. It had "SUBJECT 23" printed on it. "Doesn't that hurt?" Ollie asked.

He carefully removed the clip. The cat shook his head and smacked his body against Ollie once more. His finger brushed against paper. Something was taped onto the back of the tag. A small slip of paper. Ollie unfolded it.

Integration complete, effective for magic extraction and responsive against curses

Ollie's mind struggled to process the words. "'Responsive against curses,' huh? Does this mean you're like a good luck charm? Because to be honest, I think I need one." Ollie put the message and tag in his pants pocket in case he needed it later.

The cat meowed. Was that a yes? Or did he just want more prosciutto?

"Regardless, Subject 23 is a terrible name. I'll think of a new one for you once I get us out of this dump."

How to do so was the problem.

"Do you want to die?!" a voice roared, sending what felt like a sonic boom through the beach.

Both Ollie and the cat jumped, twisting toward the sound of the voice with wide eyes. There was a man standing in front of them, just about ten feet away. He had sickly pale skin that was almost grayed, dark circles around his eyes, and a swarm of shadows swirling around him. He wore a top hat and cape that almost made him look like a magician, but not one any person would pay to see. His face was twisted into a grotesque scowl as he opened his mouth to reveal pointed, yellowed teeth.

"Um . . . not particularly, no," Ollie answered.

"Then give that cat back," he said. "Otherwise, I'll kill you right along with him."

The cat, however, did not seem to want to go back. And Ollie did not want to give the cat to someone who just said they'd kill them both. A low growl erupted from the cat's small body as he lowered himself to the ground. Ollie could almost feel his fear, and it seemed clear that this man was the person who hurt him in the first place.

Which made Ollie mad. So mad he clenched his fists and started shaking. Ollie stood up and faced the man.

"How about you come and take him back, you discount Michael Myers–looking weirdo."

Ollie was a big fan of both horror movies and funny insults, so he was really proud of that one. He took a step forward, blocking the cat from the man.

The man turned around and took a step away.

"That's what I thought," Ollie said, standing tall with chest puffed. "Go on back to Party City and return that dorky outfit."

But the man didn't head in the direction of Backward Party City (Ytic Ytrap?), or anywhere at all. Instead, his neck bent with a *pop*. His skin extended and twisted, bones shifting underneath, until his head completely turned around to face Ollie with a sickening smile. His joints snapped in every direction, arms and legs bending like branches as they twisted toward Ollie. His finger joints snapped, the bones breaking out of the tips into claws. Gray smoke slid from his eye sockets, just in wisps so Ollie could see some white through it.

Then The Backward Man, limbs and head the only things facing Ollie, ran right toward him.

Ollie was normally a brave kid, but there were some sights that no reasonable person could remain calm seeing. That was one of those sights, and Ollie was one reasonable person.

So, he screamed.

Snatching up the cat whether he liked it or not, Ollie sprinted away from the horrifying man. He couldn't even think of any ways to escape because as the cat squirmed in his grip, his body was on autopilot. His mind was preoccupied with the very reasonable thought of AAAAAAHHHHHHHHHHHH HHHHHH!

But his legs kept running.

Thankfully, he was faster than The Backward Man and managed to put a little distance between them, but there was nowhere to hide and the man kept coming. Ollie approached the spot where he first fell into this strange world. There had to be a way out, a way back.

Ollie's foot suddenly hit something, and he tripped. His heart rose to his throat, and his stomach nearly flipped as he caught himself at the last moment, cat still safe in his arm.

He looked at the sand, where a hand was peeking out from underneath. And he screamed again.

"Ollie? Is that you?"

Ollie recognized Mia's muffled voice.

"I can pull you out," Mia continued. "Try to reach my hand!"

Ollie figured it looked enough like his sister's hand to listen.

Especially because The Backward Man was catching up to them, so close that Ollie could see his wide mouth and sharp teeth. He cringed and grabbed the hand in the sand.

"Hurry up, hurry up, hurry up!" Ollie yelled.

The cat wiggled against Ollie's chest as they started to get pulled into the ground. It wasn't exactly pleasant plunging face-first into sand, so Ollie couldn't blame him.

A sharp pain spread from Ollie's right leg as something tried to yank it back.

"Ollie!" Mia grunted from somewhere ahead, her fingers digging deeper into his arm as she pulled even harder.

Ollie kicked his other leg until it hit something solid with a crunch, and the pressure went away. Finally, he was able to push through the other side, moving the cat up first.

When Ollie finally emerged, it was darker than before, but he knew it was home when he saw Mia's worried face.

He lay on the sand, breathing heavily. The cat jumped off him but didn't run away. Ollie looked back at the hole they should have just emerged from, but the spot was entirely undisturbed, almost like it hadn't happened at all.

He could have almost convinced himself he imagined it if not for the two-tailed cat sitting next to him and the cuts on his ankle. It looked like sharp claws had gripped on to his limb, cutting through the skin just enough for tiny droplets of blood to bloom.

A moment passed.

"What happened?" Mia asked finally, something between a yell and a whisper.

"I don't . . . I'm not sure," Ollie said. He let out a sigh, trying to catch his breath and calm his racing heart. "But I think I have a cat now."

Mia looked over where Ollie gestured at the white cat with his wrapped paw. He gave a little meow, almost in greeting. "Oh," she said. "Okay. Sure." She ran both her hands through her hair. "What *was* that? I mean . . . what do we do now? Wait. Is he injured?" She squinted. "Does he have *two tails?*"

Ollie tried to get to his feet. His leg hurt, but he could still put weight on it. It was mostly just the skin that stung.

"Why don't we get him help," Ollie said, "and I'll explain everything on the way."

"Okay . . . ," Mia started.

"Just promise you'll believe me?" Ollie asked.

Mia gave a serious nod. "I promise."

5

Wishbone Carlos Di Costa the Third

"I REALLY CAN'T BELIEVE this," Mia said.

Ollie gave her a look. "You believed everything I said about the weird Backward Place with strange smoke-eyed people and The Backward Man that tried to kill me, but you can't believe we're doing *this*?"

Mia gestured forward. "Do you really think the vet isn't going to find this a little weird?"

Ollie admired their handiwork. They thought the whole two-tail thing might raise too many questions at the vet, so they'd bought a baby onesie and lured the cat into it with treats. The tails were still kind of visible under the fabric, but it was hard to tell if you didn't know what you were looking for.

"What?" Ollie said. "He's adorable."

After Ollie had time to calm down from the whole near-death experience thing, the backward beach felt far away. Ollie would deal with that later, after the cat got patched up.

"This isn't going to work out well," Mia whispered.

"Not with that attitude it won't," Ollie said. "Just act like it's normal." Before his sister had time to reply, Ollie got out of the car and brought the cat into the emergency vet building. Mia grumbled something but followed along.

Thankfully it was empty, so they were able to take the cat back for treatment right away while Mia and Ollie stayed to give the information.

"Your name?" the woman asked, looking only at the computer.

"Mia Di Costa." Mia also gave her driver's license over as a form of ID.

"Cat's name?"

Ollie thought of the cat's tails, how they stemmed from the same spot and spread into two. "Wishbone," he said. Which would have been perfect, had he not said it at the exact time Mia said, "Carlos."

Ollie glared at her.

Flustered, Mia gave a smile. "Well, both. It's . . . his full name. Wishbone Carlos Di Costa . . . the Third."

Why? Ollie mouthed. Mia just shrugged apologetically. The woman didn't really seem to care or was too tired to say anything more than what she needed to get the necessary information. When they finally were through, Ollie put on a little smile.

"I know it's an *animal* urgent care, but any chance someone could bandage me up real quick, too?" Ollie lifted his leg to show the wound.

The woman frowned. "How did that happen?"

"The cat," Mia said quickly.

The woman made a face, looking at the claw marks that were definitely not the size of a housecat's.

"The cat," she said, completely dubious.

Ollie's eyes darted over to Mia, who shrugged again, before returning to the woman. "Yes," he said slowly. "The cat."

The woman sighed.

Although there was biting, hissing, and growling of all sorts involved, Wishbone Carlos Di Costa the Third was finally all fixed up. Ollie's own leg was also disinfected and wrapped, without all the fuss (except he slipped up and swore once), so the three of them headed back to Mia's car. Immediately, Mia gripped the steering wheel and rested her forehead against it.

"How are we supposed to bring a cat home?"

"In the cardboard carrier they gave us," Ollie said.

Mia turned her head just to glare at him. "Mom and Dad will never let us keep him. They'll say it's too expensive."

She was right. Not spending money when they could avoid it was the one thing their parents actually did agree on. At least, they agreed on Ollie and Mia not spending money. Ollie had seen his parents' credit card and loan bills. While he didn't understand all of it, he could understand the huge numbers next to "amount due." There was no way they'd agree to a cat— one that already cost a couple hundred dollars in an emergency vet visit. Ollie would have to find a way to pay Mia back at some point.

"Let's just not tell them," Ollie said.

"So we're just supposed to hide a whole entire cat in your room?"

"Why not?"

"Are you listening to yourself, Ollie?"

Ollie opened the top of the carrier so Wishbone could poke his head out. "Fine, then. Tell Wishbone Carlos Di Costa the Third you named him only to throw him away." Ollie looked sadly down at the cat. "I'm sorry, little guy. My sister would rather you get hit by a car or eaten by a coyote than slightly inconvenience herself . . ."

"Shut up!" Mia started the car, inputting their apartment address into her phone to find the route with the least traffic.

Ollie smiled. "So, we're keeping him?"

Mia swallowed, giving a little smile back. "It's not like Mom and Dad are paying that much attention anyway. How hard could it be to hide one little kitty?"

The answer, they quickly learned, was very.

They were still parked outside the apartment building, not quite ready to risk it by rushing in with Wishbone. Ollie glanced at their building and almost wondered what the cat would think of it. The beige paint peeled on the outside, and some of the gray letters that were painted on the front of the building mysteriously disappeared, so instead of "1418 Ocean-view," it read, "1418 O an ew." At least the numbers were still holding on. Not that they ever really got visitors who needed to find the address.

The surrounding street wasn't a bad area. The house to the right of the apartment building was nice. There was a U-Haul parked in front, like people were moving in. The other side of them was a 7-Eleven. Maybe it wasn't the nicest view, but Ollie would rather have late night taquitos and spicy hot dogs. Nice views didn't help you when you were hungry and your parents were too busy arguing to care.

"Okay, I have an idea," Mia said finally. "Hold Wishbone."

The two of them had gotten out of the car, while Wishbone comfortably sat on the passenger seat, the cardboard carrier already unable to close since he tore off the latch. He seemed to have forgiven them for taking him to the vet, as he chewed on the plush taco cat toy Mia bought off the vet. Ollie picked up Wishbone and the toy. Mia took off her USC hoodie and put it over Ollie and Wishbone so the sleeves dangled at his side.

Wishbone shrugged his head to peek from the neck hole.

"I think that works," Mia said.

"Right, because this doesn't look weird at all," Ollie muttered.

"I'll distract Mom, and you run into your room," Mia said. "If she doesn't really take a look at you, it'll be fine." Her smile faltered. "I think."

Right. Fine. After all, what was strange about a purring cat's head emerging from Ollie's neck? He rolled his eyes. "You better have a good distraction."

They walked up to the front door, and Mia put her key in the lock but didn't twist it. Her eyes looked right into Ollie's. "I'll go in first," she said. "Don't follow until the coast is clear."

"How will I kn— Ow!" Wishbone lightly bit Ollie on the chin.

Mia swallowed, determined. "You'll know."

She walked inside, and Ollie could only just make out a quick exchange between her and their mom. Another few short moments passed before Mia let out a bloodcurdling scream. Both Wishbone and Ollie jumped.

"There's a cockroach! Mom! Heeeeelp!" Ollie heard Mia yell, followed by swearing and footsteps from his mom.

Mia had been right. He did know.

Using the opportunity of Mia and his mom shouting at each other in the bathroom, Ollie held Wishbone tightly and ran into his own room, quickly closing the door behind him. Immediately, Mia's screaming stopped.

"Oh, it was just hair. Silly me."

"Seriously, Mia?" their mom snapped.

Ollie put Wishbone down on his bed, removing the hoodie from around his neck. He also took off the baby onesie since Wishbone had sunk his teeth into the fabric, leaving little holes. "Sorry about that," Ollie whispered. "I'll be right back."

He slowly opened the door a little, where his mom and Mia

were right outside, having left the bathroom at the end of the hall. Wishbone meowed loudly from the bed. Ollie's heart stopped, and Mia froze as they looked at each other in panic.

"What was that?" his mom asked.

Ollie fished for an excuse before quickly settling on, "My stomach. I'm hungry."

He slipped into the hallway and shut the door behind him before Wishbone could draw any more attention to himself.

"Are you sure you're okay?" Mom asked. "That sounded strange."

Ollie hated what he was about to do next, but he had to distract his mom from overthinking about how she most definitely heard a meow, so he went for the worst possible subject change that he could think of. "I'm good, will Dad be back for dinner?"

A little guilt poked at him as he watched his mom's expression fall and mouth twitch in anger. It was like the mere mention of Ollie's dad made her mad all over again. Ollie knew it would. Just like he knew that Dad would not be back in time for dinner, and he and Mia would likely have to scour the fridge for something to heat up.

"I'm sorry, loves, I'm not really feeling well. Long day shift at the café." His mom pulled out a twenty from her pocket. "Why don't you two get some burgers or something?"

Mia took the bill. "Sure."

Mom gave a weak smile before disappearing back into her room. They stood still and silent until the door completely closed. Mia rubbed her temples before turning to Ollie. "We should go out anyway," she said. "We need to get some things for Wishbone, like food and litter. We can stop at In-N-Out on the way back."

Ollie really hoped Wishbone didn't need to poop in the meantime.

"I don't think twenty dollars is going to cover all that," Ollie said.

Mia nodded. "I have my savings, too."

Ollie thought back to the USC hoodie, currently covered in cat hair and resting on his bed. "You already spent a lot at the vet. And your money is supposed to be for college."

Mia gave a smile that was anything but happy. "Come on, Ollie. You know we can't afford college anytime soon. I'd rather focus on something more realistic." She sighed. "Considering it's helping a two-tailed cat you found in some creepy, backward monster world, that's saying something."

Ollie clenched his fists as his stomach twisted in anger, but not at Mia. Sure, she had a tendency to give up on things too easily, and Ollie thought she could be a little more selfish sometimes. But what he was really mad at was their situation. That even though Mia worked as many hours as she could, she wouldn't be able to go to the kind of school she wanted without student loans that added up to an impossible number. That the same would be true for him in five years. That their dreams were doomed to be nothing more than dreams, because there was only so much they could do on their own.

It wasn't fair, but all they could do was look out for each other.

Because they were family.

And according to the paperwork they had to fill out for the newly named Wishbone Carlos Di Costa the Third, the little cat was family now, too.

"All right," Ollie said. "Let's go."

6

Scary Movies to Watch with Your Cat

AFTER EVERYTHING WAS SETTLED, Wishbone was fed, and the litter box was all set up (thankfully, Wishbone had not pooped on the floor while they were out), Mia brushed off her pants and yawned.

"All right," she said. "Good night."

Ollie frowned. "You don't want to watch a scary movie?"

Just like the beach, it was practically tradition for them. Both Ollie and Mia loved horror movies, and they would always find one to watch when the day had been particularly tough and Ollie's dad went MIA.

Mia gave a sad smile and ruffled Ollie's hair. "I think you had enough horror in real life today. Next time, all right?"

Ollie didn't want to argue. Neither of them really wanted to talk more about what happened, and hadn't since Ollie's initial explanation. Mia also did look kind of tired, not to mention everything she did for him and Wishbone already that day and the issue with David and Joanie she'd been upset about earlier. He didn't want to ask again, because she'd probably go along with it, so he responded with a "good night" and watched his sister leave and close the door behind her. Then it was just him and Wishbone. Ollie grabbed a toy they bought at the pet store, a pink fish dangling from a string at the end of a wire rod. He sat on the edge of the bed and dragged it across the floor.

Wishbone's eyes went wide as he lowered himself to the floor, wiggled his butt, and pounced on the fish. Ollie lifted it up in the air, and Wishbone jumped, mouth wide as he caught the fish between his paws, not seeming to care about the paw still wrapped up. Ollie's jaw practically dropped at how high the cat was able to effortlessly jump.

"Nice one!"

A master of high jumps, Wishbone went after the fish until he was breathing out of his mouth and flopped over onto Ollie's bed.

"Well . . . do *you* want to watch a scary movie?" Ollie asked. "We don't have a TV, but it'll still look good on my laptop."

Not that Wishbone would be watching, but since Mia left him by himself, it was nice to have the company. Ollie set up his laptop in front of them. "Mia and I have a bunch of streaming services through my uncle Romeo. He's rich, like a backyard with a pool and everything. He actually has a successful business, which is probably why Dad doesn't like him." Ollie tapped on his chin, scrolling through the horror section. "What should we watch tonight?"

Ollie decided it was probably best not to watch anything with anyone moving backward in it. It was scary enough in a movie, but what he saw earlier in the day was impossibly worse. Not that his parents paid enough attention to know what he watched, but even if they didn't want him watching R-rated movies, they couldn't really say anything after what he went through today. If he could deal with the terrifying Backward Place and be okay, he could handle a movie with some blood and swear words.

His mind immediately thought of the man's twisted neck and smoky eyes, and fear pricked Ollie's spine as he felt a little sick.

Maybe he couldn't fully deal with it, but that was only more reason to have a distraction. Ollie focused on Wishbone's adorable face to block out the bad image.

Even though all two tails of Wishbone were right next to him, it was still hard to believe everything that happened on the beach was real. Ollie knew that he probably could've died, and he was still definitely freaked out, but it was like his mind refused to really accept it. And that was fine. Right?

Right. He was alive. It all worked out.

Unless, like in the horror movies, the villain came back. Ollie swallowed.

"You don't think that freaky Backward Man can come here, do you? Or any of the people from over there?" Ollie asked aloud, more for himself than for an answer. "I mean, if he could have, we'd probably be dead already, so no use worrying about it, right?" Ollie bit his lip, returning to the screen. He really needed that distraction. "Maybe a monster movie?"

Wishbone wasn't paying attention, just staring off into space with wide eyes. While he might have been looking at ghosts or a different dimension or whatever cats looked at, his gaze almost seemed to land on the poster of *The Host* on Ollie's wall.

"Ooh, I haven't seen that one in a while, and it's one of my favorite movies. It's a little old, but so good. Bong Joon-ho is a genius." It worked out perfectly because Ollie could put on the subtitled version. Mia preferred dubs, but Ollie liked reading the subtitles. It helped him focus on the on-screen events. Without subtitles, unless the movie was *super* interesting, his attention would start drifting.

Ollie adjusted his pillows so he could lean on them without hitting his back against the wall. As Ollie played the movie, Wishbone moved closer to him, curling into a circle and lazily draping his tails over Ollie's arm.

It wasn't the same experience as showing a movie to a person for the first time, or he and Mia geeking out over effects together, but it was nice. A comfortable quiet moment that distracted Ollie from everything else.

It didn't last long.

Ollie heard the front door open and his dad stepping in. Ollie silently begged for his dad to just pass out on the couch and go to sleep. No such luck. He heard his mom walk out to the living room, and the two of them immediately got into an argument.

Ollie sighed, pausing the movie and shutting his laptop.

"We'll have to finish it another time. It's not worth it when they get like this," Ollie told Wishbone. "I won't be able to hear anything, not even with my earbuds."

His mom yelled something, bringing the volume up enough that Wishbone lifted his head, eyes locked on the door. Ollie tried to pet him, but Wishbone nipped on his fingers.

"Come on, I'm trying to be nice," Ollie said. "They'll stop soon."

He made himself more comfortable, sliding farther under the covers and turning toward Wishbone. The cat's fur almost looked gray in the darkness, but his eyes still reflected the light streaming from the crack under the bedroom door and the bluish glow of the moon.

"This probably wasn't what you were expecting when we took you home, huh? Don't get me wrong, I love my parents since they're my parents and all . . . but sometimes I really hate them, too." Ollie never said that before. Maybe it was easy to tell it to Wishbone since the cat couldn't tell anyone else. It was a way to whisper the words aloud to someone, even if Ollie was the only one who understood them. "I should probably feel guilty about it, but I don't. Like, at all."

Wishbone slowly blinked his eyes. Ollie remembered reading somewhere that cats did that when they liked you. He slowly blinked back. Maybe Wishbone was saying in cat language that he accepted Ollie anyway.

"You're nice to talk to," Ollie told Wishbone, petting his soft fur.

Wishbone flexed his paws, his claws digging into the sheets as he stretched.

"I guess we don't really know each other well yet. There's not much to know about me, though. I'm trans, but I think I'm a demiboy specifically. I get in trouble a lot for having an attitude, although you can probably relate to that, Mr. Bitey Pants." Wishbone turned away, like he didn't know what Ollie was talking about. Ollie laughed and continued. "I turn thirteen next month, so I'm a Capricorn, but I honestly have no idea what that means. Aside from horror movies, I like baking a lot. I'm pretty good at it too, decorating and plating especially." Ollie lowered his voice, head flat against the pillow. "It's my dream to open a bakery someday. I want to have themed desserts based off horror movies and call it So Good, It's Scary." Even though he was talking to a cat, his face was still heated. He'd never told anyone else that before, not even Mia. "Well, the name's a work in progress. Evil Bread Rise and 28 Cakes Later are still contenders, but yeah, that's basically everything."

His parents' voices still raged on from outside the door. Ollie wouldn't be able to sleep like this. No amount of Serene Forest or Bubbling Waterfall sounds from the meditation app Mia put on his phone would save him now.

A bit of his own anger flared in his stomach. Why did he have to stay quiet and deal with it?

"Can you two please shut up?" Ollie yelled.

His parents stopped for a moment. Only for the front door to open and slam again. His dad leaving, Ollie figured. After another moment, Ollie's bedroom door cracked open. Ollie was barely able to throw the blanket over Wishbone before his mom poked her head into the room. Her eyes were watery, but Ollie knew his mom cried more when she was frustrated than sad, since Ollie did the same.

"I'm sorry, love, I didn't realize we were so loud."

Ollie rolled his eyes. "I think people in Nevada realized it."

"Come on," Ollie's mom said. "It was just a little disagreement, all right? We're all good, okay?"

Ollie didn't want to argue with his mom. Especially when Wishbone was squirming under the covers. He bit Ollie's arm, and Ollie had to try to keep still despite the sharp little pain. "Yeah. Okay. Good night."

His mom looked even more tired and sad as she nodded. "Sweet dreams, Ollie."

She closed the door just as Wishbone popped his head out from under the covers. With a sigh, Ollie leaned his head back onto his pillow.

"Can you quit with the biting?" Ollie tapped Wishbone on the nose, and the cat licked his finger. That was better than his teeth, at least. "You know, sometimes I just wish Mom and Dad couldn't fight," Ollie admitted. "That they actually loved each other."

It might have been a trick of the light, or a passing car, but Wishbone's eyes almost seemed to flash an even brighter blue. But as quickly as it happened, it went away. Wishbone stood up, arching his back with a stretch. He stepped onto Ollie's chest and sat right on top of him.

Ollie scratched the purring cat behind his ears. A bit of drool fell from Wishbone's mouth and onto Ollie. He chuckled to himself.

"Jeez, even though you're a little jerk sometimes, you must be happy to be here. Not that I blame you. Your last home was kind of a dump." A long silence passed, and Ollie thought of how it normally was after his dad left. A lot of silence, with Ollie alone in his room, begging his brain to shut down and sleep so he could leave the apartment in the morning.

With Wishbone, the room didn't feel quite so silent.

"I'm happy you're here, too," Ollie whispered. He didn't even mind if Wishbone bit him again. If anything, it made him like the cat more. It was almost like he understood Ollie in a way that Mia couldn't. She was way too nice, after all. Ollie smiled to himself, moving his fingers to pet Wishbone's head.

Before Ollie knew it, his hand flopped to the side and sleep overcame him under the watchful eyes of the strange, little, two-tailed cat.

7

Jake Remains the Absolute Worst

"MMMRREEOOOWWW!"

Ollie woke with a start, only to see Wishbone's butt right in his face. "Hey," he snapped. "Keep it down, will you?"

Wishbone sat down, right on Ollie's cheek.

"Gross." Ollie gently pushed him away, and Wishbone turned around to put his face over Ollie's, staring straight ahead as he let out another meow. Ollie looked over at his phone. It was barely past six in the morning.

"You're acting like you haven't eaten in years," Ollie mumbled. But he still got up to open a can of wet food they'd bought last night. It wasn't exactly the most high-quality option, but if Mia and Ollie lived their whole lives on a discount diet, they figured Wishbone could, too. Besides, Ollie doubted The Backward Man had splurged on Royal Canin food.

Ollie plopped the contents of the can, tuna and seaweed flavor, into Wishbone's bowl.

"Do cats like seaweed?" Ollie asked.

Based on the way Wishbone gobbled up the food, Ollie had to assume the answer was yes. Ollie quickly changed and got his things together for school. Without thinking, he looked around to double-check that no one was in the room before he kissed Wishbone on the head.

"I'll see you later," Ollie said. "If someone tries to come in, hide under the bed."

Wishbone licked tuna off his nose, not a single thought behind his bright blue eyes. Ollie bit his lip and sighed. He just had to hope neither of his parents went into his room before he and Mia got back. It didn't seem like his dad had come back home, and his mom would be leaving for work soon, so it was probably fine. Ollie left the window blinds open so Wishbone could at least look at birds or something.

Ollie walked out of his room and threw his backpack down in the hallway, immediately going to brush his teeth since it wasn't like there would be anything in the house for breakfast anyway. After fixing his hair in the bathroom mirror, he grabbed his backpack and walked out into the living room to wait for Mia.

Only his mom was in the kitchen, a large box of donuts on the table.

"Good morning, Ollie Cat," his mom said.

For a moment, he was worried that she saw Wishbone, or somehow guessed everything based on the cat hair all over his clothes, but she seemed in way too good of a mood to have found out about the pet they were hiding. In fact, she seemed in way too good of a mood in general.

"Donuts?" Ollie asked slowly. "What's the occasion?"

"Well, why not?" his mom answered, all sunshine.

Ollie slowly walked over to the box of donuts. It was from the 24-hour shop down the street. His mom even got a maple bacon one, his favorite, and chocolate frosted for Mia. Ollie grabbed a donut, sniffing it almost like it could've been poisoned.

His mom rolled her eyes, expression still light. "Come on, if I wanted to kill you, I would've done it by now."

"Ha ha," Ollie said. "Did you have too much coffee or something?"

"Am I not allowed to be in a good mood?"

Ollie almost wanted to say that no, she wasn't, not after what she and Dad made them go through last night, but he bit back the words. The last thing he needed was to set her off, especially since Dad was still out and it was a much-needed break.

Ollie was smart enough to shut up and enjoy the donut.

Besides, he knew his mom was just probably forcing it. Trying to make it up to him after last night. There was no way she'd have been *that* happy after fighting with Dad. It wasn't the first time she tried treating Ollie and Mia out of guilt.

Fortunately, a guilt donut tasted just as delicious as any other donut.

"What's this?" Mia asked, walking into the room with her backpack. "Did I forget someone's birthday?"

"I swear, the two of you. Can't we just have a nice breakfast once in a while?" Mom crossed her arms. "How hard is it to give a simple thank-you?"

"Thank you, Mom," Mia and Ollie said in unison as Mia went for a chocolate frosted.

"That's better," their mom said happily. She kissed them both on the forehead, something she didn't often do. "Have fun at school today!"

"Sure," Mia said. She turned to Ollie. "You ready?"

Ollie nodded. He took another donut for the road, and after a quick goodbye, they headed out toward Mia's car.

"Did you remember to feed Wishbone?" Mia asked once they were inside and strapped in.

"Trust me, he wouldn't let me forget," Ollie answered. "I'm pretty sure he'd bite up my ankles if I waited another two minutes. But he seems to be happy here, and his paw isn't bothering him at all."

Mia sighed as she pulled the car out from the parking spot. "We're gonna have to figure out a way to tell Mom and Dad, you know. I've been stressed about it all night."

Ollie shrugged. "That's a Future Us problem."

"Ollie."

"It'll be fine. You paid for everything with your own money. I even cleaned his litter box this morning. What are they going to say? It's not like they're allergic, so there's no reason we shouldn't keep him."

Mia didn't say anything in response to that, but Ollie could tell she was still worried about it. She wore her glasses instead of contacts and had a bit of eczema pop up on her chin and forehead, which always happened when she was really stressed. While school and the thing with David and Joanie were likely a part of it, Wishbone and The Backward Place couldn't be helping.

Ollie tried his best to give a reassuring smile. "Hey. We'll figure it out, all right? We always do."

Mia smiled at the familiar words, but didn't seem to really mean it.

After Mia dropped him off at Hillside Middle to head over to Hillside High School, the morning passed by in a blur. Ollie normally found it hard to concentrate, but it was even harder with thoughts of The Backward Man. What if he came after Wishbone while Ollie was at school? While a part of him was understandably scared, the other part of him thought of Wishbone's injured paw and wished he could punch the guy right in his backward face.

But unless the classroom floor was about to randomly open and suck Ollie through (it certainly wasn't *im*possible), he had to deal with English class first. They were spending half the class working on their partner presentations for Monday, so Ollie moved his desk next to Lauren's. She already had her notebook, laptop, and copy of the book they decided to present on. Lauren picked it because it was queer (she identified as a lesbian, which may have been part of the reason that Ollie felt more comfortable around her) and had a cat on the cover.

Ollie agreed because he liked reading about nonbinary and

trans characters and disliked wasting energy on things that weren't important to him like arguing over what book to do a report on.

"I think we should focus on the character arc part for our presentation," Lauren said. "How they start out really afraid at the beginning, but slowly learn to believe in themself and face their fears." She cracked a smile. "Or we can focus on how the cat is by far the best character."

Ollie considered showing her pictures of Wishbone. He had at least one that was a close-up and didn't reveal the cat's extra tail, and Lauren would love him. But that would probably make her want to come over and see Wishbone, and if there was anything that stressed out Ollie more than getting too close to someone, it was having someone from school see his depressing apartment. If Ollie didn't already scare people off himself, his apartment and parents certainly would.

So Ollie just flipped through his library copy of the book.

"I don't know . . . ," he said. "I think the bug monster's the best."

Lauren frowned, leaning over to look at what page Ollie had paused on. "I mean, you've got an argument, but I disagree." She swallowed. "You sure it's okay if you do most of the talking for the presentation? I won't get a bad grade if I don't say much?"

Ollie shook his head. "It'll be fine. We'll make it clear you did a lot of work on the project, and all you have to do is say a few lines so no one really notices. I'll be right next to you."

"Promise?"

"Well, yeah, where else would I be when we have English class?"

Lauren laughed a little. "I know. I'm sorry. I just really hate presenting. I get so nervous and always mess up."

"Sure, but you have me this time. And I am great in front of people. I'm kind of hilarious."

"If you say so." Lauren's teasing smirk shifted into something more vulnerable as she leaned toward him. "Thanks, Ollie. Seriously."

A few of her red curls fell onto Ollie's shoulder. He didn't like people necessarily getting into his space, but he didn't mind Lauren so much. Her hair smelled like green apples.

"Cheating on your boyfriend now, Ollie?" Jake asked, completely turned in his chair in front of them. "I'd be surprised *two* people would want to date you, but I guess even losers get lonely sometimes."

Lauren almost immediately pulled away from Ollie, who was already rolling his eyes. He didn't want to imply anything about Lauren's sexuality. Just because she was in the Queer Student Alliance and came out to him didn't mean he should assume she was out to everyone. Still, Jake made him angry.

Especially because Ollie was certain that Jake didn't have a problem with Ollie being likeable when Jake thought he was a girl. Ollie bit back that comment, because he didn't want to remind everyone of how he used to present, but he also didn't want to let it go entirely. The whole gym uniform incident felt fresh in his mind, like it happened recently instead of the very start of middle school.

"I wouldn't know," Ollie said. "Have *you* been lonely? It must be hard when the only girl that talks to you is your mom."

Jake's face grew red as some of the other kids around them giggled. He scrunched up his eyebrows. "If Lauren dates you, what does that make her anyway? Straight or gay?"

Ollie's muscles grew tense as he shot up from his desk and glared at Jake. "If I punch your teeth out, what does that make you? Dead or alive? Because I'd love to find out."

A soft pressure on his wrist pulled Ollie back. He looked to where Lauren was hunched over at her desk, eyes pleading for him to sit down. "Leave it alone, Ollie. We have to work on our project."

Ollie could hardly believe her. She wanted to just let Jake get away with saying awful things and making fun of people. Besides, their project was basically done. They were fine. What Jake was doing wasn't.

"He's not worth it," Lauren continued. Her voice was soft. "Please?"

Ollie sighed. He didn't bother looking over at Jake's annoying face before sliding back down in his seat.

"Is everything okay, Ollie?" Mrs. Easton, their English teacher asked.

Lauren's pleading eyes made Ollie sigh again. It was clear she didn't want any attention drawn to her over Jake, and Ollie wanted to respect that, even if he didn't like it. "No, Mrs. Easton. I just remembered this part of the book that got me really heated." He threw on a smile. "Huge surprise, big twist. I just got really into it."

Mrs. Easton laughed. "Well, I'm excited to hear more about the book during your presentation next week."

Ollie kept his easygoing smile until she looked away and then rolled his eyes again. He twisted toward Lauren.

"You shouldn't let him talk about you like that. It's one thing if he's trying to make fun of me, but I don't like him bringing other people into it, like you and Noah."

Lauren raised her eyebrows. "Noah? Like Noah Choi? What happened with him?"

Ollie bit his lip. Lauren was really the only person he talked to consistently at school, so he forgot she hadn't been in the library the day before. "Nothing, it's no big deal. The point is, you should let me handle Jake."

She opened the presentation on her computer, clearly wanting to change the subject. "Then you'll just get in trouble, Ollie. That's not what I want."

"Well Jake getting away with being a turd is not what *I* want."

Lauren laughed despite herself, having to cover her mouth as a few other kids looked in their direction.

The classroom phone rang then, and Mrs. Easton said a few extra-quiet words to the person on the other end of the call before addressing the class. "Jake? You're needed in the main office."

While nearly everyone made a big *ooooooohhh* sound, Ollie didn't want to get his hopes up. Jake never seemed to get in trouble. He didn't get in trouble for stealing Ollie's uniform or for the things he said the day before. It was always Ollie who got the punishment. Jake probably just forgot his lunch and had his mom bring it or something. He seemed confident enough as he grabbed a pass from Mrs. Easton and walked out into the hall.

"I appreciate you not saying anything," Lauren said once he was gone. "And it worked out."

"Not really," Ollie muttered. "It's not like anything will happen." Ollie leaned back in his seat, running his pencil back and forth across his notebook until it made an angry dent in the page. "He's the worst."

Lauren reached over to draw two dots above the mark to turn it into a slightly aggressive smiley face. "I know he's the worst," she started, "but it'll be okay."

Ollie gave her a look. "And why's that?"

Lauren just smiled. "I have a feeling he'll get what's coming to him."

8

When What's Coming Actually Comes

THE REST OF THE day went by uneventfully and wonderfully Jake-free. Ollie would've preferred to be back home, finishing *The Host* with Wishbone or, better yet, anywhere that wasn't school or his apartment, but all things considered, it wasn't so bad. The one downside was that it wasn't a baking day in his cooking class. It barely felt like a downside, though, because the chicken quesadillas they did make ensured Ollie got an actual lunch.

He couldn't complain, especially since once Mia arrived, he'd get to go home and play with Wishbone. Ollie hoped the cat wasn't too lonely or trying to chew through the bandages on his paw. At least it was Friday, and he had all weekend to spend time with Wishbone.

Most of the pickup rush already ended, since Mia had to get through the high school's after-school traffic first before making her way to the middle school. Ollie didn't mind the wait. It was honestly better than the days she had work and he had to walk home.

He sat on the steps that led up to the front entrance, watching the street.

"Hey."

Ollie turned toward the voice only to cringe a little. It was Kirk and Brian. He almost didn't recognize them without their heads up Jake's butt, but Jake was surprisingly not there.

"What do you two want?" Ollie asked. His voice probably came out a little harsh and angry, but Kirk and Brian deserved it. It's not like they cared about Ollie's feelings whenever Jake went full jerkface.

"Did you get Jake in trouble?" Kirk (or was it Brian?) asked.

"People are saying he got sent home," Brian (Kirk?) continued.

What did Ollie care if Jake was sent home? Maybe he said the wrong thing to too many people, or maybe they took one look at his unfortunate face and thought he was sick. Regardless, it had nothing to do with Ollie.

"Let me make three things clear," Ollie said, holding up a finger with each point. "One: I don't know where Jake is. Two: I don't *care* where Jake is. Three: I don't like either of you, and if you don't leave me alone, I'll give the school a reason to have *me* sent home."

Brian nervously swallowed.

"Wait, are you guys talking about Jake Barney?" At the bottom of the stairs, Nat Castelli looked up at them. She was nice enough, but kind of known for being someone who liked to talk about people and spread rumors. Still, if anyone would've heard what was going on with Jake, it would've been her. She constantly had her phone at the ready and even had friends in high school who gave her more information.

Plus, her dad was a reporter, so it sort of ran in the family.

"Yeah," Kirk (probably Kirk) answered. "Did you hear something?"

"Oh yeah," Nat answered with bright eyes. "And it's *messy*." She practically raced up the stairs to join them.

Ollie didn't really care enough to get into a whole conversation about it, but he had to wait for Mia anyway, and he didn't feel like finding a new spot, so he kept quiet and just listened.

"I have a friend who lives on the same street as Jake, and his house was on fire. Like legit, *on fire*, serious damage. And get this? His mom was arrested for it. Everyone's saying she tried to burn the whole place down on purpose because she found out that Jake's dad was dating another woman."

Kirk and Brian both had wide eyes. "Seriously?"

"Yeah," Nat said. "And it gets worse, because the woman was totally Jake's *aunt*. So, like, his mom's own sister."

Ollie snorted.

Kirk turned to him. "Do you think that's funny? What's your problem?"

"Come on, there's no way that's true." Ollie crossed his arms. "That sounds like some bad soap opera my mom would watch."

Nat shook her head. "It's real."

"Real or real like reality TV real?"

"Reality TV isn't real?" Brian asked.

Nat ignored him. "I'll prove it." She typed on her phone before showing them all a picture of the aftermath of Jake's house. It was still standing, but the outer parts of it were burnt and charred. Ash covered the grass in front. "And look, this is Jake's mom and dad." She swiped to a picture of the Barney family. "This is Jake's dad, but does that look like his mom?" There was another photo, but this time it had Jake's dad walking hand in hand with a woman who definitely wasn't Jake's mom.

Had all that seriously happened?

Kirk's face got even whiter. "And that's his aunt?"

Nat solemnly nodded. "Isn't it horrible? I feel so bad."

"It's awful."

"Right, like, I can't even imagine." Nat frowned. "That's so rough for Jake."

Ollie kept quiet. Sure, the situation was a little wild, and he wasn't necessarily happy about it, but he didn't feel *bad*. Why should he? Jake would probably laugh if something bad like that happened to Ollie. It was like Lauren said earlier, he was getting what was coming to him.

"We should do something for him," Brian said. "Like a card or whatever, or some money. His parents must be getting divorced now."

"I can totally organize it," Nat agreed. "Parents getting divorced must suck."

Ollie was getting annoyed. Jake was always terrible, but one bad thing happened to the kid and he was supposed to forget everything and write him a card? People's parents got divorced all the time. If anything, Ollie wished his parents would get divorced. It seemed like a better option.

Thankfully, Mia's car turned the corner at that moment.

"So tragic," Ollie said quickly. "I got to go, that's my sister." It was a struggle to make it sound like he cared even the slightest. "But, yeah, that card thing sounds great. You should do that."

He didn't pay attention to any of their reactions, already heading toward the car.

"How was school?" Mia asked.

Ollie shrugged. While he didn't really want to get into all the Jake drama with Mia, there was no way she wouldn't hear about it at school or in the news. "Apparently Jake Barney's house burned down."

"*What?*" Mia's eyes widened. "That's terrible."

"Yeah, I mean, the situation is terrible," Ollie admitted. "But, also, it's Jake."

"Ollie . . ."

He sighed at his sister's tone of voice. Sometimes, Mia was too nice for her own good.

"Come on. You can't expect me to cry over this. You know what he did to me. How he acts." Ollie glanced out the passenger window. "Why do I have to feel bad? It's not like he cared about me when he started being a total jerk once he found out I'm a guy."

"I feel you," Mia finally answered. "We don't need to talk about him. Maybe tonight we can watch that scary movie?"

Ollie actually smiled, one he didn't have to uncomfortably fake. "Sounds good."

Mia might not want to watch *The Host* for the twentieth time (even though they've probably watched her favorite movie, *Spirited Away*, approximately two hundred times), but Ollie had a whole list of movies they still had to watch together, so they could easily pick from there. At the top of the list was *The Thing*, after he saw a horror influencer he followed talk about how it was basically required watching, even if it was as old as Ollie's parents.

The drive home went by quickly, both of them ready to see Wishbone. Mia turned onto their street, and Ollie already felt ten times better. The U-Haul truck was no longer in front of their neighbor's house, but there was a yard sign that said, SUPPORT HILLSIDE HIGH GIRLS' SOCCER.

"Do you know who moved in next door?" Ollie asked.

"I don't know her super well, but I know it was Tiffany Choi."

Ollie's jaw dropped. "As in Noah Choi's older sister?"

"Yeah, I think so. Are you friends with him?"

Ollie made a face. Mia knew he didn't have friends like that. But Noah Choi's family moved next door? Ollie wasn't sure how to feel about that. Their house, along with all the homes to the right, looked nice.

The apartment the Di Costas lived in was a totally different story.

What if Noah thought less of Ollie because of where he lived?

Ollie's stomach sunk before he immediately caught himself. What did it matter what Noah thought of him? It's not like he was actually his boyfriend like Jake teased. Ollie felt his face heating at the thought.

Mia swore from next to him.

"What . . . ?" Ollie didn't even have to finish the question because he followed her gaze to where their dad's car was in the parking lot. He was home. Which meant either he and Ollie's mom made up (aka, went back to more-or-less coexisting and barely talking to each other) or the apartment would be tense and awkward and horrible. "Well," Ollie said. "There's always the beach."

Mia winced. "Is there? I'm not really in the mood to be sucked into that Backward Place. I don't think I'd do well in that situation."

A fair point. While it almost felt like a dream, Ollie wasn't particularly in the mood to risk it either. Bracing themselves for the worst, the two went into the house. Mom and Dad were both there, dressed up, and smiling and laughing as they stood at the counter.

Ollie and Mia shared a look. He could almost read her thoughts based on her expression alone, because he was pretty sure he had the same one.

What was going on?

Their mom giggled and kissed their dad. It was like they

didn't even notice them. Ollie couldn't stop his horrified expression. His parents had *never* kissed in front of him. He was pretty sure they didn't touch each other at all.

"Um . . . hi?" Mia said.

Both their parents jumped apart, still staying relatively close to each other as they turned toward Ollie and Mia at the front door.

"Hi, sweetie," their dad said, all smiles. "And hey, handsome. How was school?"

"Fine?" Ollie wasn't sure how to answer. He wasn't sure about anything anymore. Had they somehow stumbled into a different dimension? He had to check his phone to make sure time was ticking in the right direction, because his parents' behavior made it seem like they were in The Backward Place.

"Good," their mom answered. "We were just waiting for you to get home before we head out. There's money on the counter if you want to get delivery for dinner."

Mia looked about as weirded out as Ollie felt, her eyebrows furrowed and lips drawn slightly back. "Okay . . . I mean . . . Where are you going?"

Their parents shared a smile, reaching out to hold hands.

"It's Friday, so date night," Ollie's dad said.

Ollie and Mia's disbelief sounded at the same time. "Date night?!"

That wasn't a Friday thing for his parents. That wasn't an *any day ever* thing for his parents.

"Call if you need anything or there's an emergency." Mom

picked up her purse from the counter. "But do something fun. Watch a scary movie once you get your food. I know you two love those."

Did she . . . ? Usually their parents didn't pay much attention to what Ollie or Mia liked.

"Okay?" Mia's voice also still came out like a question.

Their parents gave them both quick kisses before rushing out of the apartment like lovestruck teenagers. There was a long pause as Mia's and Ollie's brains struggled to work properly.

"Did I die?" Mia asked finally. "Are we dead?"

"It's not April first," Ollie muttered.

Mia looked around the room. "I don't see any cameras . . ."

Neither of them had a reasonable explanation, so they just looked at each other in shock and confusion until Ollie said, "What was that? I mean . . . how? When?"

"I have no idea," Mia answered. "I kind of feel like we should just pretend that didn't happen, because I'm confused. And I'm just gonna say hi to Wishbone if that's cool."

Ollie nodded. He didn't know what else to say, and he could honestly use some Wishbone time, too. The two raced into Ollie's room, where Wishbone was trying to shake off the wrapping on his paw. Seeing Mia and Ollie, he leapt off the bed and rushed to them with a little meow.

"Oh my god, I love him so much," Mia gushed.

They both gave him lots of pets, and Wishbone happily soaked up the attention. He only tried to lightly bite them twice, which seemed like an improvement.

"He's such a good boy," Ollie said, scratching Wishbone under the chin. "When he's not Mr. Bitey Pants."

"I know," Mia agreed. "I just wish we had a better toy for him." She gestured to the three bargain-bin toys on the floor they did get.

Wishbone's eyes flashed blue. Ollie frowned, thinking of the last time he saw them do it. Last night he thought it must have been a flash of light from outside, but now it was still sunny out, the room evenly lit and bright. Was he imagining things?

A loud knock slammed against the front door, causing them all to jump.

"Are you expecting someone?" Ollie asked.

"Since when would I invite anyone *here*?" Mia snapped. She bit her lip. "I'll answer it."

Mia got up and slowly walked to the front door. Sensing a bit of her nerves, Ollie followed close behind. But when Mia threw open the door fast enough that she couldn't change her mind, there wasn't anyone there.

Only a small box with a blue paw-print logo on the top of it.

9

A Magic Cat Owner's Guide to Successful Wishmaking

MIA STARED AT THE box in shock, almost like she was too afraid to open it. Ollie immediately grabbed it, shut the door, and tore into the cardboard. It was one of those cat toys that had multiple layers, each of which contained a ball that could roll around without escaping. The top of it was a cardboard scratcher.

"This must have been delivered here by mistake," Mia tried to reason. She took the empty box from Ollie and started turning it around and around. "There has to be an address label or something so we can figure out who it belongs to . . ." But there weren't any labels, only the blue paw print.

Ollie blinked. He thought of Wishbone's flashing blue eyes and then Mia's words a short moment before: *I just wish we had a better toy for him.* "Mia. I think Wishbone granted your wish."

Mia laughed, but not like she thought Ollie was being ridiculous. More like she also thought it could be true but was kind of freaked out. "That's not— How could a cat—"

Almost like he could sense the new toy, Wishbone winded around the corner of the hallway, slipping into the living room with them. He looked at the toy with wide eyes, tails eagerly swishing.

"Is this what you wanted?" Ollie put the new toy on the floor, allowing Wishbone to flop onto his side and smack the ball around the bottom level of the toy.

"You can't honestly think Wishbone made that come true," Mia said, finally finishing her thought. "He's just a cat."

"He's a two-tailed cat from a creepy, backward dimension. You believe that, but draw the line at him granting wishes?"

Mia crossed her arms. "It's probably just a coincidence."

Ollie used the tips of his fingers to hit the ball back to Wishbone's side, the cat immediately smacking it. "Are you serious right now?" Ollie asked. "How could this possibly be a coincidence?"

"Maybe Mom and Dad found him and ordered a toy?"

She had to know that was one weak excuse. Ollie couldn't even hide the attitude in his voice. "And it arrived the same day? Even if Mom and Dad would do that, which they wouldn't, why wouldn't they say anything before they left just now?"

His parents. Leaving on date night, something they never did. Getting along, something they *definitely* never did.

"Oh my god." Ollie sprawled out on the floor. Wishbone's uninjured paw was extended, the ball just out of reach, so Ollie tapped it closer. "Last night I made a wish that they wouldn't be able to fight and loved each other. Only Wishbone was there, and his eyes did that flashy thing—did you see it? When you wished for his toy? He grants wishes, Mia!"

"I mean . . ." Mia struggled to come up with anything. They both knew there was no reasonable explanation for what happened.

"Face the facts," Ollie said. "My son is magic."

"Your son?" Mia asked. "Then what is he to me?"

"Your nephew, obviously." Ollie casually hit the ball again. "Seriously, use your brain. Plus, I think the more important detail is that he is literally magic."

Talking about magic sparked something else in Ollie's memory. *The note.* The one he found on Wishbone's ear tag. Where had he put it?

"One sec!" Ollie raced into his room and tore through his hamper to find the pants he wore to the beach. After going through the pocket, he pulled out the note on the tag. He headed back into the living room and practically shoved the paper into Mia's hands. "I found this with Wishbone. I didn't think too much of it at the time because, you know, I was running for my life, but this confirms that he's magic."

Mia frowned. "What's this part about curses, though?"

"Who cares?" Ollie asked. "That's hardly important."

"I don't know, it seems a little important."

"It says he's responsive *against* curses, so it probably just means he's like a good luck charm," Ollie reasoned. "Because he is a magical wish-granting cat, Mia!"

Mia rubbed her eyes behind her glasses. "Okay, I mean.

Okay? But we need to test it to be sure. We should wish for something super specific. To prove that it is no coincidence."

Ollie thought she was being a little extra, but he shrugged. "Go for it."

"Okay, um . . . I wish I had a cat tree that's pink, blue, and purple."

They both watched closely as Wishbone stretched out on the floor, eyes flashing. "See! He did it!"

Mia didn't look convinced just yet, but she threw a smile toward Ollie. "I'll believe it when the bisexual pride-colored cat tree materializes."

"Rude, why not trans pride colors?"

"I'm not trans."

"Well, I'm not bisexual."

"Well, it's not for you, it's for Wishbone. He could be bisexual."

Ollie studied the cat. Wishbone moved onto his back, looking incredibly cute, so Ollie forgot everything and pet his belly. "You're such a good boy," Ollie said. "A good, handsome, wonderful, sassy, potentially-bisexual-but-definitely-magic boy."

Another knock sounded on the door, causing Mia and Ollie to jump. Ollie whooped, leaping from the floor and throwing open the door with confidence, knowing a large box would be on the other side.

Only it wasn't a box. It was Noah Choi.

Ollie felt his face heat immediately.

"Um . . . hi, Ollie," Noah said, shifting on his feet. "Sorry, I didn't know this was your apartment. We just moved in next door, and we can't find a package of ours. It looks like it might have been delivered to this building, so my mom sent me over to check with everyone."

"Everyone?" Ollie asked. "If you can avoid it, don't go to Mr. Wright's place next door."

"Why's that?" Noah asked.

"He's super mean. But not like stealing-a-package mean. Just a grouchy old man who, like, gets mad at people smiling and believes having fun is a crime."

Noah snorted. "Thanks for the heads-up. But you didn't accidentally get a box?"

Ollie cringed. The package with the paw print. Had that been something the Chois ordered for their pet? Was Mia right and it all was just coincidence?

"Was it a cat toy?" Ollie asked.

Noah tilted his head. "No? We don't have a cat. Dad's allergic. Is that your cat? He's so cute!"

"What cat?" Ollie immediately said, before realizing that Mia and Wishbone were in full view behind him. "I mean, yes. Wishbone. He's my cat, yeah."

Ollie wanted to smack himself in the face. Why was he suddenly awkward? Maybe it was because of what Jake said the other day. Ollie didn't want to make Noah uncomfortable again, but Noah didn't seem bothered. He was talking to Ollie just fine. Ollie needed to cool it.

"I love cats." Noah's face broke out into a bright smile. "Can I pet him?"

It was that exact moment when a large delivery box appeared right behind Noah. Completely out of thin air, with no delivery person in sight. It had the same bright blue paw print as the box before.

Ollie internally cursed the timing.

"Um . . . we're kinda busy right now, but do you want to come over tomorrow?" Ollie blurted. He had to restrain himself from facepalming right then and there. His cheeks flamed, as he waited for the sting of whatever polite excuse to say no Noah came up with.

"Sure, I'm free all day."

Wait, what?

"I have to go back to help my mom make kimchi today, so tomorrow works better anyway."

Ollie's mind was still struggling to accept that Noah actually agreed to hang out. "Oh, I love kimchi."

"Really?" Noah's expression changed when he looked past Ollie again. "Hey, does your cat have two tails?"

"I gotta go. See you tomorrow!"

Ollie hoped his pained smile was enough for Noah to realize it wasn't a good time. He seemed to get it, turning away only to almost walk right into the box. "When did this get here?"

Mia stepped around Wishbone and rushed over to grab it. "These delivery drivers are so skilled," she said quickly. "Nice to meet you . . ."

"Noah."

"Noah, I'm Mia. 'Bye!"

She shoved Ollie and the large box inside by pushing with

her legs and gave one last friendly wave before closing the door on Noah. Ollie didn't really know how he would explain the whole two-tail thing to Noah when he came over, but that was a Tomorrow Ollie problem. Today Ollie didn't want to kill his mood. He tore open the package, Wishbone attacking and biting off little pieces of cardboard that he spit all over the floor.

They revealed a cat tree with three levels: one blue, one purple, and one pink. There were plenty of scratching posts and perches, and Wishbone joined Ollie and Mia looking at the object in wonder. He was the first to spring to action, climbing up the cat tree until he sat at the highest post.

"We have a magic cat," Mia said softly.

"I told you!" Ollie pumped his fist in the air before kissing Wishbone's nose. "Not just handsome, he's a wizard." Ollie turned around toward Mia. "What else should we wish for?"

"Wait, what if he has, like, a limited number of wishes?" Mia asked.

"I feel like there would've been some warning. And if he did, we already used three, so might as well test it with a fourth."

Before Mia could respond, Ollie's phone buzzed in his pocket. A call? Nobody *called* him. He checked the screen. *Lauren?*

Honestly, Ollie found that weirder than his cat being magic.

"Hello?" he answered. "Are you dying?"

"What? No. I mean kinda. I think you accidentally took my folder in English, and I have all my homework in there. Is there any chance I can stop by your house to get it? I need to get it done tonight. I have a bunch of annoying family stuff all weekend."

Ollie walked into the other room to check his backpack. Sure enough, the folder was there. As much as he just wanted to stay home with Wishbone, the last thing he needed was someone else coming over and seeing the cat and his two tails, so Ollie came up with another solution. "I can bring the folder to you instead. My sister can take me. Where do you live?"

"Oh, um, I'm not at home right now. I'm actually at the bakery I told you about with my mom. Can you just come here?" A small silence passed between them. "I promise I didn't do this on purpose to get you to go to the bakery with me."

"I'm not saying you did," Ollie answered, but if he hadn't been the one to suggest meeting her, he would certainly be thinking it.

"I'll text you the address. Thank you!"

Lauren hung up before he could say anything else or change his mind. Ollie looked at the folder. It literally was labeled *Homework Folder :)*, which was disturbing. Who smiled over homework?

He didn't even know how he hadn't noticed it. Ollie only had one folder he used for every class, since mostly everything was digital anyway. Of course they had to get actual paper assignments the one time this happened.

The wishes would have to wait.

10

A Bakery Experience So Bad, It's Scary

WHILE MARIE'S BAKERY DIDN'T look *bad*, Ollie thought any bakery without a pun name was a missed opportunity. The shop itself was nice, and while it was filled with people, it didn't have a Porto's-long line. Maybe he could convince Mia to buy something before they left. They walked past the glass doors into the pink-and-blue shop that had a floral, Instagram-post corner with a neon-sign, There's Always Room for Dessert!

A part of him considered taking a picture for his Instagram, but this bakery seemed a little too close to home. What if someone was able to put clues together and find out it was Ollie running the account?

Jake would never let him hear the end of it, and the last thing he needed was for all the other guys at school to see his *cute* baking creations. It was one thing when it was done in class and everyone assumed Lauren did most of the work. The idea of mixing his private baking self with his public self made his stomach twist like a pretzel. Sometimes it felt hard enough to fit in with the other guys, since most of them knew him before he cut his hair and dressed in clothes that suited him. Having a hobby that people thought was girly would set him back even more in terms of fitting in and catching up to the rest of them.

Ollie knew hobbies didn't really have a gender and he shouldn't have to prove how masculine he was, but he also knew not everyone thought that way.

And maybe Ollie felt like he did need to prove himself. Not just to Jake, but to everyone else, too.

To even himself, sometimes. It was hard not to feel a little insecure, especially when puberty and his body weren't mixing the way he wanted them to. His binder helped, sure, but it didn't get rid of his feelings about his chest. When he first got his period over the summer, it only made his body feel even less like his own and worsened the insecurities. He knew most boys didn't have to get specific period-friendly boxer briefs off the internet. It shouldn't have mattered to him, but sometimes, he felt like his own organs were betraying him. The last thing he needed was another reason for kids to question his gender.

So no one could know how much baking meant to him. Even if he was a demiboy and there were some average guy things he didn't relate to (like being gross while talking about girls or having the total embarrassing confidence of Kirk saying in health class that tampons were used to stop PMS), he felt like if he wasn't *overly* boyish, people would go back to treating him like he wasn't one.

Ollie couldn't let that happen. Even if he hated it. It was hard to prove how much of a guy he was when he wasn't even totally sure what kind of guy he wanted to be.

"Ollie! Over here!"

Ollie turned to the sound of Lauren's voice, where she sat at a table with her mom. The two of them had a spread of desserts between them, so much that even someone with a sweet tooth like Ollie thought it was a bit much. No way his mom would allow him to buy more than one thing, let alone ten or so.

Mia froze next to him, staring like a deer in headlights. "I'm gonna wait outside."

"What?" Ollie barely got the word out before she exited the store. He tried to spot what she'd been looking at and found it almost immediately. Or, rather, them. Mia's best friend, David, and her crush, Joanie, sitting at a table with the chairs moved to one side, both of their computers open but giving more PDA than Ollie would really care to see.

Like, maybe he wanted a boyfriend one day. Okay, he definitely wanted a boyfriend one day. But if that happened, they wouldn't be all annoying in public like that.

"Ollie, are you okay?" Lauren called.

At that, David and Joanie looked over at him, faces sprouting big smiles.

"Ollie-gator!" David waved, using the unfortunate nickname he'd used ever since Ollie cried five years ago at the Los Angeles Zoo when he was told he wasn't allowed to wrestle the alligators. (His attempts to get in failed, as his mom stopped him, and also the gates were pretty Ollie-proof. Trust him, he tried everything.) "How's it going?"

"Fine," Ollie answered. He liked David enough, but Ollie was always on Mia's side, so he kind of just felt awkward. Even if David didn't know there were sides to be on.

"Is Mia here?" Joanie asked, looking around. "She should join us! We're just working on college application stuff."

David frowned a little at that.

Ollie may have never been in a relationship, or had anything even remotely related to dating experience, but even he knew that you didn't invite people to be a third wheel on dates. She must accidentally ruin their dates a lot based on David's expression. No wonder his sister was confused.

"No, sorry, she's not here," Ollie said, faking disappointment. "I'm just dropping off something for a friend. So, 'bye!" He started backing away.

They might have said something else, but Ollie was already checked out from that uncomfortable situation and stepping over to Lauren's table. He held out the folder to her.

"Sorry about that," Ollie said. "My sister's friends."

"Is she okay?" Lauren asked, taking the folder from him. "She ran out of here pretty fast."

Ollie sighed. "It's a long story."

"So, I'm assuming this is Oliver?" Lauren's mom asked.

Ollie looked at her. She had the same freckles as Lauren did dusting her face. He didn't really see the resemblance past that. She wore a bright pink matching sports top and leggings, but hardly looked like she was exercising with her face full of makeup. She wasn't picking at any of the desserts, and only seemed to take pictures of them. The one thing she did seem to have taken a tiny bite of was an oatmeal raisin cookie.

While Ollie tried not to be too judgmental (sometimes), he could not trust someone who *chose* to eat an oatmeal raisin cookie. It was like the Jake Barney of desserts.

"Yep, that's me," Ollie said.

While everyone called him Ollie, he was okay with keeping Lauren's mom at a bit of a distance.

"I was not expecting you to look like this," Lauren's mom said, voice high and slow and clearly talking down to him. "You're just too pretty to be a boy!"

Ollie clenched his fists.

"Mom," Lauren muttered.

"What?" Her lips pursed. "Oh, because he's trans? I didn't mean it like that, Lauren, calm down. Oliver gets what I mean, right?"

Ollie put on his best smile. "Yes, I totally get it." Lauren's mom smiled back, not expecting Ollie to continue. "I was also surprised since you look too old to be a mom!" He mimicked the same voice she used, leaving her red-faced and gasping. "See you Monday, Lauren."

Jaw tight, Ollie rushed out of the shop to rejoin his sister. He let his anger flow through him. What a joke. He kind of felt bad for insulting Lauren's mom like that, especially since she could take it out on Lauren. But why didn't she do more to stand up for him?

They were supposed to be close. School friends, at least. Ollie was right. He couldn't trust her. Not when it counted. His eyes threatened to burn with tears. Of course, Lauren was probably mad at him for talking back to her mom. But how was that fair? Why did it feel like adults were always allowed to be angry and mean and Ollie wasn't?

Ollie forced down those thoughts and tried to think about how good it initially felt to see the shock on Lauren's mom's face. Served her right. Sometimes he needed to stay focused on the angry parts of him, because then he wouldn't be able to even think of the part of himself that was hurt.

When Mia and Ollie arrived home, things only got worse as they opened the door to see their parents looking at the massive, bisexual cat tree in the middle of the living room. Mia and Ollie looked at each other with wide eyes. At least they had moved Wishbone back into Ollie's room before they left.

Still, this was bad.

"What are you doing home so soon?" Mia squeaked.

Ollie tensed his arms without thinking, braced for an argument between his parents that likely ended their night early. Except it didn't come. They stayed close together, all smiles.

It would probably take some time to get used to that.

"We stopped in so I could grab a jacket. It got cold." Their mom pointed at the cat tree, turning to them. "What is this?"

"Oh, um, I made it," Mia said quickly. "For a fundraiser at school. For QSA."

Their dad looked a bit confused. "The Queer Student Alliance works with . . . cats?"

"Queer cats." Mia slightly winced at her own answer. "They have, like, fifty percent less chance of being adopted."

"Really?" their mom asked.

Mia's voice was high. "Sure."

Their parents shrugged, still too happy in their little bubble to really question it. Their mom patted Mia on the shoulder. "That's great, honey," she said. "Although I do wonder if it would be better to raise money for queer humans."

Mia gave a tight smile. "Hah, should've thought of that."

Ollie made a mental note to speak before Mia if something like this came up again. His sister was terrible under pressure. They were lucky their parents believed her.

"Well," Ollie's dad started, "we're going to head back out, but make sure you two order dinner. We have a lot to celebrate. Like our beautiful family, this home over our heads, and . . . bisexual cats."

"Okay, have fun, see you later," Ollie said, practically pushing his parents back out the door. Once it closed behind them, Wishbone meowed from the other room. Both Ollie and Mia ran to him.

"Are you all right?" Mia asked, checking over the cat. "How's your paw?"

Ollie was already grabbing a small can of food. "He's probably hungry."

Wishbone jumped over to his bowl. Once he started

chomping away and the two siblings had a chance to calm down, Mia looked at Ollie. "I didn't want to press you, but did something happen at the bakery earlier? You seemed upset."

Ollie swallowed. "It was nothing. But what about you?" Ollie knew it wasn't fair to deflect back to Mia, but he didn't want to talk about what happened. "I don't want to be mean, but . . . why do you like Joanie so much anyway? She seems kind of clueless."

"Oh, she can be," Mia agreed with a short laugh. Her expression lightened. "But, other times, she's the most thoughtful person ever. You know I'm not always the most loud and outgoing person in the world . . ."

Sometimes Ollie forgot that Mia was shy when she was with other people. She was talkative with him, but they were close, so it made sense. Around other people, especially ones she didn't know, Mia was like a totally different person.

"Joanie would always make sure I was included. With her, it sort of feels like I don't have to be this reserved, quiet person. Always just like watching from a distance, like I'm watching a movie. She makes me part of the scene, part of the story. And . . . it's nice to feel that way." Mia gave a small smile. "Even if sometimes she tries to include me a little too much."

Ollie made a face. "Yeah, I got that from earlier." He reached up to put an arm around Mia's shoulder. "I don't think it's bad to be a little on the sidelines. You're really good at observing and finding the best way to respond. It's way better than me, who speaks before thinking usually." Mia snorted. "But, if you want some real main character energy, I think we should test that fourth wish on our magic cat. Wish for something nice for yourself."

Mia looked hesitant. "I don't know. Does he need a break?"

Ollie gestured to Wishbone, who was licking his lips before returning to his bowl. "It doesn't seem to affect him at all, and I'm pretty sure nothing would bother him when he has food."

Mia adjusted her glasses and nodded. "Okay . . . but what if there is only one more wish or something? I don't want to use it up on just me."

Ollie mashed his lips together to think. Neither of them really got to make a wish for themselves yet. Ollie's first wish benefitted both of them, and the next two were mostly for Wishbone.

"What if we wish at the same time?"

That way, whatever happened, it was fair.

"Okay . . . count of three?"

Ollie shrugged. "Sure. One . . ."

"Two . . ."

"Three!"

"I wish we had a lot of money," Mia said at the same time Ollie said, "I wish I could look like how I think of myself looking."

Both of Wishbone's eyes flashed blue. Ollie and Mia waited, the air thick with tension.

They waited longer. Nothing happened.

Wishbone continued to noisily eat.

"Was my wish too confusing?" Ollie asked. "I messed it up, didn't I?"

"Maybe? Mine was pretty clear, though," Mia said. "Maybe the money is already in the bank?"

She logged into the account on her phone to check her bank balance, but based on her expression, it didn't seem to have any higher of an amount than before.

"It could just take a little longer sometimes," she said.

Neither of them wanted to think that they'd used up their wishes already.

Ollie bit his lip. That seemed reasonable. "Maybe Wishbone is tired like you said. It's probably tough being magic *and* the cutest cat ever." Ollie sat at the edge of his bed, and Wishbone hopped up next to him, tails happily in the air. Ollie laughed, petting Wishbone's head. "We'll just chill for tonight and try again tomorrow. Are you down for takeout and a scary movie?"

Mia grinned. "I think that's exactly what we need right now."

She ordered the food, and Ollie put on *Nope*. He had a soft spot for sci-fi horror, and aside from *Alien*, the Jordan Peele movie was his absolute favorite. Wishbone was on the bed, and Mia and Ollie sat on the floor in front of the mattress. It was cozy, nice. Ollie immediately was entranced by the movie, even though he'd already seen it. They reached a tense nighttime scene at the stables.

"Just don't jump too hard and scare Wishbone," Ollie teased.

Mia rolled her eyes. "I'm not *that* bad."

Almost immediately, the jump scare got her and she moved so much Wishbone got startled, meowing and trying to scratch her.

"I called it!"

Even Mia laughed. "It's not my fault, it's just how good the editing is! And the score! And the script." She looked almost wistful, the moving colors playing across her face as the frames of the movie changed. "Imagine being able to work on something as good as this. Piecing together the footage and shaping the film. That's why editing is so cool. Sure, you are working with what was shot and the director's vision, of course, but it is also storytelling in itself. Another perspective to come together for the final movie. How cool is that?"

Mia was different when she was talking about movies. It was like there was no shyness or uncertainty in her at all.

"It is cool, and you'll be doing it."

Her expression dropped. "Right. Yeah."

The doorbell rang at that moment. Ollie paused the movie, and Mia went to grab the food. While they didn't talk more about her dream to edit films, they did get back into the easy conversation of the movie. They were only interrupted when Wishbone stole a piece of sushi by plucking it with his claw and running around the apartment to prevent the siblings from getting it back. All the bad things—Jake and his family and Lauren and her mom and Mia's discomfort with her friends— none of them mattered in that moment.

The night may not have been magic, not exactly, but it was really, really close.

11

The New(ish) and Improved Ollie Di Costa

WHEN OLLIE WOKE UP the next morning, Wishbone was curled up between his legs, one tail tucked under him and the other draped on Ollie's thigh. The cat let out a little sigh, and Ollie made sure to be as still as possible as he reached over to unlock his phone so he didn't disturb him. His leg was stiff from being in the same position, but Ollie didn't move it. He wasn't always the best person, but he wasn't a *monster*.

Ollie focused his eyes on the screen, the time stamped over a picture he took of Manhattan Beach so he'd always have a little piece of the ocean with him.

Eleven thirty-four.

Oh no. Oh, fudge brownies, he was in trouble. How could he have slept in so late? Why didn't anyone wake him up?

Ollie's internal panic calmed when he remembered it was Saturday. Sure, it was a little out of character for him to sleep in quite so late, but it wasn't like he'd missed anything. What was more shocking was the fact that Wishbone hadn't woken him up demanding breakfast.

As if on cue, the cat stretched, sticking out his tongue as his legs extended. It looked like the dressing on his injured paw had been changed. Maybe Mia had come in earlier to feed Wishbone and fix his bandage with the instructions the vet gave. One less thing for him to worry about.

Ollie also stretched, moving his arms above his chest when he realized his chest felt different. He looked down.

"What the . . . ?"

Ollie hadn't been *big* by any stretch of the word, but there had been enough of a bump that he preferred to wear a binder or, at least, a very tight sports bra in case of emergency.

But now, there wasn't anything. His pajama shirt lay flat, exactly the way he wanted it to. He put his hands on his chest, almost in disbelief, and while it was different than what he was used to, it was a kind of different that felt natural. The way it should have been all along.

Ollie was so excited he risked divine feline punishment by moving his cat. Wishbone hissed, and Ollie narrowly avoided the cat's claws.

"Sorry, Wishbone." He jumped out of bed. "You can scratch me later."

Wishbone tried to bite his bandaged paw. Ollie gently stopped him before finally going to face the mirror.

"Whoa."

It was all he could say.

On one hand, he looked the same. He was still obviously himself. If anything, he was even more *him*—at least, that was how Ollie felt looking in the mirror. Aside from a bit more hair on his arms and legs, he also lost some of the baby fat in his cheeks. He even seemed a few inches taller. Enough that he probably had height over Mia now.

Enough that he'd be able to easily reach the top shelf to store more baking supplies.

Clearly, his wish was *practical.*

"Wishbone, are you seeing this?" Ollie asked. His voice came out a little higher in the excitement, and he probably should've included how he *sounded* in his wish, but it was hard to really worry about that when his reflection matched exactly how he felt.

He brushed back his hair to see more of his face, and his smile was bigger than he remembered it being in a while.

Ollie flopped back onto his bed to look at Wishbone. "You actually did it," he said. "You're *magic*, magic."

It was one thing to just conjure up a new item, but this was a dream come true, and Wishbone did it with no problem.

Wishbone licked his face, his barbed cat tongue scratchy against Ollie's skin. But Ollie laughed. He couldn't stop laughing. He laughed until tears formed in the corners of his eyes, and then the laughing *kind of* became more like crying, which Ollie would never admit. Like the wind by the ocean, it was another secret swallowed.

"Thank you, thank you, thank you," Ollie muttered to the

purring cat as he laughed (cried) right next to him. "You're the best cat ever."

Ollie wiped at his face to pull himself together and gave Wishbone a kiss on the head before exiting the room. He headed straight toward Mia's room and knocked loudly on her door. With no immediate answer, he kept knocking. "Mia, get your butt up!"

No such luck. Instead, his mom peeked her head into the hallway. "Good morning, sleepyhead. You slept in late! You're not sick, are you?"

"Just tired." Ollie gulped. Was his mom going to notice the difference? How would he explain it to her?

"Aw, my sweet boy." She walked up to Ollie and put a hand on his forehead, checking his temperature, then tapped his shoulder a few times. "You'll be fine."

She started to turn around, but Ollie's voice stopped her.

"You don't notice anything different?"

Ollie's mom looked at him. She bit her lip, and wrinkles formed around her eyes as she pursed her lips in thought. "Did you . . . style your hair differently?"

"Seriously?" Ollie asked. "I just woke up. I have bedhead."

His mom shrugged. "You look very handsome, honey, I don't know what you want me to say. Let me know if you are hungry, I can whip up something for breakfast." She put on a teasing smile. "Or brunch, now, I guess."

She disappeared back around the corner. If his mom didn't notice a difference, did that mean no one would? Was the change only for Ollie?

"Mia," Ollie called again after some pounding. "Miiiiiiiaaaaaaa."

"Oh my god, you're so annoying, can't I even have two minutes to po . . ." Her budding rant faded as she opened the door and took in Ollie. She had to look *up* to meet his eyes. Her face broke into an open-mouthed smile. She let out a swear word before exclaiming, "Ollie! You look amazing!"

"Right?!"

Mia pulled him into her room, closing the door so their parents wouldn't overhear. She had her headphones and laptop strewn across her bed but was already dressed in jeans and a T-shirt unlike Ollie's outgrown pajamas.

"It worked," Ollie said. "Wishbone did it."

Mia's smile was wild in what had to be a strange mix of excitement and bewilderment. Ollie could tell because he pretty much felt the same.

"Okay," Mia said. "Okay, this is awesome. The wishes probably just take a different amount of time depending on what they are."

"Did you get your money?" Ollie asked.

Mia checked her phone again. "Not yet, but it's gotta happen soon, right? How is Wishbone? I can't even be mad that he bit me this morning when I changed his bandage."

Mia held up her hand, which had a few red marks where kitty teeth broke the skin. Oh, Wishbone.

"Other than being upset I moved him off me, he's great. Still in my bed."

"I feel bad he can't come out and hang with us." Mia winced.

"I know he doesn't seem to mind, but what if Mom and Dad find him?"

Ollie snorted. "Mom and Dad seem a little oblivious to everything, especially now."

"Still," Mia pressed.

Ollie knew she was right. He didn't want Wishbone to have to hide away in his room. He wanted to let him explore, to not be stuck in one room. So, they had to tell their parents.

After they figured out how well date night went, maybe.

"Let's just enjoy it for now," he said. "We can worry when something worrying happens."

Just then, something worrying did happen. Or, at the very least, something rather strange. Right outside Mia's window was a dark gray wisp of smoke.

"What the . . . ?" Ollie started.

He didn't wait for an answer before stepping over to the window. He watched as the fog swirled around the air outside, changing shape but never changing much in size, only about as large as a sheet of paper.

Mia moved closer to watch it with him. "What is it?"

"I don't know."

Mia opened the window, as if removing the glass barrier would reveal something about the fog they couldn't already see. It was strange, for sure, but there was something beautiful about the way it moved, dancing in the breeze.

"There's not, like, a fire or anything, is there?" Ollie asked.

Mia shook her head. "Even if there was, that's not wildfire smoke."

She was right. This bit of smoke *was* different. Alive, somehow. Ollie put his fingers against the screen, inviting the smoke to come closer.

"What are you kids doing?" A yell startled the smoke away.

Ollie was disappointed enough, but looking at the face of their neighbor, Mr. Wright, made it even worse. He was normally grumpy, unpleasant, and rude—to Ollie especially—but he looked particularly terrible then. It was like he had aged ten years since Ollie saw him a few days ago. His white hair was mostly lost, only strings left hanging, and the roots looked dull and yellow. His face sagged, like even his own skin wanted to get away from him.

"Hello?" Mr. Wright pressed, looking up from the small alley between their building and the 7-Eleven. "Quit spying on me!"

Ollie made a face like he just bit into a lemon. If anything, Mr. Wright seemed like the one spying since he weirdly took his walks around the building. "I can't imagine anything I'd like to do less than *intentionally* look at your face, Mr. Wright." He crossed his arms, raising his voice slightly. "If anything, your shirt should have a content warning!"

Mr. Wright grumbled something, face turning red as he walked off toward the other side of the apartment complex.

Mia couldn't hide a small smile as she rolled her eyes. "You're going to get us in trouble."

"We're not going to get in trouble."

A knock barely sounded on Mia's door before it was thrown open. Their mom stood in the frame, hand still on the handle, looking at them with a sad expression.

"We need to talk," she said.

Ollie and Mia shared a look before swallowing.

It might not have been because of Mr. Wright, but they were *definitely* in trouble.

12

The Queer Kids Win in This One

OLLIE ALMOST FELT LIKE he accidentally wandered into The Backward Place. A family meeting in the kitchen/living room was more unsettling than birds flying in the wrong direction.

Maybe this kind of thing wasn't weird for other families, but the Di Costas had never been a family meeting kind of bunch. If anything, they were a sometimes-avoid-having-parents-meet-during-the-day-at-all-costs kind of family.

Mia and Ollie sat on the couch as their mom and dad took chairs from the kitchen table to sit in front of them. They had matching expressions of concerned-but-smiling, which made the whole situation stranger.

He had been convinced his parents found Wishbone and got mad they were hiding him. But that didn't make sense. The door to Ollie's room was still shut, and besides, there was no way his mom would hold a *meeting* to scold him about hiding a pet cat. She would present the evidence, yell at him, take away his phone, maybe grab whatever not-really-harmful object was in closest reach, and throw it.

She would not calmly and carefully fold her hands like she was doing now. "Kids, we have some bad news," she said.

Her voice was measured so it sounded like an elementary teacher. Were his parents possessed? Although in the movies he'd seen, possession usually didn't cause people to be nicer. It was more vomiting uncontrollably, being mean and distant, getting really upset at the sign of crosses . . .

"You know who's great?" Ollie said, needing to test his theory. "Jesus Christ."

Neither of his parents seemed to have a reaction other than slight confusion. Even Mia asked a verbal "what?" It hadn't hurt to check, but since the power of Christ was not compelling them, possession was probably off the table. Ollie wasn't Christian, but he studied *The Exorcist* enough to know about Christian demons.

Unfortunately, he hadn't gotten as much exposure to other demons, so maybe possession wasn't *entirely* impossible.

"Never mind," Ollie continued. "Proceed."

Their parents shared a pained look before their dad spoke. "It's your great-aunt Margaret," he said slowly. "She passed."

"Passed as what?" Ollie asked. "A decent person?"

His dad frowned as he looked for better words.

"She's dead, Ollie," Mom said.

"Oh," Ollie said. "And?"

Their mom frowned and put her hands on her hips. "Now, Ollie Cat, that's not an appropriate response to someone dying."

Ollie crossed his arms. "Who cares? She was the worst."

Sure, Jake Barney was the worst, but Great-Aunt Margaret somehow managed to be equally the worst. Like how every person thinks their cat is the cutest cat ever and each one of them is right (although Wishbone was legit the cutest cat ever. And magic. So.). Great-Aunt Margaret refused to even talk to Ollie after he came out as trans and sent Mia articles about how bisexuality was a phase and she could "choose" to be straight. Great-Aunt Margaret wasn't even related to them by blood, which would have been a relief if she didn't constantly bring up how good of a person she was for marrying into a poor family.

It wasn't much of a loss, they had to admit that.

"Well, yes," their dad finally said, "but there's more."

Was there more, actual bad news? Ollie could feel Mia tense up next to him.

Their mom took a breath. "In her will, she actually left money to us."

Ollie's jaw nearly hit his lap. "What? No way." He looked between his parents, waiting for some sign of this being a prank. "How much money?"

Even their parents had trouble maintaining their concerned and potentially grieving expressions then. "Five hundred thousand," their dad answered.

Ollie's head spun. That wasn't just money. That was *money*. Like rich-people money. That was *half a million* dollars! They were half-a-millionaires!

"We could buy a house with that!" Ollie exclaimed.

"Well, maybe not a house," their mom quickly said. "Not in Los Angeles, anyway. But this is life-changing."

Ollie and Mia turned to look at each other. They tried to bite back their smiles, but it was no use. Excited squeals burst out of them both as they leapt from the couch and hugged, jumping up and down together. Ollie turned to his parents, waiting for them to join in.

Mom and Dad were smiling, but it didn't seem to reach their eyes. It was strange, like they were pleased by the news, but not much more. It didn't make sense. Wouldn't his mom normally cry and joke about peeing her pants over that kind of money? Sure, Great-Aunt Margaret was dead and they had to act sad about that, but they'd done that already. Why weren't they celebrating like Ollie and Mia?

"This is amazing," Mia said, not seeming to notice. "I can pay for college! I can go now, right?"

She looked so happy Ollie felt his chest lighten. It was like a weight had been lifted off him with all the good news.

"Of course," Mom said. She moved her hand as if to wipe away a tear, and Ollie could swear he saw a little gray mist slip from the corner of her eye, but it was like he blinked and it was gone.

Had he seen that right? He glanced at Mia to see if she noticed, too.

"It's very unexpected," Dad said. "I didn't even know she was sick."

Mia went entirely still. Her face was practically white as paper, like she saw a ghost.

Mia grabbed on to Ollie's arm and pulled him away. "Give us a minute," she said before closing them both into Ollie's room.

"Did you see the smoke thing with Mom?" Ollie asked. "Is that some kind of eye infection?"

"What?" Mia asked.

Ollie blinked. "Is that not why you pulled me away?"

"No. I pulled you away because I'm freaking out!" Mia ran her hands through her hair. "I killed Great-Aunt Margaret."

Ollie reached over to pet Wishbone. "What are you talking about? She lived all the way in Pittsburgh. You couldn't have killed her."

"Think about it." Mia paced around the room. "You wished for Mom and Dad to stop fighting, and then news drops about your bully's dad running off with another woman."

Ollie grimaced. "I'd hardly call him *my* bully. He's just a jerk."

Mia didn't listen, going on with her pacing and her point. "We wished for new stuff, and the Chois had a box that went missing during their move. Remember? You wished to look more like how you want, and suddenly Mr. Wright looks like a corpse. Or, more of one, at least. I wished for money, and now we have an actual corpse in Pennsylvania because *I killed Great-Aunt Margaret with my wish.*"

Admittedly, what she was saying made sense. There did seem to be a clear connection between what they had been wishing for and some of the other things going on. Did Wishbone's magic really cause all those other things? Ollie pressed his lips together.

Mia's eyes were wide, her breathing coming out shallow with panic. "I think that for every wish that comes true, something bad happens to someone else."

A bit of panic rushed through Ollie, but he tried not to focus on it and instead went to help Mia. Ollie could recognize the signs of his sister's anxiety attacks. He gently sat her down on the edge of the bed and put her hand on Wishbone's fur. He reached out to rub her back. "It's okay, you're going to be okay. You're safe, Mia, we're safe." He led her in a slow breath, and she followed, nodding along as she pet Wishbone.

"Right. I'm okay, we're okay."

After a few more breaths, it seemed like the worst of it was over.

"Everything that happened was our fault, Ollie. We can't ignore that." Mia's eyes were still glassy, even if her breathing slowed.

Ollie felt a hollowness in his chest. Was it really their fault?

"I mean, we didn't know . . . ," Ollie started.

"This must be the curse thing that the note mentioned," Mia gasped. "I told you that was important! It literally mentioned curses, and you didn't want to listen!"

Ollie's jaw clenched. Why was Mia blaming *him*? Why was he expected to know everything when a magic cat was involved? One that *he* found. It wasn't fair. There was no way he could have known random bad things would happen. It wasn't like he did it on purpose.

The familiar flame of anger swiped through his stomach,

igniting the empty space where his panic and guilt had been before.

Even if he had known, why should he be responsible for things happening to other people? They weren't even good people! Well, the Chois seemed like good people, but maybe the lost package was something evil? Regardless, one missing item wasn't that bad. As for the other things . . . Ollie had to deal with bullying and mean comments from Jake, Mr. Wright, and even Great-Aunt Margaret for years now. Didn't they basically deserve what happened to them?

Ollie swallowed, trying to keep his voice calm.

"So, maybe the magic has a bit of a side effect. Is it really that bad?"

Mia halted her slow breathing. "Um, *yeah*. It is. We can't just ignore someone dying."

He rolled his eyes. "She was *old*, Mia. Old people die. It happens." He didn't mean to sound quite so harsh and upset Mia, but it was the truth. "I mean, it seems like the bad things are only happening to bad people. Jake Barney? Sucks. Mr. Wright? Sucks. Great-Aunt Margaret? Also sucks." Ollie frowned. "Well, sucked, anyway. But good things happen to bad people all the time. And bad things happen to good people constantly." The two of them knew that better than most. "Isn't it kind of nice that bad people are finally getting some of the bad, too? I think we've had enough of it, and I'm tired."

Ollie could tell that Mia was listening to him. He knew that she was tired, too.

"Maybe it's not fair for us to make these wishes," Ollie continued. "But you know what else isn't fair? That I have to deal with people saying ignorant and plain mean things about my gender all the time and I'm still expected to be polite about it." His eyes threatened to sting, so he blinked, gesturing to Mia instead. "That you have to work all the time and still can't go to the college you want to even though you'll for sure get in. That both of us have to sneak around our own home sometimes. That you're the one taking care of me when our parents should be taking care of both of us. None of that is fair." Despite his best efforts, a few tears fell. Ollie sometimes cried when he was angry, which was almost more annoying than crying when sad, because it just made him angrier. "Look, I've seen all the movies. I know that stopping is the right thing to do. But when do things start going right for *us*?"

Mia just sighed. Ollie sat down next to her and Wishbone.

"It's always been the two of us against the world. Now it's the three of us. Don't think about anything else," Ollie said, physically waving his hands like that could dispel Mia's worries. "Life is always unfair, but us queer kids are gonna win this time."

Wishbone meowed sharply. It almost sounded like a *yeah*.

"See? Even Wishbone agrees. He probably is bisexual."

Mia laughed. She shook her head a little, like she couldn't believe what she was going to say next. "Okay."

Ollie gave his own excited smile, picking up Wishbone and putting him on his lap. "Okay?"

"You're right." Mia took another breath, scratching Wishbone behind the ears. "As long as it's only happening to bad people, it's not like we're doing it directly. It's like the universe righting its wrongs."

Mia was right. It was the universe. And with Wishbone, it seemed like the universe itself was finally on their side.

13

A Guide to Monster Cakes
and Making Friends

THE REST OF THE afternoon was spent trying to keep Wishbone quiet when he had the zoomies (a near impossible task) and almost getting caught when Ollie's mom came to ask him if he wanted to go to the grocery store with her. Ollie loved grocery shopping, as long as the store wasn't ridiculously crowded. Something about the bright colors and the way everything was neatly stocked was satisfying, plus he could admire the bakery. Normally, when they went to the store, it was very in and out, racing to get a cheap dinner or splurge on a rotisserie chicken (if there was a deal). He would all but beg for baking ingredients, and his mom would give a sad "Sorry, kid."

This trip was different. Ollie's mom was the one who browsed the baking aisle, grabbing flour and sugars and spices and even equipment that Ollie was never able to have. "You definitely need piping tips," his mom said, adding them to the already-stocked cart.

"Um . . . yeah," Ollie said. "Thanks."

Even if his mom was possessed from the wish or whatever, he kind of liked it that way.

Ollie looked over the wall of baking supplies. He lifted a silicone spatula with a cat printed on it that looked just like Wishbone. "This is cool."

His mom added it to the cart.

Ollie was already brainstorming all the things he could make later. With the new piping tips, a cake would be fun to decorate. Maybe he could do his nonna's old recipe for cassata cake. His mom's side of the family all lived in Cleveland, so he hadn't seen them since his nonna's funeral (an actual loss, unlike Great-Aunt Margaret), but she left behind a lot of recipes Ollie was able to copy.

"Can I go back and get strawberries?" Ollie asked.

"Sure thing," Ollie's mom said.

Ollie still almost expected her to say no and felt his heart skip at the permission. He weaved through the aisles to get back to the produce section.

"Hey, Ollie! Dude, what's up?"

Ollie twisted around to see Kirk and Brian. He made a face despite himself. Why were they smiling and talking to him as if they were friends?

"What do you want?" Ollie snapped.

"Nothing," Kirk answered. "Just wanted to say hi."

Brian nodded. "My mom's taking forever with shopping, and we got bored, so we came to see when it rains on the fruit, you know?"

Almost like it was on cue, a mist shot over all the produce.

"Dope," Kirk said, nodding in approval. He grabbed a handful of the twist ties used to close bags and started bending them into stick figure people. "By the way, those are really cool shoes."

Ollie had to stop himself from making a mean comeback. Did Kirk just . . . compliment him? He didn't seem sarcastic at all. Ollie tilted his head to the side. "Thanks?"

"Yeah, of course." Brian rocked on his own sneakers. "Hey, man, you know, we're sorry we haven't really defended you before. Jake has been our friend since kindergarten, so, you know, he's our boy, but he can be kind of a jerk. We should've said something, even back when you two first started fighting. Not that it was your fault. I probably would have thrown my lunch on him, too."

Even back when Jake and Ollie were friends, he hadn't been part of the same crowd as Brian and Kirk. They were Jake's *other* friends, not Ollie's, so he kind of understood why they chose Jake over him. It didn't mean they were *good* guys, but Ollie could almost respect how loyal they were.

Almost.

"We're really sorry," Kirk emphasized, finished with one twist tie stick figure and moving on to the next. "You're cool. For real."

Ollie wasn't sure what to say. He usually defaulted to insults with people like Jake and his goonies. He wasn't prepared for **them** to be nice. Especially because it didn't feel forced, like **they** felt they suddenly had to treat Ollie differently. It felt authentic. "Um . . . thank you?" Ollie grabbed two containers of strawberries. "I should get back to my mom, though."

Kirk and Brian both fist-bumped him as a goodbye. Even though neither of them were exactly his favorite people, he kind of felt like one of the guys in a way he didn't before. Mostly everyone at school was cool with him, but the other boys almost acted like they had to be careful around him, or something. Like the fact that he sometimes used the all-gender bathroom if it seemed like the boy's bathroom was full made him just different enough to treat differently. Ollie hated that. Maybe he wasn't *exactly* like other guys, maybe there were parts he didn't really *get*, but he didn't want people to walk on eggshells around him. He wanted to be just a bro, and have the other guys tease him and not care if they farted or burped in front of him and ask him to join them for the weird stuff boys did when they were together, like trying to see who could smack the wall above the stairs the highest and force each other to eat the gross concoctions they made by mixing up the worst of the cafeteria food.

He didn't want to be noticed, not really. He wanted to blend in with the rest of them. He knew there were some differences, that he was a demiboy and sometimes thrived in the space between, but he didn't want to be treated like it.

When people kept noticing him for reasons he didn't want (his transness or queerness), it was better to make them notice him for other things (being funny or, when necessary, willing to fight).

Now that he had a glimpse of being treated like just another guy from school, he felt a flutter in his chest. It was so easy. So nice.

Sure, maybe he couldn't totally feel like a part of the group when he didn't have friends, but it was a start. It was *something*. And regardless of his loneliness or gender feels, Ollie didn't really want *Kirk and Brian* as friends (he wasn't that forgiving).

But, despite that and because of them, he was happy.

He had to hide a smile as he went back to find his mom.

They had barely finished unpacking the groceries when Ollie cleaned his new equipment and got to baking. He basically rushed his mom out of the kitchen (he liked to have the space to himself when he baked) and was so excited to get through the recipe that before he knew it, the cake was cooled, the strawberries were prepped, the frosting was whipped, and everything was ready to assemble. Seeing it all come together was so satisfying.

He took a progress picture to share to his story.

Gonna call this deconstructed strawberry cake and sell it for $30 to fancy LA food influencers 👻

Ollie added a small dollop of frosting on the platter for the cake to stick to before carefully placing the bottom layer.

Then came frosting, strawberries, and a few repetitions of the process. Once it was all together, he used his new offset spatula and scraper tool to frost the crumb coat of the cake.

Then it was the part he was waiting for. The literal icing on the cake. He grabbed the new piping tips his mom bought. Not only was there a large assortment of designs, but he had actual piping bags, too. Not a sad sandwich Ziploc in sight.

He mixed frosting in different colors, various shades of blues and pinks, and piped them all over the cake. It was a swirl of rainbow, bright and eye-catching, textured and almost fuzzy.

Fuzzy. Hmm. Ollie could work with that.

He grabbed two Oreos from the pack Ollie's mom bought for Mia, and piped some white frosting and black frosting in circles to make little eyes. He put those at the top of the cake. Flattening a section of frosting on the front side of the cake and using more of the black, he made a mouth. Ollie cut the leftover strawberries into sharp triangles and arranged them like teeth.

The finished result was a cake, sure, but it also was an adorably grumpy monster.

Ollie could be hard on himself at times, but even he had to admit that it looked awesome.

He took a photo of the final product and posted it to his feed.

My favorite thing to do when I'm angry is eat dessert. This sugary monster might always look grumpy, but he's sweet on the inside. Promise. (He's even got trans pride colors!) #baking #cakedecorating #coolcakes #kidbakers #queerbakers #transbakers

Immediately after posting, he got a few likes. Someone even commented, "omg so cool." There were also two practically instant "promote this on welovebaking" comments from bots, but Ollie deleted those. His urge to watch his notifications roll in was interrupted with a sharp knock on the door.

Normally, Ollie would yell for Mom or Mia to get it, but he was in a good mood and Mom was helping Mia with her financial aid application (even with Great-Aunt Margaret's money, USC was expensive), so he opened the door himself.

To reveal Noah Choi, standing outside with a large jar in his hand.

"Um, Noah, uh, hey," Ollie blurted. "Are you still looking for that package?"

Noah gave a bit of an awkward smile. "I'm here to hang out and see your cat, remember?" He ran a hand through his hair. "We sort of made plans yesterday, but I guess we didn't really say what time. Is now okay?"

With everything that had been going on, Ollie totally forgot about telling Noah to come back the following day. Today. Ugh. Ollie wanted to punch himself for being so obvious about how he forgot and not just welcoming Noah.

"Yeah, totally, sorry."

Ollie stepped aside so Noah could walk in. He held out the

jar to Ollie. "This is kimchi my mom made. I remember you said you liked it, and we had a ton of extra, especially with the new jars we made yesterday, so I thought I'd bring some. For you. Not that it was only because there's a lot, I mean, I wanted you to have it." Noah bit his lip. "Should I just put it in the fridge?"

Noah almost looked more handsome when embarrassed, although the thought made Ollie's face hot. He willed the threatening blush to stay away. He could hardly believe that Noah even remembered that he mentioned he liked kimchi, let alone brought a jar for Ollie to have.

People were normally all talk and empty promises.

Apparently . . . Noah Choi was different.

Ollie's chest felt a little weird, but not necessarily in a bad way. Maybe he was hungry?

"Oh, that's awesome!" Ollie said. "But, yeah, sure."

He was even more grateful for the grocery trip now. Had it been a normal day, Ollie probably would have put the kimchi in the fridge himself to avoid Noah seeing the embarrassing lack of fresh food (and, sometimes, food in general). Now, Noah didn't bat an eye as he placed the jar in the fridge door. But when he turned and saw the counter, his expression totally shifted.

"Whoa! That cake is sick. Where did you get it?"

Ollie felt his face heating. "I, um, I actually made it."

Noah's jaw dropped. "You made it? Like from scratch?"

Ollie nodded. Whenever he imagined telling people about his baking, it seemed embarrassing. But Noah was being so nice. Ollie didn't feel embarrassed—he felt kind of . . . proud. "Yeah,

I really like baking. Especially decorating. I just did this one for fun. I already took pictures, so we can eat some if you want."

"That's so cool," Noah said, leaning in close to the cake to examine it. "You're like an artist. If you ever want to join the drama club, you could probably help with the sets. I bet you'd make some amazing props."

While Ollie knew he would probably always prefer food that could be eaten, the idea of making realistic props kind of sounded fun. It would be something different, maybe a little challenging, that could help him get even better at decorating desserts. And it would be a reason to keep hanging out with Noah.

"Yeah, maybe," was all Ollie said, though. "If it would help."

"It would definitely help." Noah continued to examine the cake. "Like, this is seriously incredible. How'd you come up with the idea to make it a monster?"

Ollie bit his lip. He wasn't sure how to answer that. He just kind of started without a plan and waited for inspiration to strike. He finally shrugged. "Well, I love monster and horror movies, so I generally like making things spooky."

He also liked piping flowers, but that really didn't seem as cool, so he kept that part to himself.

"Seriously?" Noah asked. For a moment Ollie was worried he said too much, but then Noah broke out into a big smile. "I am obsessed with scary movies. It's basically my dream to star in one. Something that's creepy but also emotional, like *Train to Busan*."

"I love *Train to Busan*!" Ollie said right away.

"No way!"

Ollie had already liked Noah—it was hard not to—but he hadn't expected him to be a horror fan. It was cool to have someone to talk to about scary movies who wasn't his big sister. He loved Mia, of course, but she did constantly close her eyes during really creepy parts or fangirl over the editing, which Ollie only kind of got. Plus, it was different when it was someone who wasn't literally forced to spend time with him, even if they did like each other.

And Noah seemed different in a lot of ways. A lot of good ones.

Even the idea of getting dropped off at the theater and sitting right next to him in one of the recliners sparked a little excitement and hope in Ollie's chest. He could even imagine reaching out and taking Noah's hand at a jump scare. Would it be softer than his, which had some burn scars and a few cat bite marks thanks to Wishbone?

"Ollie?" Noah asked. "I asked if you've seen *28 Days Later.*"

Ollie's face heated entirely. What was he *thinking?* If Noah knew, he'd probably be weirded out and the whole thing that happened with Jake in sixth grade would happen all over again. Only worse, because Ollie never liked Jake like that.

Not that he liked Noah like that.

"Yeah," Ollie said quickly. "It's great." He hid his face by turning to grab some small dishes from the cupboard. "It's actually one of my ideas for a baking horror store name. 28 Cakes Later."

"Wait, I'm obsessed with that. What about the Hills Have Pies?" Noah thought for a moment before brightening up. "The Éclair Witch Project!"

As if Ollie didn't already have enough reasons to like Noah Choi.

But not like *that*.

He was pretty sure.

The two kept talking horror movies while Ollie moved around the kitchen. Ollie cut two pieces from the cake, and although Noah visibly cringed, they brought the plates into Ollie's room. Once the door was opened, Wishbone jumped off the bed and rushed toward the two of them.

"Be careful," Ollie warned quickly, "he bites!"

But Wishbone didn't bite. In fact, he rubbed his head against Noah's legs and dropped down onto his back, exposing his belly entirely. Ollie's jaw dropped. Traitor.

"Wow," Ollie said. "He really likes you. He's never like this with anyone."

Sure, Wishbone loved Ollie *now*, but it had taken a lot of hissing and prosciutto. He and Mia still got the occasional attitude when Wishbone didn't get his way, even if he gave cuddles the rest of the time. But he immediately loved Noah. Unfair.

But, Ollie couldn't lie, a little understandable.

Noah quickly set his cake down and let Wishbone sniff and rub against his fingers before petting his belly.

"He's adorable," Noah said with a huge smile. He ran his hand along the length of Wishbone's furry body, stopping when he reached his tails. "That's so wild that he has two. Do you know why?"

Ollie didn't have a prepared answer for that question. Or, really, any answer. So, he told the truth: "Magic."

"Ha ha." Noah playfully rolled his eyes. "Magic or not, it looks awesome."

"Yeah, he's the coolest," Ollie agreed. Although Noah didn't know the half of it.

For a moment, Ollie almost considered telling Noah everything. Or, at the very least, some things. The cool things. Like, Ollie didn't know a lot about making friends, but a literal magic, wish-granting cat seemed like something that couldn't miss. Ollie opened his mouth, the words buzzing over his tongue and excited to enter the air.

But he stopped them, clamping his jaw shut so they slammed against the inside of his lips.

He shouldn't get Noah involved. He liked Noah well enough, sure, but he couldn't exactly trust him yet. What if Noah told other people and someone came to take Wishbone away? Ollie had seen enough movies to know what would happen then. Some bad guy would catnap him and use his magic for their evil agenda. If Wishbone was lucky. If he wasn't, the government would take him away to some secret center in the middle of the desert where they'd do horrific experiments, like what they did to Eleven in *Stranger Things*. And that was only if they didn't cut him open! Ollie felt sick at the thought.

Other people couldn't find out. Ollie didn't even know

where The Backward Man was lurking or looking, but if word got out that Wishbone was magic, it would probably go so viral even The Backward Place would hear about it.

He couldn't trust Noah. He shouldn't.

He had trusted Jake, and then Jake turned on him. He trusted Lauren, and she let her mom get away with being terrible toward Ollie. Sure, that wasn't *entirely* her fault, but she hadn't even texted an apology or anything.

Ollie couldn't trust someone again.

Not even someone as cute as Noah Choi.

Sitting on the floor next to Wishbone, Noah picked up his plate of cake again and took a bite. "This is so good," he said, frosting already staining his mouth a dark blue. "Can I bring a piece to my sister? She's got a bigger sweet tooth than me."

Ollie nodded. "I think there's enough for both of our families." He paused for a moment. "While I could eat half of it myself, I definitely *shouldn't*."

Speaking of, Ollie sent a quick text to his Mom and Mia, still holed up in Mia's room, saying he had a friend over and that they could help themselves to the cake on the counter.

Noah laughed. "I mean, it really is that good. It doesn't just look great, it tastes amazing, too. How did you get so talented?"

Ollie had been called a lot of things in his life: weird, annoying, loud, distracted, temperamental, snarky, disrespectful, confused. He couldn't, however, remember a time that someone called him talented and seemed to mean it.

"A blood sacrifice every full moon," Ollie deadpanned in response to Noah's question.

"You know what, I should try that," Noah responded, also fake serious. "Your demonic altar or mine?"

Ollie scoffed. "It's always Bring Your Own Demonic Altar. You should know this."

Noah laughed. "I wish I would've known you were into horror earlier. It wouldn't have taken me so long to really talk to you then."

"What do you mean?" Ollie asked.

Noah looked away. "I just . . . well, we haven't totally had the chance. It's not like you're intimidating . . . although the way you almost beat up Jake Barney was pretty cool." Noah cleared his throat. "Thanks for standing up for me, by the way."

Ollie was already mid-bite into a forkful of cake. He hoped it hid any embarrassment. "Oh, uh, sure. I mean, you stood up for me first. I should be thanking you."

"I couldn't help it. It was messed up of him to be so loud about . . ." Noah trailed off.

"Me being a demiboy?"

Noah's face reddened. "Yeah."

Ollie shrugged. "It's fine. It's just how I feel. I like the term. It makes sense to me, you know? It's not like it makes me less of a boy or anything like he said." Ollie looked down then, suddenly feeling a little shy. He didn't really open up like that to anyone besides Mia. Ollie liked to keep his emotions close, but being around Noah made it easy to just say whatever was on his mind. "I'm sorry you got dragged into the whole thing. Jake was just making fun of me, I know you're not gay."

Now it was Noah who looked away from Ollie. "I am, though."

"What?" Ollie felt his heart skip a beat.

"Well, I guess I don't really know how I identify or anything," Noah started, eyes locked on the cake and Wishbone. "But, uh, I do like boys. Like that."

"Oh," Ollie said. "Cool. Me too."

Ollie cringed. Why did he say it like that?

"Cool," Noah said softly.

Ollie swallowed another bite, desperate to change the subject. "Do you like any horror video games? I downloaded this short one that's really scary if you want to play."

Noah's smile was wide again. "That sounds awesome."

Ollie grabbed his laptop and sat next to Noah, Wishbone snuggled up between them. He immediately fell asleep, paws and tails occasionally twitching. Ollie and Noah focused on the game, reacting to all the jump scares and accidentally annoying Wishbone. It was great.

Ollie knew he really shouldn't get too close to Noah.

But while they were sitting and playing together, screaming and then laughing, Ollie found himself forgetting all the reasons why.

14

When Everything Is Finally Okay

AFTER A WHILE NOAH had to head home for dinner, but before leaving he exchanged numbers with Ollie. After his own family's dinner, Dad took Mom out for another date and Mia went to stare longingly at college websites or whatever she was doing for applications. So Ollie went back to his room to hang out with Wishbone and continue to text Noah. Despite his best efforts, Ollie found himself smiling every time a notification popped up on his screen. Even though only Wishbone was around to see it, he still dropped the smile immediately.

"It's not like I care *that* much," Ollie said. "Like, we're neighbors now. We're going to be close, literally. That doesn't mean I have a crush on him or something."

Wishbone side-eyed Ollie, almost like the cat didn't believe him.

"I'm serious," Ollie said.

Wishbone jumped down from the bed and went to lick leftovers from his food bowl. Ollie leaned back against his pillow in bed and unlocked his phone.

if you had to be in a horror
movie, which kind would
you want to be in?

Ollie bit his lip, thinking it over.

def not apocalypse horror
i'd be first to die

Noah was a super-fast responder, which was nice. It made Ollie feel less embarrassed for practically never looking away from his screen, waiting for a reply.

really? why?

I couldn't live like that
no running water, no ollie
no wifi, no ollie
i'd just let the zombies take me

omg noooooo that's like
the worst way to go

but if i eat some brains, i might
finally be able to get an A in math

Noah responded with a bunch of skull emojis.

i'd want to be in a slasher
movie obvi
sure, they are gory, but the
killer is just some guy
so your chances of survival
are way better

Not that Ollie had any reason to believe he could fight off a grown adult with a penchant for harming kids at summer camp or whatever, but at least he'd have a shot. It's not like you could punch ghosts. At least, Ollie didn't think so.

i'm going to say vampire movie

are you kidding?????

no, vampires are OP

VAMPIRES????

yeah if I can't beat them, i can
just become a vampire

they are not OP. They have like
so many weaknesses. Crosses,
holy water, wooden stakes,
THE LITERAL SUN, NOAH

I'm a night person anyway

I have garlic in the kitchen
right now
you're done
OP. When my pasta could kill you

Wishbone jumped back up on the bed and sat next to Ollie, his paws pressing into Ollie's leg. He kept putting his claws out and pinching Ollie, so Ollie had to keep gently removing them from his pants. After a few times, he gave up and just held both Wishbone's paws in one hand, his phone tight in the other. He tried to be extra gentle with the injured paw, even though it was healing nicely. The feeling of the cat's little toe beans against his palm was nice. Almost as nice as the conversation with Noah. Mia wasn't fun to argue with, she could take things a little too personally.

ok what monster would
you be then?

                              not a sparkly weirdo,
                                    that's for sure

i'm waiting ???

                                obviously a demon

how is that obvious?

                       because they are actually OP.
                      the lore is different in different
                        movies, so they can have like
                            whatever power you want
                                plus the weaknesses
                                   aren't that bad
                        it's literally so easy to avoid
                       churches I've done it all my life

hahaha
you're just jealous I'd make
a hot vampire

Ollie's face heated as he read the last message. He wasn't
about to start thinking about what Noah would look like as a
vampire, no sir, not that day . . .

He was totally thinking about it. And had a sinking feeling
that Noah was right.

In order to combat his heartbeat quickening, Ollie downloaded a picture of Nosferatu and sent it to Noah.

lolol i hate you

                                   lies you do not

definitely not

Then he sent a green heart.

Ollie practically flailed around in his bed, rolling over away from Wishbone to bury his face in his comforter. What did that *mean*? A heart almost made it seem like Noah was saying he *liked* Ollie, but did the fact that it was green mean that he didn't *like* like Ollie and just thought he was a friend?

Wait. Why was Ollie even worried about that when he wasn't supposed to have feelings for Noah anyway?

"Wishbone. Why are people so confusing?" Ollie asked.

Wishbone yawned, clearly not caring about Ollie's totally-not-a-crush.

Ollie peeked back at his phone, but Noah hadn't sent anything else. Was he waiting for Ollie to respond? What should he say?

Then Ollie noticed the time.

If he didn't stop now, he'd be late for movie night.

> **haha i actually have to go, movie night with mia and wishbone talk later**

That time, it took Noah a bit longer to respond.

yeah np ofc

Ollie sent a ghost cat that was smiling and locked his phone. Ollie scooped up Wishbone in his arms and walked over to Mia's room. He used his foot to knock on the door with a few kicks. After a moment, Mia opened it, her glasses falling down her nose and one earbud still in.

"It's movie time," Ollie said.

"Oh! Right. Let me just finish this one application thing," Mia said.

Ollie smiled. "Are you almost done?"

Mia nodded. "Sending it in tonight. Mom got all the financial aid stuff together, so between that and the inheritance, if I get in, I should be able to go."

Ollie did a little dance with Wishbone. "Mia the Trojan. *Fancy.*"

Mia blushed, giving him a playful shove. "Stop. I didn't get in yet."

"You're such a nerd, how could they say no?"

Mia rolled her eyes. "Shut up and start the movie."

Ollie rushed into the living room with Wishbone, placing him on the couch. With their parents gone, he figured they could venture out of his bedroom. In front of them was a new, shiny, beautiful, fifty-inch television. Dad had bought it that afternoon, even saying how it would be perfect for movie night. Mia said it was another credit card purchase, but at least their parents could actually pay off all that soon. Ollie turned on the TV before walking over to the kitchen to grab some popcorn and a tuna treat for Wishbone he hid on the lower shelf.

By the time all the snacks were ready, Mia finally joined them.

"What are we watching tonight?" Mia asked.

"There's some new haunted house movie that's supposed to be really good," Ollie said. What he didn't say was that Noah was the one who gave the recommendation. Mia would ask too many questions about that, especially since she already gave him a knowing look when Noah left earlier. If a cat who didn't understand him hardly seemed to believe Ollie wasn't getting too close to Noah, there was no way his nosy older sister would.

Mia leaned back on the couch, Wishbone curled between them, right in front of the bowl of popcorn. He didn't pay much attention to the salty snack, instead still licking up his tuna puree. Ollie started the movie.

They barely got a few minutes in when the door opened, revealing both of their parents. Ollie, Mia, and Wishbone all froze.

A long moment passed as their parents took in the sight and, notably, the two-tailed cat going wild on a tuna treat.

"I thought you were going to be out late?" Mia asked.

"We were late to our movie, so we thought we'd just skip it and join your movie night," their dad started.

"Is that a cat?" their mom asked.

Ollie's stomach dropped all the way into the cushion. He paused the movie before looking at Mia, who was too stunned to speak. Would their parents yell at them for lying? Would they have to get rid of Wishbone? Ollie refused to let that happen. The cat had changed his life—not just through granting their wishes. He became a presence he could count on. It was all too easy to adjust to the sassy cat, and now, Ollie could hardly believe there was a time when he didn't have him. In just a few short days, Wishbone had become his best friend. He didn't have a lot of competition, obviously, but if a best friend is someone who listens and is always there for you, then that was Wishbone.

Panicked, Ollie looked into Wishbone's blue eyes. If he had to, Ollie could just wish that his parents would be okay with keeping him. Or maybe wish that his parents thought they always had Wishbone as a pet.

Whatever he had to do, he wouldn't give up Wishbone for anything. But he wanted his parents to love Wishbone even without magic making them do it, just like him and Mia. So he draped his arm around the cat's small frame. "He showed up today, and he doesn't belong to anyone, so . . . he's our cat now," Ollie said.

His mom crossed her arms. His dad pursed his lips. He could practically feel the tension build in the room and just waited for either one of them to explode.

"I've heard that's how you get a cat," Ollie's dad finally said. "The cat distribution system, they call it."

"You have a litter box and everything, right?" Mom walked into the room, dropping her purse on the table. "Oh! Mia, please tell me you kept that queer cat tree. He would look just darling in it."

"Yeah," Mia said, still looking stunned but probably for a different reason than being caught. "I did."

"What's the little guy's name?" Dad asked.

"His name's Wishbone." Wishbone perked up at Ollie's words.

"Because of his tails!" His dad chuckled. "Clever."

They were taking it all so well—too well. It was suspicious, but Ollie didn't want to worry about it. It worked out for them, so what did it really matter?

"What are we watching?" Mom sat at the end of the couch, next to Ollie. She nudged him with her arm and put on a low voice. "Something spooooky?"

Neither Ollie nor Mia seemed to know how to respond at first. Their dad also joined them in the living room, taking a seat on the old armchair and kicking up his legs.

"Don't make fun of me if I close my eyes at the terrifying parts," he said with a teasing smile.

Ollie blinked a few times. Were his parents joining them for the movie? Together? Ollie knew things were different after the wish, but it was like his mind still refused to accept *how* different. It felt kind of . . . nice?

"Wait." His mom suddenly got up. "I think there are some chips and M&M's in the cupboard. We might as well go big, right?" She walked over to the kitchen side of the room and started pulling out bowls and snacks.

Mia turned to Ollie, giving him a disbelieving look. Ollie just smiled and shrugged. So, Mia smiled and shrugged back. It was weird, for sure—much different than what they were used to— but also a heck of a lot better. Why question a good thing?

While his mom finished getting more snacks, Ollie decided to check his Instagram. With Noah coming over and them texting most of the evening, he hadn't even thought to see how his post of the monster cake was doing. When the app opened, his heart almost stopped. His notifications were going wild. Ollie clicked on his most recent post of the monster cake.

Ten thousand likes????

He checked his follower count. It had jumped to nearly five thousand. Ollie started to scroll through the comments. They were all complimentary, people loving the cake and saying it was cool how he was already so talented. Ollie had to suppress a squeal. What had happened?

He looked at his mentions. A bunch of people shared the post to their stories, including Miss Sugar N' Spice herself.

This kid is killing it! she had written on her story.

And she also *followed* Ollie.

"MIA." Ollie practically shoved his phone in his sister's face. "MIAAAAA."

She swatted him away, causing Wishbone to jump off the couch and sniff their dad's shoes. "Calm down, I can't see when you're shaking . . ." She held his hand steady. "Miss Sugar N' Spice liked your cake? OLLIE."

"RIGHT?"

"What's going on?"

Mia and Ollie turned toward their dad, who was now petting Wishbone, purring happily on Dad's lap. What was it about dads that cats loved so much?

"Ollie's baking Instagram is blowing up." Mia pushed up her glasses as the words tumbled out in excitement. "A literal celebrity shared his cake!"

"The monster cake from earlier?" his mom asked, walking back to the couch with a bowl of chips and a large bag of M&M's. "It was delicious, honey, that's amazing."

"We know how hard you've been working on your baking," his dad said. "I'm so proud of you." His voice got higher as he looked down at Wishbone. "You came to the right house, Cat. My son's going to be a *celebrity baker*. He's gonna be friends with . . . Gordon Ramsay!" His dad looked up. "I don't know many famous food people. Gordon Ramsay doesn't yell at kids, right?"

"Gordon Ramsay could yell at me any day," their mom said.

"Ew," Mia responded. "Can we start the movie now so I can replace that mental image with something less terrifying, like a ghost or dead body?"

Ollie laughed. As he started the movie and they all settled in, it was something like a dream. His mom and dad both with them, happy and cracking jokes, nearly spilling snacks at the jump scares, even Wishbone making himself at home in the new room.

Of course, they had always been related, but that night was the first time Ollie truly felt like he had a real family.

15

When Everything Is Actually NOT Okay

OLLIE OPENED HIS EYES to a harsh orange sky. A sense of dread filled his entire body as the initial panic of not knowing where he was struck.

The last thing Ollie remembered was his eyes fluttering closed on the couch as his family put on a second, and much less interesting, movie. The night had started out great, but he had become a little annoyed. Part of it was the choice of movie, but a bigger part was how it took almost thirteen years for him to have a normal family night like that. He tried to push that thought away and enjoy himself, but he must have still had a sour expression on his face because Mia kept giving him weird looks until Ollie decided to just close his eyes. But he didn't remember anything otherwise. He figured he fell asleep at some point, because nothing else could explain why he was currently not in the living room.

He blinked, but the orange didn't go away. Instead, gray

smoke spread, violently swirling around in it. Crows flew backward overhead, coughing out metallic *caws* as they passed. Ollie's chest tightened painfully as he took in the sight.

No. No no no no.

He sat up, but the scene didn't change. Instead, he felt the concrete sidewalk under him and the inky vines that rose through the cracks. He wasn't on the beach where he found Wishbone, but that didn't bring much comfort.

Ollie was back in The Backward Place.

Oh no, oh no. This was bad. It was worse than bad. How did he even get there? He couldn't remember being pulled through like he had been on the sand. Was it possible to just *wake up* there?

Ollie's breathing was shallow and too quick as his heart pounded in his chest. He had to get out of there. Ollie scrambled to his feet. How had he left last time? Mia had pulled him back up.

What if no one was around to get him this time?

He shoved aside the fear. He couldn't think like that. He'd find a way. Someone back home would hear him.

"Mom?" Ollie called. "Dad?"

He had to wave off bugs that flew backward toward his face, practically smacking into him. It almost looked like he was in his neighborhood, but it wasn't quite the same. The street was just like his, and he recognized the apartment and the Chois' house and even the 7-Eleven, but it seemed abandoned, practically destroyed.

"Mia?" His voice shook. "Wishbone?"

No one answered. He was alone.

How had he even gotten back there? Did the couch somehow swallow him up like the sand had? He searched the ground for holes, anything that might be able to send him back home. But there was nothing except hard concrete.

He rubbed his bare arms to warm them up. At least he had put long pajama pants on before the movie. The air held a faint scent of smoke and pine, but it didn't seem to come from any one point.

There had to be a way out of here. He turned toward the apartment building that looked like his, aside from the crumbling exterior and protruding vines.

Well, mostly the vines. The crumbling wasn't anything new.

Maybe his family was inside? He rushed into the apartment that seemed to be theirs (the number was backward), the door opening easily, and called again. "Hello?"

Like the rest of The Backward Place, everything in the apartment looked almost the same, but also . . . wrong. Unsettling. It felt like there was more dust than air, and debris filled each room, the vines covering every corner and interlocking across the floor. Between the dust and crumbling walls and torn-up fabric, it looked like the place had been broken into. Then his eyes landed on a shadow of someone on the couch.

"Mom?" Ollie asked.

He slowly walked over the vines, breath caught, as he

approached the shape. He was already too close when he saw that it wasn't his mom, dad, Mia, or Wishbone. It wasn't even an odd, backward version of any of them.

No, unfortunately for Ollie, it was far worse.

It was what could only be described as a monster. But none of the scary movies he'd watched could have prepared him for this.

It had the body of a lion, but most of its fur was patchy and gray. Instead of a normal tail, a snake sprouted from its rear, twisting in the air to bare its fangs at Ollie. But the most terrifying thing was the head of the beast, which was something like a wolf and a deer sloppily sewn together. Its antlers, fur, and mouth were all matted with blood, which Ollie could see all too well as the monster growled, digging its claws into the fabric of the couch as it turned toward him.

Ollie screamed, and the beast lunged forward.

He only just escaped the outstretched claws by taking a sharp turn toward the door as the creature slammed into the television, shattering the screen. Ollie ran out of the apartment and away from the building, but the monstrous being following him was a lot faster.

Running wasn't going to work. He had to hide somewhere.

Ollie took a hard left into the Nevele-7, vines overtaking the place, all the food rotten and products thrown from the shelves. He jumped behind the counter and tucked himself into a tight, concealed corner. Holding his breath, he watched the door through a small space near the floor.

Ollie held back a groan as he saw the door swing open, followed by the monster's claws scraping across the tile. The creature gave off a low growl, sniffing the air with an open mouth. It then turned in Ollie's direction.

No no no no no.

Ollie was rethinking his love of scary movies. On second thought, they seemed like the worst genre and he deeply regretted sometimes rooting for the monster—especially as the one he was currently dealing with crept closer to his hiding spot.

Ollie cringed as the creature slowly climbed on top of the counter, opening its split face to reveal the sharp, bloody teeth inside. Even the snake on its tail hissed. Ollie didn't want to know what those teeth would feel like closing on his head, so he had to think fast.

He reached into the hot food warmer and snatched the spicy hot dogs.

"Fetch!" he called, throwing them across the torn-apart store.

Was it the most creative idea Ollie ever had? No. Was it the first one he could come up with? Yes.

And, miraculously, it worked.

The creature sprinted after the hot dogs, its claws sliding on fallen Twinkies (or, rather, Seikniwt). Ollie stood shocked for half a second, hardly believing a couple hot dogs were enough to distract the monster from his much meatier almost-thirteen-year-old body, but he didn't have time to be insulted. Ollie flung himself at the exit, pulling a rack of snacks after him in an attempt to block the door as the creature gobbled up the hot dogs.

Ollie ran down the sidewalk, trying to get as much space between him and the monster as possible—and hoping he wouldn't run into another one. Luckily, he only saw people as he ran, but it wasn't much of a comfort. All of them had that gray smoke pouring from their eyes. Ollie kept his distance. "I have to get out of here," Ollie said, hoping that saying the thought out loud would make an escape route magically appear.

No such luck.

Ollie's pace slowed as he glanced around the street. Most of the houses had those weird people in front of them, watching him with their smoky, eyeless sockets. He had nowhere to go.

One large house loomed at the edge of the street that Ollie didn't recognize from his world. Unlike the rest of the homes with broken windows, peeling paint, and black vines bursting through them, this one looked relatively put-together, and none of the smoky-eyed Backward Place residents stood outside. There also seemed to be a light on.

Was that Ollie's way out?

Sure, he knew that it was the kind of decision that could get him killed in a horror movie, but he also knew it was the kind of decision the final girl would make, and they were the ones to stay alive until the end. The horror-movie obsessed friend who was cautious and knew all the tropes usually ended up dead.

Ollie had to be a final boy and take the risky route.

He heard the window of the convenience store crash as the body of the monster shoved through it.

And he had to do it *now*.

Ollie ran up the front porch of the house, each step creaking under his socks. The front door was wide, muted red, and (of course) slightly ajar. Ollie was either going to make it home, or end up in some murderer's freezer. A roar sounded through the air. Ollie pushed inside and closed the door behind him, deadbolting it.

The interior of the house sort of made the ending-up-in-a-freezer option seem realistic. It was old and falling apart, with dust that swirled around in the streams of light. There were books and papers scattered all over the wooden floor, most of the pages filled with symbols Ollie couldn't understand. He stepped closer to what appeared to be a dining table.

It was littered with dark feathers and dried blood.

"What the . . . ?" Ollie started, unable to help his face twisting up.

Gross. It was all creepy and gross and not the kind of place to explore randomly in pajamas. What would a way out look like, anyway? Some kind of big, obvious portal would've been nice. Ollie glanced around the annoyingly portal-free house. A warm light rose from behind a cracked door.

Ollie did not want to go toward the light.

But a final boy would.

Ollie slowly approached it, quietly pulling the door open. A set of stairs led down.

You didn't even have to be a horror movie fan like Ollie to know scary stuff *always* happened in the basement. And as much as Ollie knew everyone watching him in a movie would be begging, *Please, Ollie, do NOT go into the super-scary basement!* he took the first step. Then the next.

Nothing would be solved by staying in the same place, and whatever was down there probably wouldn't be worse than the deer/wolf/lion/snake nightmare waiting outside.

Fortunately, the door didn't immediately slam shut behind him. Unfortunately, the wood of the stairs was scarred with claw marks. That certainly didn't suggest anything good.

Ollie peered around the corner at the bottom of the steps— the coast was clear. There was a sharp smell in the air, like chemicals and cleaners. It made his nostrils twitch.

The basement was some combination of a library and a lab. Books were stacked in piles on the floor, some of the bindings broken and pages scattered around them. There was a counter with a variety of different potions and lotions in a rainbow of colors. Behind them, on the wall, were little boxes and jars filled with plants and powders and pieces that Ollie couldn't make out.

A squeaking sound pulled Ollie away from the strange books. It was frantic and high-pitched. He moved to the other side of the room, the lantern above blinking off and on. When he was close enough, he jumped, a bit of bile rushing up his throat.

Above a wooden desk were dozens of cages filled with mice.

But these mice didn't look right. One mouse had red veins bulging from its body. Another had a tail coming out the middle of its head and a second mouth on its side. Some were too large, some too scrawny, some a level of terrifying that words would struggle to capture and was probably better left to the imagination.

But all of them had a thin trail of gray smoke rising from the corner of their eyes.

The same smoke all the backward people outside had. The same smoke he'd seen outside Mia's window. The same smoke he'd sworn he'd seen seeping out of his mother's eyes.

Ollie wanted to open the cages and let all the mice out, but he also saw enough zombie movies to know that was how people got infected. He glanced down at the desk below the cages and scanned the pages of notes. They were filled with different drawings of animal creatures, parts from different beings sewn together. Was the person who lived here the one who made the thing outside?

Each page seemed to be worse than the last, with diagrams that showed more medical information about the monsters that were created. Ollie's heart pounded. He flipped to another page, and it almost stopped altogether.

There was a drawing of a two-tailed cat that looked exactly like Wishbone.

Had *this* been where Wishbone came from? Was he supposed to end up a part of one of the monsters like the one that almost killed Ollie?

Eyes wide and stomach churning, Ollie picked up the page.

Day One: Subject 23 received first dose of magic via injection. Initial reaction of increased aggression, restraints were put in place.

Day Ten: On the tenth injection, Subject 23 has started to grow what looks to be a second tail. Process appears to be painful to the subject, restrained to prevent biting the area.

Day Twenty: With most recent injection, the subject attempted escape. It was shut away. Irritation noticed at injection site, will use new site beginning injection twenty-one.

Day Thirty: The magic is almost fully integrated into Subject 23. With one more injection, the cycle will be complete and the subject will be the first successful lab-made magic being.

Ollie felt his eyes burn. Just what had Wishbone gone through before Ollie found him? Ollie had kind of assumed he was some fantasy creature that was born with magic. But no. He was a regular cat who was victim to some messed-up experiment. No wonder he seemed so eager to leave.

Guilt flickered in Ollie's chest. What if using Wishbone's

magic *did* hurt him? If this was how he got it, was using it just as painful? The cat didn't seem to mind, but he couldn't exactly complain either.

Then anger bloomed. Who would treat Wishbone—treat any animal—like this? What kind of monster could do this?

The Backward Man.

He was the one who ran after Wishbone, who *hurt* him. Ollie hadn't known how much, but now tears formed in his eyes as the rage within him built.

A loud *thud!* sounded from upstairs. Ollie's heart shot to his throat. Footsteps, followed by the basement door creaking open.

Oh no. That was *bad*.

As much as Ollie would have loved to punch him in the face right then and there for what he did to Wishbone, if The Backward Man found Ollie . . . there wasn't exactly anywhere to run like on the beach.

Ollie needed a way out and fast. But where could he go? The creature could still be waiting for him outside.

The first steps creaked with weight as Ollie desperately searched the room for an escape, but it was pointless. He would have to hide. He opened up the door of a thin cabinet. Fortunately, it was empty with a few slits at the top of the door to let air in. Unfortunately, the inside was covered in bloodstains.

Ugh. He was going to die, wasn't he?

Ollie looked back where the shadow coming down the stairs grew. He internally groaned but quickly got inside the cabinet and closed himself in. He barely made it as The Backward Man turned the corner. Gray smoke rose from one eye as he scratched at his gray skin, hands and feet still turned the wrong way. He moved in the direction of the cabinet. Ollie could feel his heart in his throat, so loud it practically thudded in his skull.

The Backward Man paused. He scanned the room slowly as if looking for something out of place. His eyes landed near the cabinet, and he snarled, "What are you doing here?"

OH NO. ABORT MISSION.

Ollie's muscles tensed as he waited for The Backward Man to approach and throw open the cabinet, but he stayed in place as another voice answered.

"That's how you greet me now, *Mage*?"

Ollie struggled to see through the slits in the direction of the second voice. He could just make out some movement in a shadowy corner of the room. Then, a monster stepped forward. It looked human, almost, but its skin was entirely a chalky gray, all its limbs bent in the wrong direction, its head entirely twisted backward. Both eyes were completely gone, replaced with that rising gray smoke.

It was something out of a nightmare. A hundred times worse than The Backward Man or the other people Ollie had seen outside. And if it had been there the entire time . . . it knew about Ollie.

Ollie's skin prickled all over. He thought things had been bad before, but it turned out it was worse than he could have even imagined. The monster opened its mouth again, revealing rows of pointed teeth. "You should leave," it said, looking directly at the cabinet where Ollie hid.

Thanks, freaky monster. Wish I'd thought of that! Ollie was stuck in a cabinet and The Backward Man was directly in his path to the stairs. Where would he leave?

"My own house?" The Backward Man asked. "If anyone should leave, it's you, *witch*."

"It's not too late," the monster (Witch?) said softly. "To let it go."

"Let it go?" He laughed, low and bitter. "This is all your fault. Sealing up magic like that, thinking it would stop me. You're lucky I still had that little bit left or I would've killed you already."

Ollie's brow furrowed. If magic had been sealed up, how did The Backward Man inject it into Wishbone? And if he only had a little left . . . why put it in Wishbone at all?

The Witch almost looked sad, but its voice remained even. "You let most of your magic slip away. That's not my fault."

A low rumble came from the chest of The Backward Man, a sinister cross between a chuckle and a groan. "Slip away? No, no. It was *stolen*. And don't you think for one minute I won't get it back. After I tear apart the *boy* that took it, limb from limb."

He spat out the last words, and Ollie's heart froze. Fear rushed through his veins, panicked and pulsing. It didn't take a lot of logic to realize that Ollie was the boy in question. The Backward Man didn't just want Wishbone back.

He wanted revenge.

"I won't let you," The Witch said.

"You can't stop me!" The Backward Man roared. He slammed his fist against the desk, causing Ollie to jump and accidentally hit the side of the cabinet with a thud.

Even the frantic mice stilled and grew quiet as The Backward Man turned in Ollie's direction. Ollie's entire body was frozen, breath caught, but his mind was racing. Would he be able to get past the two of them to run up the stairs? If he did make it, where would he go from there? Back to the jaws of the beast outside?

Ollie's stomach sank as he realized just how stuck he was.

Helphelphelphelphelp, he found himself repeating, even though he didn't know who he was asking.

The Backward Man walked up to the cabinet door, more smoke spewing from his eye as he curled back his lips in a wide smile, revealing the sharp teeth stained with dried, brownish blood. He reached out toward the handle of the door as Ollie made a desperate wish. As the door was thrown open, something yanked Ollie back.

16

Monday Always Comes Too Fast

A SCREAM CAUGHT IN Ollie's throat as he was pulled, but instead of facing The Backward Man, he was greeted by his mother. "What were you doing shut in the closet?" she asked. "Wishbone was pawing at the door, and I thought he wanted food. Nearly gave me a heart attack when I saw you in there."

Ollie blinked. He was in the hallway of their apartment—the real one, not the one in The Backward Place—standing in front of the open storage closet. He looked back at his mom, who was watching him like he was about to go off the handle, and Wishbone, who was sitting next to his mom but now rubbed against Ollie's legs.

He couldn't explain to his mom what happened. He wasn't entirely sure what was happening himself, and what he was able to tell her would probably get him sent to a psychologist.

"Um . . . I was going to get litter, but I kind of dozed off."

"While standing?"

"I'm really tired," Ollie lied. Although it made sense. It had to be, what, like three in the morning?

"Let me make you some tea," his mom said. "You've got to get ready for school."

"Yeah, I could have some . . . Wait, *what?*" Ollie looked at his mom. "But it's Sunday."

His mom made a face. "Well, you must be still half asleep. It's Monday, love, Sunday was yesterday."

"No, we watched the movies on Saturday night . . ."

"And then Sunday happened, we went to sleep, and now it's Monday, yes, dear, that's indeed how the days of the week work." She put on a smile, tapping Ollie twice on the back. "Now, come on, before the bus leaves without you."

Ollie frowned. "Why do I have to take the bus? Is Mia staying home sick or something?"

His mom went still for a moment, face scrunched as she tried to think. "Mia, of course. She'll drive you to school. Not sure where my mind is this morning. Maybe we're all forgetting things. Now, where did I put my phone?"

She walked off into the kitchen. What was happening? First Ollie almost died, then The Backward Man threatened his life, and now he'd forgotten an entire day? He raced back into his room and checked his phone. Monday. And underneath, a notification that he had Instagram messages. He opened his Instagram and almost passed out.

Twelve thousand followers.

Ollie's DMs were filled with random people messaging

him. At first, most of the messages were positive and uplifting, but something happened Sunday in which the tone totally shifted. There were messages insulting Ollie, his parents, even actual threats just because he'd used hashtags with "trans" in them and had the trans flag in his bio.

"Right, you jerks really care about protecting us kids. That's why you're spending your time coming after me just because I made a cake," Ollie mumbled. The flicker of rage burned in him.

Ollie tossed his phone across the room, his brain being pulled in different directions and all of them making him more angry. He'd barely survived The Backward Place, lost a whole day of his life, all to come back to *this*?

Ollie wanted to hit all those transphobic commenters with a bat. Or a car. A part of him almost wanted to specifically wish for terrible things to happen to each of them, but unlike some people, he didn't *seriously* wish to cause harm to strangers. Could he give them cold and wet socks for life, at least? A curse to step on a LEGO whenever they walked into a new room? Something?

Ollie sighed. They weren't even worth a scrap of Wishbone's magic. In fact, they weren't even the scariest thing to threaten his life that morning. He glanced at his phone on the floor. What else had happened yesterday? Did he miss a message from Noah?

Ollie raced over to pick it up. There were new messages from Noah, but he had already responded to them. They had a whole conversation he didn't even remember.

He scrolled through with a smile until he reached the last few messages.

did something happen?

> it's fine, I just got into a
> fight with Mia

I'm sorry. I fight with Tiff all
the time and you two seem
really close
so I'm sure it will be okay
do you want to talk about it?

> it's fine
> I just wish I didn't even
> remember it

Oh no. Did the wish come true from *typing* it next to Wishbone, or had Ollie actually made the wish aloud? His mind struggled to remember, but it was all gone. Totally out of reach.

"I hate everything," Mia said, pushing into Ollie's room and flopping on his bed, already dressed and ready for the day. For a moment, Ollie figured she was guessing *his* thoughts, but his sister was visibly upset. Wishbone jumped onto the bed after her, biting at her fanned-out hair. "Well, not you, Wishbone. Why are you looking at me like that, Ollie? Are you still mad about last night?"

"No, but only because I don't know what happened last night. I'm mad because I somehow ended up in The Backward Place and barely got out alive and the scary Backward Man wants to kill me and I thought I was only there for maybe thirty minutes, but I think I accidentally wished to forget the fight I don't remember us having because I've forgotten everything that happened yesterday."

Mia's jaw dropped open before she winced a little. "Well, now the thing I was going to complain about seems silly." She sat up. "And it was nothing, just . . . I was worried about making more wishes, and we were a little unfair to each other . . . Don't worry about it. But how did you end up in The Backward Place?"

"I don't know! The last thing I remember, we were watching a movie on the couch, and then suddenly I was there. What happened after our fight yesterday?"

Mia shrugged. "You went to your room and slammed the door, and I got ready for bed. I thought you just went to sleep, too, but I don't know. We were both pretty upset, so I thought it would be best to just let each of us cool off alone."

Ollie's stomach hurt with how freaky it was to have no clue what he did. Apparently he was angry, and maybe made a wish, but that didn't explain why he woke up in The Backward Place. But his memory wasn't even their biggest problem. "I almost got killed by some terrifying animal hybrid thing and escaped into this creepy torture basement where The Backward Man experimented on Wishbone, which, by the way, is why he's magic and has the extra tail. So that's already terrible, but to make it more terrible, The Backward Man mentioned tearing me limb from limb to take back Wishbone and almost found me when I suddenly woke up here." Ollie dropped his hands. "Well, not *here*. In the closet? I don't know, it's all weird, and to make matters even *worse*, because apparently that's still possible, while all this is happening, I was getting mean messages from random bigots on the internet! So I'm the one that really hates everything now!"

Mia scratched her neck, still red from her most recent eczema breakout. "I'm sorry, Ollie. People are the worst." She lifted a finger. "That being said, we're both allowed to hate everything."

"*Mia*."

"I'm just saying!" Mia pushed up her glasses before petting Wishbone. "That's . . . a lot, though. So you saw The Backward Man's house?"

Ollie thought back to it, even though some sights (namely, the mice and the hacked-up feathers on the dining table) were something he'd rather forget. "Yeah, it was at the end of our street. But not *our street*. The backward our street. And it was more evil lair than house. Oh! I almost forgot, there was also a monster witch thing, and it called him Mage."

"I don't think his name really matters, but sure, The Mage. The Backward Man. The Evil Piece of Crap. Whatever." Mia's face grew pale. "And he said he was going to kill you to take back Wishbone?"

Ollie nodded. "Yeah. He clearly meant it, too."

"Why does he want Wishbone back so bad?"

"I don't know." Ollie ran both hands through his hair. "He mentioned something about The Witch sealing up magic, so I think Wishbone has the only magic that's left. I guess he needs the magic for something?"

"But what?" Mia asked.

Ollie was getting frustrated by all these questions he didn't know the answer to. "I don't know, Mia! Evil stuff! He's an evil backward wizard, so I'm sure he wants to do evil backward wizard stuff!"

"You don't have to yell," Mia yelled back.

"I'm stressed!"

"Well, so am I!"

"Yeah, but is the evil backward wizard trying to kill *you*?" Ollie snapped.

Both of them took deep breaths, calming down. Mia was flushed, looking slightly embarrassed. "Sorry, you're right. But we can't let him get Wishbone. He's our family."

Ollie's eyes stung. "I know, and . . . he really hurt Wishbone there, Mia. Like really bad. We absolutely can't give him back." Ollie wiped his nose before carefully petting Wishbone. He had to wonder where the poor cat had the magic injected, as he didn't want to accidentally hurt him if the spots were sore. Wishbone accepted the pets, though, leaning into Ollie's hand. "He experimented on him. Other animals, too. Like I think he made the gross lion deer snake wolf thing that almost ate me."

"The what?"

Ollie sighed. "I got away. Thanks to hot dogs. It's a long story."

"Did anything follow you? Back to our world, I mean?"

Ollie shook his head. "I don't think so. I don't think The Backward Man, or Mage or whatever, even really saw me, he just knew that *someone* was there."

"Oh, good." Mia put her forehead against Wishbone's back. "We can hopefully just avoid him and that place in general."

At first, Ollie agreed.

But would it really be that simple?

When The Mage threatened Ollie, he didn't seem to have any concern over not being able to find him. Besides, if his house was really on the same street, only in The Backward Place, it wasn't exactly far. If The Mage was able to cross over like Ollie did, it would only be a matter of time before he found them.

Ollie couldn't let that happen. The Mage wouldn't stop wanting to come after them, that much seemed clear by the anger Ollie witnessed earlier. He couldn't count on hiding forever. He'd have to stop The Mage first.

"We just have to figure out how to cross back," Ollie said. "Then I can find him."

Mia shot up with wide eyes, scaring Wishbone. "Um . . . why would we ever *intentionally* go there? Did you already forget he wants to kill you?"

"Have you paid literally any attention to any of the movies we've watched?" Ollie asked. "Since when does the bad guy just give up? We stole his experiment. Of course he's going to come after us! We know where he is, so we have the element of surprise if we go after him first."

"No." Mia shook her head. "*No*. First of all, you literally just said he is a mage and he's friends with some terrifying witch and has deadly, messed-up pets. That means they have *powers*, Ollie. We do not. Wishbone has magic, but it sounds like he was basically tortured. We can't bring him back there."

Ollie's stomach sunk to his feet as guilt rose up in its place. He hadn't even thought of that. Of course Wishbone wouldn't want to be there again. It would be traumatic. Ollie didn't know everything Wishbone had gone through, but what he did know was terrible enough.

He practically dove down to pull Wishbone in a hug, burying his face in his warm fur. "I'm sorry, Wishbone. I won't make you go back there, I promise. We'll figure it out, but whatever happens, we'll keep you safe, okay?"

Wishbone didn't know what was going on but started purring. He lightly bit Ollie on the nose. It was a loving bite, at least.

Ollie eyed Mia. "Why were you so upset, though?"

Mia's face grew extremely red. "Well, it's nothing compared to evil mages and forgetting time . . ." She sighed under Ollie's look. "David said I can't go with Joanie and him to prom anymore. We were supposed to go as a group, but now he's saying it's weird if I go with just them and I'd need to find a date or I just shouldn't come."

"Ew," Ollie said. "Why is David being such a jerk? And why should you need a date? Also, I'm sorry, but since when do you care about prom?"

Mia wasn't exactly a school dance kind of person. She barely even hung out with the other kids in her grade, even blowing off David and Joanie when they invited her to parties.

Mia groaned. "It's not about prom really. It's the fact that we promised we'd go as a group. I already got a dress and everything. And what's his problem? I'm agreeing to third wheel so we can go together, and *he's* the one making it weird. Like if I had been the one to ask Joanie out first, I wouldn't treat David like this. I would've still gone as a group like we *promised*."

Ollie thought for a moment. He didn't like seeing Mia upset ever, but especially not over Joanie and David. In this case, David really wasn't being fair to Mia. Was he jealous of her or something? It did kind of seem like Joanie liked Mia too, maybe even as more than friends. She was always asking about her, it seemed. It's just that David beat Mia to her.

"What if you *were* the one who asked her first?" Ollie said slowly.

"What?"

"You can wish for it."

Mia shook her head so fast her glasses almost flew off. "No, I can't."

"Why not?" Ollie sat up. "I accidentally made that wish last night, but nothing *that* bad happened to anyone because of it." Assuming his wish was unrelated to being pulled into The Backward Place, of course, which Ollie was pretty sure it was. "And I didn't think it through. Or, at least, I don't *think* I did. But Wishbone seems okay. It's not fair how he got the magic, but using it doesn't seem to bother him at all. And David will be fine. He's a straight boy with a car, he can get someone else. You deserve to be happy, too. To get what you want."

Mia bit her lip. "I can't just waste a wish like that."

"It's not . . ." Ollie rolled his eyes. "Fine, I'll waste one, too. One that won't have any easy consequences. I'm sick of people making me angry when I have bigger problems to deal with, so I wish no one could say anything mean to me. There. Done."

Wishbone's eyes flashed, confirming it.

Mia's mouth was open in horror. Ollie shoved her. "It's *fine*. I used a wish for a totally selfish reason, and see? We're good, Wishbone's good, and now I can focus on what's important: saving our cat from a creepy mage."

While she still seemed a little unsure, Mia was always too easily convinced by Ollie. She closed her eyes and spoke quickly. "I wish I had told Joanie I liked her first and we were dating instead."

Another flash of blue. No loud bangs, curdling screams, or sirens in the distance. They were all good.

"Now, let me get dressed, and we can worry about The Mage after school," Ollie said. "I've got a presentation today, so I've got to actually look decent."

"Right," Mia said. "Hurry up."

As if she wasn't taking her sweet time talking to Ollie.

"Don't worry so much," Ollie said as Mia left his room. "It's gonna be fine."

His phone buzzed.

sorry it's so last minute but can
I get a ride to school with you?
Tiffany has a college visit
please save me from the bus?
you know if a zombie virus breaks
out everyone on the bus dies first

Ollie couldn't help but smile. Sure, he had The Backward Place and the magic monstrous people (and literal monsters) inside it to deal with, but in that moment, Ollie felt like he could deal with anything.

Things weren't just going to be fine. He had a feeling they'd be even better.

17

When You Remember Saying Everything Will Be Fine Usually Results in Things Becoming Not Fine (Whoops)

WHEN OLLIE FOLLOWED MIA outside the apartment, Noah was already there, waiting in the parking lot.

Butterflies fluttered in Ollie's stomach. Did Noah look better than normal that day? Or was it because they had been texting so much, finally seeing him again felt a little different?

"Good morning," Noah said, dimples showing. "Weather today sucks, though. Huh?"

Ollie honestly hadn't been paying attention to the weather at all as his eyes had been so focused on Noah. He glanced up at the sky.

Not only did it seem foggy, but the color of the sky was deepening, too. It looked a sickening, almost unnatural gray.

"Huh," Ollie said, waving bugs away from his face. "Maybe we'll actually get some rain." He slapped a particularly large mosquito that landed on his arm, leaving a tiny spot of blood behind.

Usually there weren't this many flies and mosquitos this late in the year. Ollie looked to the sky again. Did this have something to do with the strange fog?

Mia gave him a look that was half annoyed and half panicked. She got into the car anyway, and Ollie and Noah followed.

"Something's not right," Noah said from the back seat. "Things feel . . . off. Is there about to be an earthquake or something?"

Normally, Ollie slept through earthquakes, but the one he actually remembered didn't give any warning. It certainly didn't affect the *sky*.

"It's just foggy," Ollie said.

But the longer he looked up, the more the sky kind of reminded him of The Backward Place.

Was it possible that The Backward Place was starting to invade their world? Could that even happen? Ollie didn't want to think about what would happen if The Mage's creatures crossed over, too. If that was a possibility, it would be even more important that they stopped The Mage before things got worse.

Mia braked at a red light. "What's up with those crows?"

Ollie looked out the windshield to where she was staring. There was a group of crows perched on the telephone wire, but all of them were twitching. It seemed like a glitch in a video game.

Moving to open his camera app and record a video, Ollie watched as the time on his phone flicked from 7:27 to 7:26.

His eyes widened. He'd only seen his phone do that once

before, and that realization sent an electric jolt of fear through him. But before he could say anything to the others, everything seemed to happen at once. The crows took off, wings pulling them backward, and a swarm of bugs started to fly backward against the car. Little splotches of liquid pooled on the windshield, insect legs still visible on them.

"What's happening?" Mia asked, panic lining her voice.

Bugs kept coming, hitting the front of the car like rain. More crows appeared in the sky, flying in the wrong direction with their tail feathers leading the way. The smoke in the air seemed to churn a little bit faster.

One of the crows flew directly into their windshield with a sickening *smack* before bouncing off. Ollie jumped, Mia swore, and Noah let out a particularly bloodcurdling scream.

Then the clock moved once more: 7:27.

Then, almost like nothing had happened, the air seemed to clear and the stoplight switched to green. The car behind them honked, prompting Mia to turn on the windshield wipers to clean the bug guts and feathers away and drive. Ollie kept one eye on the clock as the silence in the car stretched on: 7:28.

The tension was uncomfortably thick, so Ollie glanced back at Noah. "That was a great scream, though. You really would make a good final boy."

"That's the best compliment anyone has ever given me," Noah said seriously. "And I'll definitely be using this moment as inspiration when I can act in horror movies because what *was* that?" He ran his left hand through his bangs, eyes wide. "The birds and bugs were going backward, right? That crow hit us? I wasn't just seeing things?"

Some of the crows already seemed to have disappeared, but the ones that remained were flying correctly now, moving forward or perching on the power lines without any glitching.

Ollie looked at Mia. Her knuckles were white on the steering wheel.

"Maybe it was the Santa Ana winds," Ollie said. "Strong winds might have messed up the flying patterns. Or something."

It was the best Ollie could come up with. He almost felt bad for thinking Mia had terrible excuses under pressure. But what was he supposed to say? If he explained The Backward Place to Noah, he'd have to get into everything: Wishbone, his magic, The Mage . . . It still wasn't worth risking Wishbone's safety.

"Ollie, it's not even a little bit breezy today," Noah said. "And the Santa Ana winds are strong, but they don't do *that*."

"Climate change is scary," Ollie mumbled, but even he knew Noah wasn't going to buy that excuse.

"I need a coffee," Mia said firmly. "I'll buy you both donuts."

"Won't we be late then?" Noah asked.

"If that's the case, I'll pretend to be both of our moms and call in with a valid reason, like the fact that we were in some freak incident and now the front of the car is covered in bug goo."

When his sister put it like that, it really *was* a valid reason to be a little late to school. Besides, after sharing a look with Noah, it seemed like neither of them wanted to pass up the opportunity for donuts. If anything, Noah just seemed relieved that he hadn't imagined it all.

Ollie's jaw was tight. He kind of wished that he had.

Mia stopped at their usual donut place, Donut Skip Dessert! (Ollie appreciated both the pun and their maple bacon bar), and Ollie and Noah exited the car after her. Ollie noticed that a few other cars had unfortunate bug stains, too, mostly on the front. It was almost comforting to know it wasn't just their car that had been pelted. But still, the tightness in Ollie's chest wouldn't go away.

What had happened?

And, more importantly, would it happen again?

Ollie tried to push down the feelings of worry and focus on the donuts. Mia was the one who worried, not him. There had to be some reasonable explanation, and even if there wasn't, what did it matter? No one was hurt, they were fine. And now they had breakfast. While Mia didn't seem calmer, the coffee at least got her to stop shaking so much.

"Seriously, what do you think that was?" Noah grabbed some napkins from the counter before turning back to Ollie. "Was it maybe some kind of . . . I don't know, sound wave or something?"

"No idea," Ollie said, even though in some ways it felt like a lie.

They exited the donut shop, and getting out of a car was probably the last person Mia wanted to see right then. Joanie. Her curly hair was tied back, and her dark brown eyes widened as she broke into a sunshine-filled smile. Mia, on the other hand, looked white as a ghost.

Especially when Joanie walked right up to Mia and kissed her.

"I didn't know your sister had a girlfriend," Noah said.

Ollie's jaw dropped. "I don't think any of us did."

"What?"

Ollie took a bite from his donut. "Nothing."

Ollie had almost forgotten about Mia's wish from earlier. Apparently, Mia had too, although Ollie hadn't expected it to happen this quickly.

Mia reached up to touch her lips in disbelief. "Um . . . Joanie? What are you doing?"

"Is it weird to kiss my girlfriend? You should've told me you were getting donuts, you know I'm always down for a morning iced coffee." Joanie blinked, looking between them like they had started moving backward. "Is everything all right?"

That was a difficult question to answer at the moment.

Mia struggled to find words but was finally able to speak. "I mean, no. Wait, yes. We're all right, but . . ." Her mind seemed to be moving a mile a minute when she finally blurted out, "Where's David?"

Now Joanie looked especially confused.

"David?" she asked. "Who's that?"

Mia was already panicking, but Ollie could tell it had gotten worse since Mia had practically run away from Joanie at the donut shop and hurried Ollie and Noah back into the car. Now, she kept scratching at her neck, even as they drove away.

"David's going to kill me." She bit down on her lip. "I didn't think Joanie would completely forget him!"

Ollie tried to smile. "If it makes you feel better, this could have been because of my wish last night. Maybe they were the ones who got punished and forgot each other. They have been pretty unfair to you."

"That doesn't make me feel better, no," Mia snapped.

"Hold on," Noah started from the back seat. "What's happening?"

Ollie looked at Mia. He almost forgot Noah was with them for a second. "Do I tell him?" he whispered.

Her voice was also low and frantic. "I don't know, do you think we can trust him?"

"I'm pretty sure. Wishbone loves him, and he probably only likes good people."

"Does he? Because Wishbone loves you."

Ollie glared at her. "Is now really the time for teasing?"

"I'm sorry. Ollie, I'm on the brink of a breakdown."

Noah coughed a little from the back seat. "You two realize I'm literally right here?"

Ollie sighed, giving one last glance at Mia. She seemed to understand, nodding quickly. "It's a long story, and you might not believe it . . ." Ollie made a face. He couldn't believe he was about to tell Noah everything, and he still wasn't sure it was the best idea, but whether he liked it or not, he accidentally dragged

Noah into it. The least he could do was tell the truth. Ollie took a deep breath. "The short version of this is that Mia had a crush on the girl her best friend was dating, and he was being a bit of a jerk, so she wished they were together instead. But apparently now Joanie forgot about her boyfriend entirely."

Ollie looked back at his sister. "Ex-boyfriend?"

"I think that's a little too short of a version," Mia muttered.

Noah opened his mouth a few times before speaking. "What do you mean she *wished* for it?"

Right. Ollie had to go back further than this morning.

"Um. So. The thing is . . ." Ollie tried to think of a good way to say it, but there probably wasn't one. "Wishbone is a magic, wish-granting cat. Some evil mage guy forcefully gave him powers, and he wants to come from his creepy backward world to kill me and take our cat back because I *maybe technically* stole Wishbone from him, but he sucked! So, yeah. That's everything."

Ollie finished with a smile, but Noah didn't seem to return it. "*What?*" he asked.

Ollie sighed. "Look, I know this is all unbelievable and seems like a joke, and I will totally prove it to you and everything, but I think right now we need to focus on the fact that Joanie doesn't remember David." Ollie twisted back in his seat to look at Mia. "I'm sure he's okay, though."

Mia tossed her phone over to Ollie. "Can you text him for me? Just to check?"

Ollie opened Mia's messaging app and started to type in

David's name, but nothing popped up. "Isn't he saved in your phone?"

"What? Of course he is."

"Well, it's not showing up." Ollie switched over to Instagram, but David's account wasn't coming up either. Had he gotten so mad he deleted everything? Ollie didn't want to make Mia panic, but it was hard not to think that *something* was wrong.

"So . . . you're saying Wishbone is like a cat genie?" Noah asked from the back.

"Yes, but no," Ollie answered. "Just give me a minute, I swear I'll explain." Noah's mouth was a flat line, but he nodded. "Mia, all his stuff is gone."

"What?" Mia turned on the street that led to Hillside Middle before pulling over on the side of the road. She went through her phone, hands only shaking more as everything Ollie said was confirmed. "I'll call his mom. I have her number in case of emergencies." Mia pressed on a contact and put the phone on speaker. A woman picked up.

"Hello?"

"Hi, Ms. Carlson. It's Mia Di Costa, can I talk to David?" Mia sounded worried and desperate, her eyes glassy.

"David?" the woman repeated.

Tears started forming in Mia's eyes as she threw her free hand against the steering wheel. "Yes, David, your son, David! Can you put him on? Or tell him to call me?"

"I'm sorry, you must have the wrong number," the woman said. "I don't have a son."

The call ended and Mia stared at her phone with an open mouth. Ollie felt his own stomach twist. They had been right about the wishes causing curses, but this felt especially bad. The curse didn't make it so that Joanie forgot about David. The curse made it so that David didn't exist at all.

"We can fix this," Ollie said immediately.

"How?" Mia snapped. "I told you something terrible would happen! Now it's happened!" She wiped her eyes. "The bad things were only supposed to happen to bad people, but David didn't do anything, and now he's gone."

Ollie forced his face still. The last thing he needed was to get upset like Mia already was. Nothing was solved when everyone panicked. Besides, he already felt bad enough for Noah, who was watching them in the back seat with an especially nervous expression.

"Wishbone made this David guy *disappear?*" Noah asked, sounding a little panicked. Ollie really needed to take control of the situation.

"Let's just go wish David back. We should show Noah how Wishbone's magic works anyway. He's a part of this now," Ollie said.

Mia blinked, almost like she hadn't thought of that at all, but a bit of determination seemed to creep back onto her face.

"Sorry, boys," she said, starting the car. "We're missing school today."

Neither Noah nor Ollie could argue with that.

18

The Care and Keeping of Your Magic/Cursed Cat

WHILE MIA PUT ON her best mom impression to call them out of school, Ollie filled Noah in on the missing details, trying to answer any questions he had. Noah seemed to take it well. Probably because of the whole freaky-crows-and-bugs-time-stop situation from earlier.

Thankfully, Mr. and Mrs. Di Costa had already left for work by the time they made it back to the apartment. Ollie and Noah could hardly keep up as Mia rushed inside.

"Wishbone?!" Mia called out as she opened the front door. "Wishbone, where are you?!"

Wishbone's head popped up from where he was sprawled out on the living room couch. Mia hurried over, Ollie and Noah crowding behind her.

"I wish David was back," she said immediately.

Ollie waited for the familiar flash of Wishbone's eyes, but it didn't come. Instead, Wishbone let out a breath. It sounded almost . . . upset. A bit of panic rose in Ollie's chest. Ollie scratched Wishbone behind his ears to comfort him.

"Hey," he said softly, "you okay?"

Wishbone didn't even try to playfully bite, which had to be a bad sign.

"Did he not hear me?" Mia asked, refreshing the feed on her phone. "I wish Da—"

"No!" Ollie interrupted, holding on to Wishbone protectively. "I don't want to hurt him. Something was wrong with that wish. It didn't work."

Mia's eyes were glassy. "Why didn't it work?"

Ollie bit his lip, still petting Wishbone and giving small kisses to the top of his head. The cat seemed calmer. He nipped at Ollie's chin. "I guess we can't undo our wishes?"

"So now there are rules to this thing?" Mia snapped. She collapsed on the couch, burying her head in her arms. "I can't believe this is happening."

"Maybe it just takes a while?" Noah suggested.

"No, that's not it. I mean, they do take a while sometimes, but Wishbone's eyes were supposed to do a flashy thing," Ollie said. "Here, make a wish."

"Ollie," Mia warned.

"It's fine as long as we don't try to undo something, I think." Ollie turned back to Noah. "Just try to wish for something simple that wouldn't lead to someone dying or being erased from existence."

"So, no pressure," Noah teased. He gulped but looked at Wishbone.

"I wish we all knew how to fight really well. Um, please?" Wishbone's eyes flashed brightly, the blue of them shining.

"See?" Mia mumbled. "They were supposed to do that."

"You wished we can fight?" Ollie asked. "Seriously?"

Noah held up both his hands in defense. "You put me on the spot, and considering some evil wizard guy might be after us, at least it's something useful!"

He had a point. While Ollie wasn't sure that The Mage seemed like a hand-to-hand combat kind of villain, it couldn't hurt.

"How do we test it, though?" Noah asked. "Like, how do we know it worked besides the flashy eye thing?"

Ollie shrugged, then stepped in front of Noah. "Punch me."

"*What?*"

"It's fine, I'll try to avoid it, so go for it." Ollie stood tall. "It's okay if you hit me, we have to prove it, right?" He gave an easy smile. "Just try to avoid my face, it's my best feature."

Noah smiled at that comment, but it dropped quickly. He looked uncertain. Finally, he nodded. Noah threw a punch toward Ollie, but Ollie was able to quickly dodge it. He responded with sending a low kick toward Noah's leg, body basically moving on its own, but Noah checked the kick. He then lowered himself and rushed into Ollie, executing a perfect double-leg takedown. Noah landed on top of Ollie, fortunately on the carpeted floor.

It was at that moment that Ollie realized just how close they were. Face heating, he scrambled away and got back to his feet. He couldn't even look Noah in the eyes, desperate to hide any blush. "So, yeah, Wishbone's still magic."

"What do we do about David?" Mia asked, still not moving her face from her arms, so the words came out muffled.

Ollie frowned. "Just because we can't wish him back doesn't mean nothing will. We just have to figure out what to wish for that will work. Worst case, we might find an answer in The Backward Place."

That got Mia to look up. "You almost got killed both times you went there."

Ollie didn't remind Mia that neither of those times had he *chosen* to go to The Backward Place.

"I'm just saying. There are people there besides The Mage. Sure, they're a little . . . odd, but someone could know how to get David back."

"What if someone here knows?" Noah asked. "Like if they posted online."

Mia crossed her arms. "We can't exactly look up what to do when your magic cat accidentally pulls a Thanos with your best friend."

"Well, the Avengers got everyone back," Ollie muttered. He didn't like how Mia made it sound like this was Wishbone's fault. If anything, it was the way she made her wish. She should have been more specific. Also, they didn't know if David no longer existed. Maybe he was someone or somewhere else, perfectly happy and not missing out on anything. Mia was being a little dramatic. One would think she was the actor instead of Noah.

"There could be something." Noah shrugged and then reached for his backpack to take out his laptop. "There are over seven *billion* people in the world. Someone had to have experienced something similar and posted about it." He turned on his computer and grinned. "We just have to find it."

Mia and Ollie exchanged a look. After a moment, Mia sighed. "It's better than going to The Backward Place."

Better, but not easier. Seven billion plus people might have been alive on the planet, but none of them seemed to be particularly good at documenting rules of magic. There wasn't *nothing*, but there wasn't a lot that actually seemed credible.

Ollie scrolled down the thread he was on to check the comments.

"I can't believe I'm researching on Reddit," Ollie sighed. "There's nothing helpful. Tons on made-up fantasy stuff, or paranormal sightings, or the Mothman hanging around Chicago, but nothing we can use."

They were all spread across the kitchen and living room area, after taking a break to get lunch (researching was hard enough when you were still full of donuts), but more hours of looking up articles and even watching videos on YouTube still gave them nothing close to what was actually happening. Mia was curled up on the couch, looking on her phone and occasionally taking control of the TV. Ollie and Noah sat on the floor with their laptops, a bowl of chips between them.

"I found a guide on taking care of magic cats," Noah said, "but I'm pretty sure it's a fiction book."

Ollie's eyes were already getting tired from all the reading, and the fact that they weren't finding anything made it more frustrating. In the movies, people always just went to the local library and found some archive or did a quick search and got a full how-to on performing an exorcism. Yet they spent the entire day trying to find something on The Backward Place or an actual experience with magic and curses, and it was all just wild conspiracies that didn't make any sense.

"Maybe we should keep track of what we do know." Ollie opened up a blank document on his computer and started typing.

MAGIC / CURSES FACTS (?)

1. Magic seems to come from Backward Place. That was where Wishbone was injected with magic to get powers
2. Magic seems to automatically work when you make a wish out loud in front of Wishbone
3. When it is effective, eyes flash
4. For each wish, a separate but related curse happens to someone else
5. Curses might have something to do with gray smoke/fog (comes from eyes?)

When he was finished, he stepped over to Mia to show her the list. She quickly scanned it.

"None of these really seem like *facts*."

Ollie yanked his laptop away from her. "Well, it's all we got. So, facts or not, this is our starting point."

"Wait." Noah jumped up from his spot. "I think I found something!"

Ollie practically fell over himself. They hadn't found anything worthwhile, so what Noah uncovered had to be amazing. "Let me see!"

He scrambled over to Noah, Mia following. They all looked at the screen, but as Ollie read the title, his smile faded.

"'An Evil Wizard Turned My Brother into a Bird Man'?" Ollie looked at Noah. "Seriously?"

Noah shrugged. "Okay, sure it seems just like a bad story . . ."

"It's literally posted on a thread for scary fiction," Mia said, sounding equally disappointed.

"I know," Noah continued, "*but* some of the details seem kind of similar. Just read it. I know a lot of writers from my theater camp, and, trust me, they all steal stuff from their own lives. It could be based on the truth."

Ollie and Mia shared a dubious look before scanning the story on the screen.

You're not going to believe me at first. I don't blame you, I wouldn't either. But there will come a time when you realize I'm telling the truth. By then, it will be too late.

My brother had this friend. Let's call him John. John was sort of a troubled kid. He had a single mom who didn't really seem that close to him, and he'd act out a lot. But my brother, Pete, he was always the nice guy that wanted to be friends with everyone. To not exclude anyone. So he sort of took John under his wing.

But John wasn't well. One day, he started getting worse. Changing. He would disappear for long periods of time, and when he came back, he started telling John about how he found this power, this magic, and soon, he'd be able to get revenge on everyone who ever hurt them. I only found out about this after, when I noticed how worried Pete was.

It just got worse and worse until John came over to our house. He didn't know that I was home. He thought it was only him and Pete. I heard him telling Pete how he was going to use these curses to unleash monsters on everyone who teased him, who teased Pete for being friends with him. Anyone who would stand in their way. I honestly thought he was a little weird. Pete was clearly uncomfortable, and got mad at John, saying he was wrong and needed help and Pete was going to turn him in. But then it got scary.

Smoke started pouring out of John's eyes. Like the inside of his skull was on fire. His head twisted around. A crow literally flew into the window out of the blue, and then John lifted his hands and some smoke came from his palms, too. He killed the crow and then slammed it and the smoke into Pete.

Pete's body started changing, he was sprouting feathers

and his face split open and a beak grew out. He kept screaming
as he turned into a monster: half man, half bird.

I tried to keep quiet, but it was too horrible.

I met John's eyes, right as he snatched Pete's arm and
disappeared into the floor.

Top Comments:
Scarystorylvr42: this writing is trash
Ghostgirrrrl: where did the bird even come from?
Chickennugget: idk I liked it, hope you write more
Friendofanimals: how DARE you kill the bird!!!!

Ollie's stomach churned as he finished reading. While the
story definitely read like fiction, Noah was right. There were too
many similarities to what was happening to them to ignore. The
crow flying into the window. The evil wizard. The hybrid animal creature. Was it possible that the story was true, and this
John guy was The Mage?

Ollie could feel his heart pounding. If The Mage was able to
use curses to turn people into freaky animal monsters like he
did in the story, he could easily do that to any of them. It might
even be the real reason why he wanted Wishbone back. To finish using him for some gross experiment.

Ollie felt sick. He reached out toward Wishbone, not wanting to turn away from the cat for a second.

"Can we DM the user who posted it or something? Ask if
any of this really did happen?" Ollie asked. "Maybe he knows

something about The Mage's weakness. Or how he was able to control these curses."

Noah scrolled for a second before his shoulders sank. "User not found. He must have deleted his account."

"This is bad," Mia whispered. "This is really, really bad."

That felt like an understatement. Both Noah and Mia looked at Ollie.

"What do we do?" Noah asked.

Ollie didn't have an answer. Before he could even try to give one, he was interrupted by a loud banging on the apartment door.

19

So Maybe Ollie Really Messed Up

OLLIE, MIA, AND NOAH all looked at one another, the tension in the room thick. Even Wishbone shot up, eyes wide and alert and ears pulled back.

"Is that the scary mad scientist wizard?" Noah stage-whispered.

"I don't know," Ollie said. "Stay quiet."

The hairs on his arms were standing on edge, skin completely gooseflesh. Was it possible that The Mage was able to find them, just like Ollie somehow found him? Sure, he expected to have to face him again, but not so soon and not at home.

Ollie slowly got up, trying not to make any noise. On the balls of his feet, he took careful steps to the door and glanced through the peephole. No one was there.

"I don't see anyone," Ollie whispered.

Another knock sounded, and the three of them jumped.

"Oh crap," Noah said. "Are we going to die?"

"We're not gonna die," Mia said quickly, despite not looking convinced.

"Should I open the door?" Ollie asked.

"No, you should NOT open the door," Mia whisper-shouted. "Do you want to get murdered?"

"You just said we weren't going to die!"

"Because I'm not ridiculous enough to open the door!"

Noah shushed the siblings. "It's going to hear us."

"Ollie?" a voice said from the other side of the door. "Are you there?"

It certainly didn't sound like The Mage, or a monster at all. It sounded a lot like a seventh-grade girl, and Ollie was pretty sure he knew which one. Despite a quick protest from Mia, Ollie opened the door.

Lauren stood there, still wearing her helmet and holding on to her teal-green bike. In the other hand, she had a plastic bag. "I heard you were super sick, so I got your address from the school directory and I stopped at my favorite deli to get you matzah ball soup . . ." She seemed to take in the sight that was Ollie, Mia, and Noah, all staring with confused expressions. "Wait, what is Noah doing here? Are you . . . are you not sick?"

Ollie blinked. Why was Lauren even bringing him food? He thought they hadn't been talking after he insulted her mom. It wasn't like she had reached out. Was this apology soup? That made him feel even guiltier about being caught lying. "Uh . . ."

"You left me to do the group presentation *alone* so you could play hooky?"

Ollie's stomach dropped. Oh no. He had completely forgotten about that.

"Lauren, I'm sorry, I can explain—" Ollie started, but she cut off the rest of his words.

"How could you?" Lauren snapped. "After I told you how nervous I was about having to talk in front of class? You said you'd do most of it and I just had to do a few lines!"

Ollie's fingers clenched. He did make that promise, sure, but with everything going on, school had been the least of his worries. If she would just let him explain, she'd have to understand. "Lauren, if you calm down, I can exp—"

"Calm down? Seriously? It was so embarrassing! People were laughing at me because I kept messing up! The teacher made me start over *twice*." Lauren made a motion like she wanted to throw the bag of soup, but instead carefully set it on the floor. "I thought you were sick, so I tried to be understanding, but turns out you're just a selfish jerk who ditched me to hang out with your new popular friend and the complete *worst*."

Ollie knew he should feel bad, but instead he just felt annoyed. Sure, he was a little guilty, and he understood why Lauren was upset, but she wouldn't even let him talk. Ollie hated when people yelled nonstop and wouldn't even allow for an explanation. It was what his parents would do. Or, at least, what they had done for most of his life up until recently. And it wasn't like Ollie really did anything *wrong*. Yeah, he left

Lauren to do the presentation by herself, but all the work had already been done, and he couldn't have asked Mia for a ride to school for one English class that didn't even matter in the grand scheme of things when David was gone and they were all in danger.

But he didn't get to say any of that.

Because in the middle of yelling, Lauren started gasping, clutching at her throat.

"What's happening?" Noah asked. "Is she choking?"

"I don't . . . I don't know!" Ollie said, panicking.

Mia pulled Lauren inside. "Call for help!" she commanded Noah, examining Lauren for anything that could be causing this.

Lauren began shaking violently, eyes practically rolling back in her head. All Ollie could do was stand and stare.

Noah's phone finally connected to the emergency line, but before he could say anything, Lauren stopped shaking and choking. Her mouth split into a bright smile as if none of it had happened. Noah dropped his phone onto the floor, leaving the person on the other end to hang up.

"Lauren?" Ollie asked. "Are you okay?"

"I hate you, Ollie," she said with a too-big smile, cheery voice—and wisps of smoke rising from the corners of her eyes.

The apartment was silent aside from Lauren's shoulders shaking behind her big smile.

"I don't understand," she said in a tone that matched Mia's "customer service" voice. "What's happening to me?"

It was eerie, to see her face and tone of voice suggest one kind of emotion, but for her eyes and words to communicate something else entirely. Clearly magic—a curse—was behind this. It wasn't like Lauren had wished for anything during her rant, and none of the wishes they'd made today would have—

Oh no.

"You were mean to me," Ollie muttered under his breath, realization dawning on him.

Noah twisted to Ollie, confused. "Is this a wish? Did you wish for this to happen?"

"No!" Ollie ran a hand through his hair. "Not directly anyway."

"Oh my god," Mia groaned. She sat on the couch, head in her hands again.

"I didn't mean for this to happen! I just wished that no one could say anything mean to me, that's all."

"You *what*?" Noah asked as Mia groaned again.

Ollie threw his hands up in defense, even though he knew it wouldn't help. "I was fed up with getting transphobic comments! And I wanted to prove to Mia that the magic was okay."

"Well, it's clearly not okay," Mia muttered.

Ollie rolled his eyes. "Yeah, thanks, very helpful. It's not like I expected it to turn out like *this*. Just like we couldn't have known we would un-exist David with your wish."

"Don't put this back on me. That could have been your wish that you *forgot*!"

Ollie tried to bite back his anger by chewing lightly on the inside of his lip. It wasn't working. Why did Mia keep blaming him? He was doing his best to protect *them*, to figure it out, like they always did.

Yet everyone was acting like he was some kind of monster himself.

"I'm not saying it's on you. I'm saying it's no one's fault. It's not me either, it's just . . ." Ollie let out a breath, trying to keep his frustration under control as he grasped for the right word. "A little mistake."

A few sniffles sounded, and it was only then that the three all seemed to remember that Lauren was in the room. Finally, her forced expression had begun to relax. There were still no traces of anger on her face or smoke in her eyes, but instead of the clownish smile was only confusion and fear.

"Can someone explain to me what is going on?" Lauren asked with a shaking voice. After the first line got out, more followed like she couldn't hold any of it in anymore. "Why are you talking about wishes? What was wrong with me? Suddenly I was choking and everything hurt, and then I couldn't stop smiling, and now I'm randomly okay? And you are all acting like this is normal?! It's not!"

Mia moved first, grabbing a tissue from the cluttered coffee table, and offering it to Lauren. "I'm sorry, uh, Ollie's Friend. It's a lot to explain."

"Lauren," she said, taking the tissue.

Ollie figured Lauren wanted to be anything but friends with him at the moment, but she didn't say anything about it.

Instead, after blowing her nose, she looked between them. "Can you at least try to explain it to me?"

They didn't really have much of a choice. Starting from the beginning, Mia and Ollie told her everything they could.

When they finished, Lauren was silent for a moment. Then finally she offered a simple, "Huh."

She was seated on the couch, no longer in her helmet, but with her hands folded in her lap. Ollie could tell from her expression she didn't believe them. Of course she didn't.

"We have to show her a wish," Ollie said.

"No, bad idea." Noah waved his arms for emphasis. "The wishes are what's getting us into this mess."

"We agreed that we wouldn't," Mia added. "We don't know what it will do."

Ollie waved that away. "I didn't agree to anything. We can keep it small. It's fine."

"It's not fine," Mia said, her voice raised. She cleared her throat and took a deep breath as if to calm herself down. "We can't keep making exceptions, and I'm the grown-up here, so what I say is final."

Since no one wished that *Ollie* couldn't get mad, he found his frustration rapidly building up again. Mia was being unfair. It was one thing to disagree, but she didn't have to treat him like some little kid, especially in front of Noah and Lauren.

"You're not a *grown-up*," Ollie snapped. "I'm the one who rescued Wishbone, so I should get final say. He's *my* cat. Just because our parents suck doesn't make you my mom."

It was one of those angry statements that only felt good for about a second before regret immediately took over. Ollie knew he went too far based on the way the words echoed around the room, slapping him back in the face. Mia's own expression was pale, and her eyes were shining. It wasn't something that Ollie should have said in front of Noah and Lauren, who were friends but not *friend* friends. It probably wasn't something he should've said at all.

"You're right. It doesn't," Mia said finally. Her face was forced into a smile, but she kept going. "Maybe I'm not an adult yet, but someone had to act like one. Why do you think you're able to act like a freaking toddler now? Because everything falls onto me." Mia's voice was calm, which was so much worse than if she'd been yelling. Her bright smile didn't match at all with her words, and even the magic couldn't completely erase the hurt behind them. "You want to make another wish? Fine. But you have to take responsibility for whatever happens because of it."

Ollie knew there was more she wanted to say. Probably years of stuff. He also knew that he likely wasn't the person she really wanted to say it to, but even if their parents were home, they wouldn't understand. Not with how they were now. Not with how they were before either, if he was really being honest. Conflicting emotions bubbled and fought within Ollie. But his annoyance was starting to outweigh his guilt.

Either way, Noah and Lauren were clearly uncomfortable.

"Lauren," Ollie said. "Maybe you should make the wish. You're the only one here who hasn't."

She had been completely still on the couch but looked up at Ollie's words like a startled animal. Her red curls fell into her face as she quickly shook her head. "No way. This is already freaky and weird, and I don't want anything to do with . . ." She paused, her hazel eyes looking off in the distance like they could find the right words there. "These wishes."

Ollie sighed. Everyone was looking at him like he suggested they sacrifice a puppy instead of making a wish. The bad thing wasn't Wishbone or his magic, it was the person who did this to him—The Mage. *That* was what they had to focus on stopping, and they'd need magic to do it.

"Okay, fine," he said. "I'll wish for something simple, like an item. One that will help us." He bit his lip before looking back at Lauren. "If you had to fight an evil wizard guy, what would you want to bring with you?"

Lauren shrugged. "A sword?"

"A *magic* sword," Noah corrected. "He's a wizard, after all."

"That's true," Lauren agreed. "It's probably got to be magic."

Mia sat on the floor, holding her head in both her hands. "What is even happening today?"

Ollie was just glad that some of the tension seemed to clear from the room. It was a good distraction, so he didn't completely lose his temper. Sure, he made a mistake in wording some of his past wishes maybe, but it wasn't like he had tons of experience in what to do when your magic cat's wish-granting powers caused unexpected issues.

There was a *lot* going on, and Ollie thought he'd been doing a pretty good job handling everything, considering.

"I'll wish for that then," Ollie said. "An item should be fine. If somebody else loses a sword or something, it's not a big deal. Okay?"

Despite asking the question, Ollie didn't wait for anyone to answer. He walked over to Wishbone, who slowly blinked at him. The cat seemed oblivious to the hectic happenings around him.

"I wish we had a powerful magic sword that could defeat evil wizards or magicians or . . . really anything evil, I guess?" Ollie looked over to Noah, who shrugged but then gave a thumbs-up.

Wishbone's eyes flashed as he walked over to sniff Lauren's shoes before hissing at her.

"Sorry," Ollie said. "He's nervous around new people."

"He wasn't like that with me," Noah said.

Lauren glared at him. "Well, I guess we can't all be perfect, *Noah.*"

Noah blushed. "I didn't mean—"

"Ollie, this is a really bad idea," Mia said.

Ollie turned to her, his anger boiling back up again. "Why? Because it's my idea? Wishes have only been making good things happen to us. *That's* what's important. Now, we're going to have a weapon we can use against the actual bad guy, so stop treating me like *I'm* the problem when I'm the only one making any sense!"

Ollie's voice echoed through the room, his biting tone lingering behind. No one said anything. A knock on the door broke the uncomfortable silence. Mia checked through the peephole before opening it to reveal a long box. She quickly pulled it in and shut the door, clicking the lock loudly.

"Is that . . . ?" Lauren asked.

"The magic sword? Yes," Ollie said smugly. "See? I told you. A simple wish. Absolutely nothing to worry about. You all need to *listen* to me because, like I said, we're all good."

It was right after that statement that Ollie felt a little dizzy. He also felt a wetness under his nose. He placed his fingers on the skin, then pulled them away to see fresh red blood on his fingertips. He thought the others were calling his name, but they felt so far away.

The world around Ollie's vision went too bright, everything framed in white, and then immediately cut off into black.

Which, perhaps, was something to worry about and definitely not good.

20

The (Terrifying, Awful, Buttfaced) Monstrous Mage

OLLIE AWOKE TO THE orange-and-gray sky of The Backward Place and cursed to himself. Not again. Crows cawed as they flew backward overhead. He was flat on his back on the ground where black vines ran through the dry and yellowed grass. Ollie lifted his head enough to see that he was right in front of The Mage's house, which towered over the rest of the houses on the street.

Great.

He didn't even have the sword.

Ollie scrambled to a standing position. His nose seemed to stop bleeding, at least, but dried blood caked the edges of his nostrils.

How had he ended up here again? And better yet, how was he supposed to get back home? It wasn't like something specific happened either time that gave him a clear idea of what to do. He was either pulled or pushed through, but that didn't really help if there was no one to pull or push him. He hoped the monster wouldn't make another appearance . . .

To the left of the house, a shape moved, and Ollie's stomach flipped. But it looked like a person, one entirely in the right direction, not like The Mage, and way less gray than the rest of The Backward Place people. Had someone come with him?

"Hey!" Ollie yelled. "Wait up!"

He rushed after the person, who was running away. Ollie pushed himself to move faster. The closer he got, the more features he was able to make out, seeing that the person looked exactly like—

"David?" Ollie asked aloud.

Still far ahead of him, David turned. His face was twisted into a smile, and gray smoke rose from his eye sockets. Oh no. Was this actually David or just a Backward Place version of David? Either way, Ollie needed to do something.

Would this David hurt him, though?

Before Ollie could decide if he wanted to take a step forward, one of the black vines wrapped tightly around his ankle.

Not this again.

Ollie's leg was yanked, causing him to fall right on his butt. His skin stung as he was pulled across the ground. He glanced ahead, where he saw that the vine wrapped around him was coming from the base of The Mage's house.

Ollie dug his fingers into the ground and kicked at the vine, but it wouldn't budge and his clawing hardly slowed it down. The door to the house opened, and The Mage stepped out. On both sides of him were two beasts, different from the one Ollie had encountered the last time. One was smaller, a rough-looking cat that seemed like two different cats put together, and had a giant scorpion tail protruding from its rear. The one on the right was much larger, mostly a bear, but with gills on the side of its neck and a large rhino horn. Both creatures bared their teeth, circling Ollie.

The Mage was facing forward but looked terrible. His skin cracked and peeled, revealing a stony gray underneath. Smoke slipped from around his eyes, and his hat was tattered and falling off in pieces.

The vine pulled up Ollie by the ankle, dangling him upside down in front of The Mage. He could see the animal hybrids ready to pounce from the corner of his eyes.

"Welcome back, thief," The Mage said. "My chimeras are quite impressive, are they not? I heard you've met one already. You know how neighbors love to gossip." Ollie couldn't glance back to see the smoky-eyed residents who apparently snitched on him. The Mage was all too happy to continue speaking, anyway. He looked at Ollie's empty hands, dangling just above the ground, riddled with broken glass and bloodied feathers. "I see you didn't come to return what you stole. A pity. I suppose I'll have to wait to kill you until after I get the cat."

Ollie grimaced. "I'll never give you Wishbone, you butt-faced freak."

The Mage laughed. "Quite the mouth on this one. And you named Subject 23. Cute." The Mage leaned in closer so Ollie could smell his metallic, rancid breath. His stomach turned. "Now where is the cat?"

Ollie kept his mouth closed. More smoke poured from The Mage's eyes as they narrowed. If The Mage didn't know where they lived in the real world, maybe that meant he couldn't cross over? Either way, it seemed like good news.

"I'll ask nicely once more. Where. Is. The. Cat?"

Ollie spat in his face.

The Mage chuckled, turning away. His monsters were ready to jump, but he stopped them by holding up his hand. There was a moment of quiet as their growls silenced, Ollie looking at The Mage's back as he swayed from the vine. A crow landed tail-first onto the ground, giving Ollie a curious glance. It pecked at a large piece of glass close to Ollie's fingers.

Just then the silence was broken by a sickening *pop*.

Ollie looked up as The Mage's bones cracked and his head spun backward, quickly enough that a glob of spit flew off his mouth as he faced Ollie. The Mage's right arm snapped backward along with it, snatching the crow between his fingers before it could fly off.

"I don't think you understand what's happening here," The Mage snarled. "I am going to disembowel that cat to get the magic out, and then do the same to you for fun."

He squeezed the bird, which let out frantic caws. Ollie's fingers clenched below him. He was dizzy from all the blood rushing to his head.

"I won't let you," Ollie snapped. His fingertips brushed the glass the bird had been interested in. A plan started to form in his mind. "Besides, you can't even get to my world, can you? If you could, you would've killed us already. There's nothing you can do."

The Mage laughed. "I can't get there? You're practically rolling out the red carpet for me, kid. The more magic you use in that world, the more curses unleash. Once your whole town is cursed, I won't even need magic to come through. And then you, the cat, your entire world . . . everything will be mine."

Ollie tried to make sense of what he was saying, but his thought process was cut short when The Mage bit the head right off the crow. Ollie choked back a panicked cry but took the opportunity to grab the piece of glass. Twisting his body and using all the core strength he had, he stabbed the vine wrapped around his ankle. It reared back, dropping him onto the littered dirt. The fall knocked the breath out of him, and tiny pieces of glass stung his skin, but Ollie didn't have time to worry about that. Adrenaline took over, and he got to his feet and ran.

"After him," The Mage called out. "Feel free to hurt him, but keep the boy alive."

Ollie didn't turn back. He didn't have to. He heard the heavy steps of the two chimeras, moving fast behind him. As Ollie's feet pounded across the pavement, running past his backward apartment, he knew there wasn't a chance he was faster than the beasts. The growls and pants were getting louder, and his legs were already starting to ache.

He'd always been pretty good at sprints in gym class, but Ollie was no long-distance runner. He still didn't turn back, afraid he would look right into the wild eyes of the monsters after him.

A beach was in front of him. It wasn't Manhattan Beach (Hcaeb Nattahnam?) where he and Mia usually went, but it was a beach nonetheless. Ollie pushed himself harder. The beach had been his safe place with Mia. If he made it there, maybe everything would be okay. Maybe he'd somehow make it home.

Just as his feet hit the sand, they were pulled out from under him. The bear/fish/rhino stepped over him, Ollie flat between its four legs. Ollie scrambled onto his back, but he couldn't get away, there was hardly any space to shimmy out from under the chimera. It lowered its head, roaring and revealing its sharp teeth. With a low growl, it moved mere inches from Ollie, drool spilling onto Ollie's face.

His heart was pounding. Tears sprung up in his eyes, and he had to actively try not to pee his pants.

Ollie was going to be torn apart.

The monster reared back, ready to bite. Ollie closed his eyes and braced himself.

But nothing happened. Instead, he heard a whimper.

Cautiously, Ollie opened one eye. The chimera had been tossed aside, whining with sad puppy eyes as it looked up at the elongated gray form of The Witch. The Witch held the other chimera in its hands, calmly petting the monster as it happily purred.

Ollie blinked. He quickly got up to his feet, taking a step away from all of it. The Witch looked at him, or at least seemed to, and moved closer.

"Stay back!" Ollie yelled, hands outstretched in front of him. (Maybe Noah's wish to be able to fight would actually come in handy.)

"You aren't ready," The Witch continued, stepping toward Ollie. "Not yet. Look at you, still trying to do everything on your own."

Ollie slid back. "I said stay away!"

The Witch stopped where it stood, and Ollie got his first good look at the creature outside the poor lighting from The Mage's basement. It was even worse than The Mage. Thick smoke poured from its eye sockets. It moved in a strange way, like every angle of its elongated body was double-jointed, perhaps explaining how it moved backward with such ease. Its neck was entirely twisted, like a sickening corkscrew. Its pale whitish-gray skin looked tight around its bones as it opened its mouth to reveal spiked teeth in a complete circle around the lipless hole.

Ollie slowly backed farther away, trying to see which direction he could run to.

"I'll catch you if you run," The Witch said, "or one of my friends here will, but I'm not the one looking to hurt you."

Ollie glared at The Witch. "I'm supposed to believe that? You're with The Mage. Those . . . beasts were just trying to kill me, and you're calling them *friends*?"

He couldn't help but wonder if there was a person in either

of the chimeras like the story from the internet. But both of them seemed entirely animal.

Either way, Ollie tasted bile at the thought.

"They didn't ask to be made like this. To be cursed. They're quite friendly when he's not influencing them," The Witch said. The cat chimera gave a happy meow, shaking its scorpion tail.

Ollie blinked. "You're lying. You just want to kill me and take Wishbone."

"You're just like him. Always angry, always thinking you know better. Wanting to push everyone else away." The Witch's smoking sockets seemed to lock right on Ollie, almost like they could see through him. "But at the end of the day, you're just a scared little child that wants to be loved, aren't you?"

Anger burned inside Ollie. It was like The Witch peered into the parts of him that he hated the most, the parts that he didn't want anyone else to see.

"Shut up, you don't know me," Ollie said. "Who even are you?"

"I am Lost," The Witch said simply. "I am Cursed. But, once, I was human."

Ollie blinked. He rubbed his hands over the bumpy skin on his arms. It was hard to believe that this monster had ever been human. Ollie almost needed the confirmation, like he had to have heard it wrong. "You were human?"

"Like you," it said. "Like him. A human who tried magic, and thought it tasted so sweet that they didn't mind the curses. A human who craved power, and wanted it so much, they lost themself to it." The Witch crouched down, twisted head level with Ollie as it crawled forward. "A human, a human, a human."

"Him?" Ollie asked, almost stumbling over his feet.

"The one called The Mage," the monster said. "The one with the lab, who comes for you and your two-tailed friend."

"I'm nothing like him!" Ollie defended quickly.

A part of him wanted to add that he was also nothing like The Witch either, but something told him it wasn't a good idea to risk offending a creature of nightmares with a throat full of pointed teeth. It was bad enough that he made The Mage angry. The Witch seemed scarier.

"Are you nothing like him, child? Is there any human that is different?"

Ollie wasn't sure what The Witch meant by that.

"I would never hurt Wishbone," Ollie said, "he's my friend."

"Ah." The Witch released the syllable in a long breath. It finally stopped moving closer to him. "But you would hurt someone who wasn't your friend?"

Ollie couldn't deny it. He would. He had. He hurt Jake and Mr. Wright and Great-Aunt Margaret—and he'd do it again. But they *deserved* it.

"A human, a human, a human," The Witch repeated, claws tapping the sand. There was almost something wistful about the way it said the words, like if it didn't repeat them, it would forget the meaning.

The Witch turned its head back at Ollie as the chimera jumped from its arms. "Am I your friend, human child?"

"If I say no, are you going to kill me?"

It was almost like The Witch wanted to smile, but without the lips to do so, it just widened the hole of its mouth, revealing teeth that continued to spiral down its throat.

"I don't plan on it, no."

"Well, your friend clearly wants to."

"I wouldn't call him my friend."

Ollie crossed his arms. "Then what would you call him?"

The Witch didn't answer. Instead, it turned to the distance, back in the direction of The Mage. "He's growing more powerful. Soon, he may be able to cross over. I tried to prevent it, but I had no idea some of the magic slipped through."

Wishbone. The Witch had to be talking about him. Ollie kept his voice steady. "What do you mean? Why does Wishbone have the only magic left? The Mage must have some."

The Witch shook its head. "He can only use curses now. I cast a forbidden spell to seal up all the magic in this place. I needed to keep it away from The Mage," it said simply. "The only way to release it is with more magic. Curses may give us power, but they alone can't break the spell. I thought I stopped him for good, but I didn't realize he had some magic stored away for his experiments."

"But why does he need to unlock the rest of the magic so bad?" Ollie asked. "He seems to be doing pretty all right with just curses."

The Witch sighed. "When you are fully cursed like we are, you can use curses, yes, but you can no longer use magic. But magic is required to pass through to the normal world, just as curses are required to come here. He wanted to put magic in one of his chimeras and use it to cross over."

The Mage wanted to go to the real world. Clearly not just to kill Ollie, if that was the reason he had been after Wishbone in the first place.

Ollie gulped. "What will he do when he crosses over?"

"Nothing good."

It was difficult to think about. If The Mage crossed over, he'd probably bring all his chimeras. And they wouldn't be docile like they were with The Witch. He'd use his curses to stop anything that got in the way.

It wouldn't end with Wishbone and Ollie.

He would destroy the whole world.

"But why? What does he have against the regular world?"

"That is a complicated question. One that I'm afraid I cannot answer. What I can tell you is curses stem from negative emotions. They are connected. That's why we were all drawn here," The Witch said, gesturing to the world around them. "Loneliness. Hopelessness. Frustration. That's what brings us to this place."

"So all the people here, they came because they felt those things? But doesn't everyone?"

"Not everyone. Not like this." With its long claws, The Witch lifted sand and let it fall between its fingers. "This realm, it invites in people like that. I'm not sure why it chooses only certain people but there's one thing they all share. They are lonely, angry, broken souls. Like I was. Like you are now."

Ollie glared at The Witch. "I'm not like that."

Even though, he had to wonder if he was. If curses came from negative feelings, Ollie certainly had his fair share of those. His heart pounded in his chest. Was that why he kept getting pulled into The Backward Place? Because he couldn't control his anger and annoyance and frustration?

In that sense, he was no better than his parents.

Ollie bit his lip. No. He couldn't think that way.

"I'm not like that," he repeated, but his voice was softer. Unsure.

"You will be. If you don't stop him. If you don't break the cycle. The curse."

That didn't make much sense. If magic was all the good stuff they wished for and curses were all the bad stuff that happened as a result, there were a lot of curses that had to be broken.

"Which curse?" Ollie asked.

The Witch reached out a clawed hand and touched it to Ollie's chest.

"Yours."

With that, it pushed Ollie down, down, down as the sand fell beneath him, and he was once again buried under its weight.

21

When Getting Parents Involved Is Not Helpful

OLLIE CAME TO WITH a start, his hand outstretched, and grasped on to Mia. His body was between the couch cushions, and Noah grabbed his other free arm to pull him out the rest of the way. Ollie glanced back at the couch, even moving the cushions, but there seemed to be no way he could have fit in there.

"Did you pull me out of the couch?" Ollie asked.

Mia, Noah, and Lauren all looked equally freaked out. Wishbone gently bit and licked Ollie's hand, as if making sure he was okay.

"You had fallen through the floor, somehow?" Noah sniffled. "These vine things pulled you. Then, a few seconds later, your hand was peeking through the couch."

Ollie's heart raced. He had definitely been in The Backward Place longer than a few seconds. Time moving backward there must have a weird effect. His breathing came out faster. His muscle soreness and panic caught up with him, and his legs shook and gave way, causing him to fall onto the couch.

Thankfully, vines didn't emerge and pull him back into impossible depths.

"So you were actually in that Backward Place?" Lauren asked. "It's actually real?"

Ollie nodded. "I saw The Mage. He's coming for us."

"What does that mean?" Noah asked.

"It means he wants Wishbone, and I'm not going to let that happen," Ollie said. He picked up Wishbone and held on to him, almost like letting the cat out of his sight for a moment would put him in danger. The Witch had been right. Ollie hadn't been ready to face The Mage. He didn't have any weapon or plan or way to defend himself. But that didn't mean he couldn't get ready and face him for real. If The Mage was preparing to cross over to their world, Ollie wouldn't have a choice. A shining glint caught the corner of his eye. "Is that the sword?"

It was leaning up against the side of the couch. The sleek and thin sword had an intricate hilt with dark gray extensions that would wrap around the wielder's hand. Instead of a typical silver, the blade shone an array of purples and blues like the galaxy itself. When Ollie leaned forward, Wishbone stepped off him and onto the couch, so Ollie grabbed the hilt. It felt light in his hands. Perfect.

"No, it's the *magic* sword," Noah corrected.

"It's super awesome," Lauren added.

Ollie could only nod in agreement. It *was* super awesome.

This combined with his new ability to fight would make him able to take on the vines and even The Mage and his chimeras. Hopefully. Ollie stood up, sword firm in his grip.

"I'm going to find a way into The Backward Place, and I'm going to stop The Mage before he comes here."

Mia's face lost some color. "He's coming here? As in, our world here?"

"That's been his goal all along. From what I learned in The Backward Place, Wishbone's magic was his way to cross over, but, apparently, if things here become cursed enough, he can cross whenever." Ollie sighed. He knew that Mia was going to I-told-you-so him, and he didn't want to deal with that, so he stood firm in his past decisions. "But I still think making *smart* wishes was a good idea. We can't go up against The Mage and his curses without magic."

Mia looked like she wanted to say something not so nice to Ollie by the way her mouth was beginning to twitch up at the corners, but Lauren spoke first.

"So how do we get to The Backward Place?"

Ollie's eyebrows scrunched up. "Um, *we* aren't going anywhere. You stay and protect Wishbone. I'm going to handle this alone."

Mia, Noah, and Lauren all opened their mouths in protest, Wishbone even giving what sounded like an annoyed meow. But before anyone else could speak up, the front door swung open. Mr. and Mrs. Di Costa walked in. Ollie looked over at them. It would be bad enough if they found out Mia had called them out of school, but Ollie was currently holding a literal weapon. How would he explain that?

"Uh . . . ," he started. "Hi, Mom. Dad."

Mia gave a seemingly innocent smile. Noah and Lauren tried to follow suit and awkwardly waved.

Wishbone's fur bristled as he hissed in the direction of Ollie's parents. Ollie gave him a reassuring pet on the back, smoothing his coat. It seemed extra, even for Wishbone.

Mom and Dad took in the scene with wide eyes. Ollie tried to remember to breathe. Maybe it was a good opportunity to come clean. His parents weren't exactly reliable, but maybe they could help watch Wishbone while Ollie went to The Backward Place.

"Who are all of you?" Mom asked.

"Oh, sorry," Ollie said. "This is Noah, and that's Lauren—"

"How did you get in here?" Dad interrupted.

"Our . . . key?" Ollie answered.

"You two aren't being funny," Mia said to their parents, clearly having no patience left after everything that'd happened that day.

Their parents maintained looks of complete confusion. Stepping into the apartment, they let the door slowly close behind them. When both of their eyes landed on Ollie, there was no spark of recognition. Even when his parents were mad at him, they never looked so cold and unfeeling. The muscles of their faces began to twitch uncontrollably before settling into large smiles.

Their mom spoke first. "But what are you all doing in our home?"

The tone of her voice was steady, but it didn't match the twitching smile.

"Are you kids lost?" Dad added. He stepped forward, his smile faltering at times before turning back into full force.

"Dad, you're freaking me out," Mia said.

"What are you talking about?" he said. "I'm not your dad."

Their mom kept up her smile. "We don't have kids."

There was a long silence in the room. Ollie felt slightly dizzy and nauseous.

"What's going on?" Noah asked.

Lauren stepped toward Ollie. "Those are your parents, right?"

He could only nod. His mom's forgetfulness that morning made a lot more sense. He looked over at Mia. "Well, I think I officially wasn't responsible for David disappearing."

Mia looked crushed, and Ollie didn't blame her. He felt his own mouth twitching and eyes threatening to burn. While he had figured something else must have happened because of his wish to forget his fight with Mia, he never would have imagined his parents would forget them altogether.

Ollie's chest felt hollow. Maybe he really did mess up.

"We're going to call the police," his dad said slowly, "and get you kids home."

That was the last thing they needed. They *were* home, even if it hadn't always felt like it. The police coming would just cause more trouble and delay Ollie from getting to The Backward Place and they would probably take his sword away, too. Not to mention, seeing his parents look at him like that hurt more than he'd care to admit.

He had to fix this. Before his parents ruined everything. Maybe he couldn't directly undo the curse, but he could try to stop the worst from happening in the meantime.

"I wish Mom and Dad couldn't see us!" Ollie blurted.

His heart hurt at the thought, but they already didn't remember him. Besides, while things had been good recently, would being invisible to his parents really be that different from the way it used to be?

Wishbone meowed from the couch, eyes flashing.

"Ollie! No!"

Mia's words were drowned out by the ominous feeling Ollie got in the seconds following his wish. It was like the air changed, got heavier in the silence.

Then both his parents turned to him in synchronization.

They looked like puppets, heads slightly dangling, all smiles, eyes wide. Then they started shaking. Their limbs bent, and their eyes rolled back, and the two collapsed to the floor.

"Mom!" Ollie rushed over to his mom first, kneeling at her side, dropping the sword onto the floor. She had to be okay. She had to. "Mom?" Ollie gently moved her shoulder.

Her eyelids lifted, but not to reveal her normal hazel irises. Instead, the thick, gray smoke rose from the empty sockets. Her smile was still on full force. Ollie's chest hurt as he blinked back tears.

"Mom?" he asked. "Are you okay?"

"Of course I'm okay," she said in a perfectly pleasant voice. "But I'll be even better once I kill you, dear."

Her wrists bent in the opposite direction, fingers snapping backward before they reached out to Ollie's neck.

22

A Real Dysfunctional Family

OLLIE'S MIND WENT BLANK for a moment as his mom's fingers wrapped around his throat. Panic surged through him at the initial pressure. While the person in front of him looked like his mom, it wasn't. It couldn't be. Not with that too-big toothy smile and those smoky eye sockets. She was becoming cursed, just like the man in the post.

"Mom, stop!" Mia yelled.

Mom kept her pressure as her head snapped toward Mia. "Oh, I'll kill you, too, dear. After I rip your brother lovingly limb from limb."

While he was still in a panic, Ollie tucked his chin and used both hands to pull on his mom's arm. Breaking the choke hold, he kicked his mom away.

"Sorry, Mom," he yelped as she fell backward.

Maybe Noah had been on to something with his fight-knowledge wish.

His mom's and dad's bodies continued to crack and shift,

joints popping in the wrong direction. Their necks twitched and extended, entirely spinning around to face the group once more, smiles still wide and eyes replaced with rising gray smoke.

Everyone screamed, aside from Ollie. While he was also very freaked out, he at least had the experience of seeing The Mage all backward before.

Ollie's dad grabbed on to his wrist, holding so tight Ollie worried he'd break a bone. What would his dad do with him in his clutches? Literally rip off his arm like his mom suggested? Try to bite off his head like The Mage did to the crow? Even if it didn't seem possible as Ollie wasn't crow-sized, the thought of it made him squirm anyway.

Then Noah jumped onto Dad's back, his elbow at the center of Mr. Di Costa's twisted neck as he closed a choke hold. "Sorry, Mr. Di Costa," Noah said quickly. "Sorry, sorry, sorry."

Finally, Mr. Di Costa passed out, and Noah stepped over to Ollie. "I'm sorry I choked out your dad," he said.

"It's okay," Ollie answered, heart pounding. "You probably just saved my life."

Ollie's mom started to get to her feet again. Mia picked up the sword from the floor and pointed it at their mom. "We gotta get out of here," she said. "Get to the car."

"Grab Wishbone!" Ollie called.

Lauren scooped up the cat into her arms. Despite the danger, Wishbone still tried to bite her hands, but she held tightly on to him anyway. Alongside Noah, she rushed outside. Ollie looked between his parents and Mia.

"What if they come after us?" Ollie asked. It didn't even seem like Ollie's wish had worked—clearly his parents could see them well enough to try to kill them, and he really didn't want to have to hurt his parents if they tried again.

Mia hit their mom in the head with the hilt of the sword, causing her to crumble to the floor. "Let's shut them in the bedroom," Mia said. She winced as she looked down at her mom. "Sorry. But this backward thing is way too freaky." She turned toward Ollie. "Their necks aren't, like, broken, right? They'll be okay when we fix this?"

He was glad she said *when* and not *if*. Knowing her anxiety, it meant a lot that she still believed in him, and this was one change in his sister Ollie appreciated.

"The Mage seemed to go back and forth, so I don't think it actually hurts them."

"Freaking curses," Mia muttered. She swallowed. "Okay. Let's lock them up."

Working together, Ollie and Mia dragged their parents into the primary bedroom and closed them in. It took a lot of legwork, and Mia was out of breath by the end of it, but they managed. With the door closed, they shoved the large kitchen hutch in front of it. Thankfully, the bedroom door opened outward.

"Do you think that's heavy enough?" Mia asked.

"We have to hope it is," Ollie said. "At the very least, it should slow them down."

Ollie and Mia rushed out of the apartment to join Noah, Lauren, and Wishbone outside.

Things had gotten substantially worse. There was a pressure in the air that seemed to push down on Ollie's skin. Both Noah and Lauren had their heads turned up to the sky. Ollie followed their gaze.

"Oh no," he mumbled.

The sky was a swirling gray that was practically unheard of in sunny Los Angeles. They weren't typical rain clouds either, or the kind of May gray/June gloom cloud cover they'd get in the spring. It was smoke. The same kind of smoke that came from his parents' and The Mage's eyes.

It was the curses.

A flock of crows moved backward across the sky.

"You know a group of crows is called a murder?" Noah said, trying to crack a smile. "It seems fitting."

"What is *happening*?" Lauren asked, voice quivering.

In her arms, Wishbone chirped at the birds.

"Get in the car," Mia said. "We have to get out of here." She was looking at the birds too, but cleared her throat and repeated the command in a stronger voice, pushing Ollie toward the passenger door while Noah opened up the back. She gave Ollie the sword and he tightened his grip around it.

With the door closed, Wishbone sat between Noah and Lauren.

"We can't exactly buckle in Wishbone, can we?" Noah asked.

They really should have bought a carrier.

"We'll hold on to him," Lauren promised. "Does he bite a lot?"

"Kind of," Ollie admitted. "But usually not hard."

While Mia was holding it together, it seemed like she crumbled entirely at that point. Tears started streaming from her eyes as she gripped the steering wheel too tightly.

"What are we supposed to do?" Mia sobbed.

"Hey," Ollie said softly, "it'll be okay. We'll figure it out, right? We always do."

Mia twisted toward him. "No we won't, Ollie. Not this time. You didn't listen to me because you're so stubborn and always put yourself first." Her face began to shift into that weird, twisted smile. It didn't stop her from continuing. "Now look what happened. Mom and Dad didn't just forget us, *you* cursed them, and now they want to kill us. And the entire city is messed up. I mean, look around. What can we do to fix this?"

Her eyes were entirely rimmed in red, and Ollie could see past the forced-happy expression to the complete hopelessness. A part of Ollie felt the instinct to comfort her, but it was buried under his discomfort. He was a little guilty, partially ashamed, but he still felt angry. Betrayed.

Mia was supposed to be the one person who was always on his side. The one person he could always count on. From the beginning, they had been in it together. They both took care of Wishbone, they both agreed on the wishes and benefitted from them. But she was blaming him for everything.

The flames lit inside him, lapping up against his chest and making everything burn.

"*I* cursed them?" Ollie snapped. "That's what I hate about you, Mia! You always act like you're so nice and good and so much better than me. But you're not. You made wishes, just like I did. You got your money for college and our parents, and you didn't care about what was happening to other people. It's supposed to be me and you against it all, but it turns out I can't even trust you. I can't trust anyone because everyone keeps turning on me. That's all people want to do. Make me the bad guy, the problem, the *monster*."

Ollie's voice cracked on the last word, a bit of smoke slipping into the corner of his vision. His breath came out shallow and quick. He looked directly into his sister's eyes, hoping he hurt her even more than she hurt him.

"Well, fine," Ollie continued. "I'll be the monster. Because sometimes, that's what it takes to win."

"Um . . . Ollie?" Lauren said from the back. "I think you should calm down."

Ollie spun toward her. "*What?*"

She was using her free hand that wasn't holding on to Wishbone to point out the car window. Ollie followed her to see the black vines crawling up the side of the window. They were completely coating them, a web encircling the entire car, blocking out all the windows. Noah tried to open the door, but it wouldn't budge.

"What are these things?" he asked.

Ollie swallowed, fear extinguishing his anger. "A big problem."

With that, all the light was blocked as screams echoed in Ollie's ears and the slithering vines swallowed them whole.

23

Back to Backward

THE CAR LANDED WITH a heavy crash that sent Ollie jumping in his seat and smacking against the door. Wishbone hissed, and Lauren let out a yelp, but Ollie couldn't actually see anything. The vines were still blocking all the light. Finally, the car seemed to settle in place.

"Is everyone okay?" Ollie asked.

"I think so," Noah answered first.

Wishbone hissed again.

"I'm sorry!" Lauren's voice said from the back seat. "Stop trying to bite me!"

"Wishbone, *bad boy*!" That was Mia.

Well, everyone was still alive at least. But what had happened?

The vines slowly slithered back down, peeling away from the car. Ollie could only watch in horror as orange light poured in through the window. It was their same street, the exact spot they were in before. But it was different.

The Backward Place.

Ollie's blood turned cold. This wasn't how they were supposed to enter The Backward Place. They weren't ready at all! They had just been trying to get away from his basically possessed parents, and they only had the magic sword, and Ollie hardly had a real idea of how to use it. Sure, he had been really upset at Mia, but—

Ollie swallowed. He thought back to his conversation with The Witch. Was it his anger that sent them all there?

"Ollie?" Mia asked next to him. It seemed like their fight was momentarily forgotten in the sheer horror of the situation. "Is this . . . ?"

"Yeah," Ollie said. "We're in The Backward Place. We have to move."

Mia slammed her foot on the gas pedal. The engine revved, but the car wouldn't budge. The vines that had pulled them down through the ground held them firmly in place, and the vines began to crawl out from the A/C vents, stretching toward them.

Mia, Lauren, and Noah all wore expressions of pure fear, but none of them really had a chance to say anything else before something smashed into the left side of the car. Noah gave his impressive Horror Movie Star–worthy scream, and Lauren soon joined him. Ollie's own scream was caught in his throat as he looked at the mouth of the chimera attacking them.

It had the head of a tiger, but with large, bloodstained tusks splitting from both sides of its jaw. Patches of fur were gone from its arms, revealing scales underneath. From its back, large porcupine quills broke out of the skin.

The chimera smacked against the glass, shaking the entire car.

"We got to get out of the car," Ollie said.

Mia turned to him. "Get out?! Are you joking? We'll get eaten!"

The chimera crashed into them again, a crack forming on the window next to Noah. He and Lauren were holding on to a puffed-up and hissing Wishbone.

"We'll get crushed if we stay here, so we have to take the chance!"

Noah, who seemed particularly ready to get away from the deadly beast at his window, nodded. The chimera dug its claws into the metal of the car, and Ollie saw their moment to escape.

"Now!" Ollie yelled.

He rushed out of the passenger side door. Lauren exited next from the back with Wishbone, and Mia and Noah quickly followed, climbing across. They were barely out the door when the chimera leapt on top of the car, smashing the metal roof into the seats below.

Ollie swallowed and tried not to think about what would've happened if they were still inside. The chimera crouched low, baring the fangs behind its tusks as it let out a sound that was a cross between a hiss and a rattle.

Ollie stood between the monster and everyone else, gripping the sword and holding it out.

Maybe the chimera wasn't evil, like The Witch told him, but it certainly acted as if it wanted to kill them. Ollie had to hope magic swords also acted like regular swords in desperate times.

Not that he knew how to use it against an animal hybrid that looked specifically designed to hunt and eat people.

"Everyone, keep back," Ollie said. "I'll hold him off."

"Very heroic of you," Lauren started, "but there's a big problem with that."

Growls sounded from behind Ollie's shoulder. He looked back quickly, only to see that they were cornered. There were multiple chimeras surrounding them from every side, and none of them looked particularly welcoming.

They were trapped.

Wishbone squirmed out of Lauren's arms and leapt over to Ollie. His bandage was red with blood, the wound on his paw slightly reopened. Seeing Wishbone like that broke something in Ollie then. He didn't want to face it, but he was the reason they all ended up in The Backward Place. He was the reason they were all going to get ripped apart by the chimeras. He was the reason Wishbone was hurt again. Ollie couldn't even think about anything else. He dropped the sword and picked up his cat.

"Ollie, what are you doing?!" Mia asked, not moving the sword herself, as if afraid of spooking the chimeras.

Tears rolled down Ollie's cheeks as he hugged Wishbone. "I'm so sorry, Wishbone. I'm so, so sorry. This is all my fault."

Ollie yanked off a piece of his shirt, ripping the fabric and tying it around Wishbone's bandaged paw, but not before a drop of blood fell onto the ground. It hit one of the vines, causing it to flash the same blue as Wishbone's eyes.

Oh no.

Ollie had the feeling that was definitely not good.

A low laugh sounded, reverberating throughout the air. It seemed to come from every direction, almost like it was amplified. Smoke swirled in the air, thick and heavy. It began to tunnel, like the start of a tornado, before shooting down into the ground in the middle of where Ollie, Mia, Noah, and Lauren stood. They were thrown back by the force as the ground where they'd just stood caved in, forming a deep hole. The vines crawled and circled around it, smoke filling the space until it started to glow a sickly orange and red.

"What is that?" Mia shouted from the other side of the hole.

Ollie didn't have the chance to answer—someone else beat him to it.

"That is how the end of the world begins," The Mage said. "And you kids helped make it happen."

Ollie turned, heart racing, toward The Mage. He brushed past the snarling chimeras, stopping only a few feet away. His full height towered over Ollie and Wishbone, so long and thin he hardly seemed human. Although his gray, cracked skin, bloody grin, and smoky eyes mostly caused that effect.

"Nice to see you again, thief," The Mage said. His head jerked to the side as his gaze locked on Wishbone. "Ah, yes. And hello to you, old friend. Thanks for the bit of magic. Unfortunately, it's not quite enough to fully open my portal, but props on the good start. Looks like I'll still need to bleed the rest of it out of you."

With Wishbone sitting at his feet, paw fully wrapped, Ollie picked up the sword. He held the blade in front of him, pointed toward The Mage. He moved in front of Wishbone, ignoring his own heart pounding in his throat. "I'm not going to let you take him, creep."

The Mage laughed, loud and clear. *"You?"* His already strained neck twisted farther as he swooped his head toward Ollie. In one swift motion, The Mage reached out and dug his fingers into Ollie's hair, lifting him up by it so his toes brushed the vine-covered, cracked concrete. Ollie's scalp screamed along with his sister.

"Ollie!"

She jumped forward, trying to get around the hole to them, but The Mage flicked his overextended wrist, roughly throwing her back onto the pavement.

Mia groaned from the ground, and anger boiled up inside Ollie. He lifted the sword and swung, but The Mage's limbs were so long that even the point of the blade couldn't reach him.

Ollie tried to twist out of The Mage's grip, but only succeeded in tiring himself out. Ollie's arms felt so heavy. Too heavy. With one final swing, the sword slipped from his hands and plopped onto the dirt.

The Mage's smile was bright. "Give up now, boy. What were *you* going to do, anyway? You're not the one with magic

in you. No . . . there's only one thing you can do, *Oliver*."
The Mage leaned in, his horrifying face mere inches from
Ollie. "Die."

He reached out toward Ollie, and screams sounded, but
Ollie's vision went entirely white.

24

We Interrupt Ollie's Incoming Death to Be a Cat

OLLIE DIDN'T FEEL LIKE himself when he opened his eyes. He wasn't sure where he was, and everything looked strange. Colors weren't the same, his senses felt too sharp, and his body wasn't quite right. Wasn't quite . . . human.

Weird.

He tried to step forward, but he couldn't move. Glancing down, he saw that he was wrapped up tightly in something. It made him feel terrible. Trapped. He squirmed, struggling to get out, but none of it worked. He still couldn't move.

A shadow blocked some of the light, and Ollie turned his head toward it.

It was The Mage. But he looked different. His skin and eyes were completely human, all his limbs the normal length. However, he was *huge*. At least compared to Ollie, who had never felt so small in his life. What was happening? Ollie struggled against his restraints.

The Mage pressed a button on a voice recorder, then held up a large needle. "Day One, about to inject Subject 23 with the first dose of magic."

He approached with the syringe, and Ollie hissed.

⸺

Ollie was in pain. His body hurt. He tried to lick his fur, but it was difficult to move. He was mad. He wanted to bite and claw and hiss, but his muscles ached. He was tired.

A strange feeling formed near the base of his tail.

What was going on?

Ollie was scared. He was so scared. There were others that had strange growths, that were crying out before they were stitched together and turned into something new. Was that what was happening to Ollie? Maybe not. Because there were others that faced something even worse . . .

Like Subject 22. Who used to hold Ollie down and groom him. Who playfully wrestled Ollie in their little cage. Until he was taken away, given the shots, and then he wasn't himself. Ollie didn't want to think of how Subject 22 was at the end, but his mind couldn't forget it. The way that his paws bent in wrong directions. The way smoke poured from what were once green eyes. The way The Mage yelled and then Subject 22 was never seen again.

And then Ollie was pulled from the cage next to screaming mice and given a number:

23.

Ollie was tired.

His tail and whiskers twitching, the world faded to black as he dreamed of eyes that held beautiful colors.

Ollie was in the lab, but time had passed. He felt different, stronger in some ways, stranger in others. He jumped down from the counter but stumbled on the landing. He was still trying to get used to his second tail. The door to the outside was closed, as it always was. It was riddled with claw marks from him and all the other cats and creatures before him.

The ones that didn't make it.

He needed to get out. There were no cracks in the lab, no secret passageways. No matter how much he meowed and pawed at the door, it mysteriously refused to open.

He was trapped. And if he didn't escape, he would be hurt and hurt again, until he became like Subject 22. Like all the subjects before. A number that would be buried out front or cut into parts to be put onto someone else.

Ollie didn't want that. He wanted to get out. He wanted to escape.

He wanted, more than anything, to be loved.

So, desperately, he wished for it.

The Mage stomped down to the basement, and Ollie backed into a corner, his paws light on the floor. He knew he couldn't hide. The Mage always found him. Sure enough, once he turned the corner, a slightly smoking eye landed right on him.

"You're ready, Subject 23. I think you'll be the first successful experiment." The Mage wrote down his update and taped it to the annoying thing on Ollie's ear. Ollie tried to scratch it, but it was just out of reach. "We're almost done now." The Mage grabbed him by the scruff on the back of his neck. Ollie went still. "Just one last thing . . . a little bit of curses to balance out the magic. Let's hope it doesn't kill you."

The Mage lifted his palm, smoke swirling inside it. He moved it closer to Ollie's face. The smell was strong, ash and charred wood. Ollie wanted to twist away, but he couldn't move.

He pictured joints snapping and shifting. Smoke pouring from eye sockets. Teeth bared back and ready to rip into skin. Vicious. Feral. Lost.

Ollie couldn't let that happen. He had to get away. He let out a low growl.

"You'll listen to me, Subject 23," The Mage said, "because if you don't . . . Well, I only need your magic to cross. After that, there's no use for you."

He held a knife in his other hand, tapping it against his chin. Ollie needed to go then or he'd end up like all the others. No. Worse.

Then Ollie realized something. He hadn't heard the door shut when The Mage walked downstairs. It might've been left open. So he made a desperate wish and, perhaps, a terrible decision. While he wasn't cursed yet, he decided to act as if he was.

Just as the smoke shot up his nose, Ollie launched into action. He ignored the burning sensation and scratched The Mage's face and chest, peeling off skin with his claws. The smoke filled his vision for a moment, but it almost made it easier to feel his anger, to enjoy the blood rushing from The Mage's face. The Mage fell backward, dropping Ollie as he held up the knife to defend himself. It slashed Ollie's paw, but the sharp sting didn't stop him. With The Mage unbalanced, he ran up the stairs. The door was open and his heart soared. He sneezed, a bit of smoke coming out. His head felt a little dizzy from inhaling it, but he couldn't stop. He had to get away.

Outside the house, Ollie almost tripped over his paws when he saw The Witch. He didn't recognize it, and fear shot through his veins. The Mage's yell followed him from the house. He heard growls, roars, thundering paws, the others were going to come after him. He looked at The Witch with wild eyes.

The Witch studied him. "You wished for this, didn't you?"

Ollie couldn't answer.

"Go," The Witch said. "I'll hold them off."

Ollie didn't have to understand its words. He ran. He kept running, even though his paw ached and left drops of blood behind him. He made it to sand, water rushing in the background, and started to walk on three legs, giving his injured paw a break. He was tired.

He was HUNGRY.

He wanted to be safe. Ollie spotted a hole, a dip in the sand. He could rest for a moment. Carefully holding his hurt paw up,

Ollie leapt into the hole and curled up. There was something immediately comforting about the small, closed-in space. Only then did he allow himself to cry.

After a few moments, he smelled something new. A shadow loomed over. Ollie looked up and saw a boy. Himself. Well, his human self. Scared, Ollie bared his teeth and hissed.

Human Ollie laughed. "Smart cat. You shouldn't trust anyone." Human Ollie knelt down and held out something in his hands. It smelled *delicious*. "I'm only trying to help, I swear. I'm not going to hurt you. I'd only hurt someone who deserved it, and something tells me you didn't do anything to deserve that, huh?"

Cautiously, Ollie lifted his injured paw again and walked closer to the wonderful-smelling piece of meat. He eyed Human Ollie but sniffed the meat. Oh, man. He licked it once, and then once more.

It was wonderful.

Maybe this Human Ollie wasn't so terrible after all.

Then, suddenly, he wrapped up Ollie, trapping him. Ollie panicked. Would he get another injection? Would he get hurt?

Human Ollie tied something around his bleeding paw and let him go. Ollie twitched his paw. That felt weird. He hissed again at Human Ollie, to clearly let him know that was totally uncalled for and he did not approve. Then he went back to the delicious meat.

Human Ollie kept talking at him, but Ollie didn't mind. He kind of liked the sound of his voice. Compared to The Mage, it was softer, smoother. Kind. Human Ollie reached out his hands, and Ollie wanted to thank him for the snack, so he sniffed his fingers (a nice smell, also unlike The Mage) and bumped his head into Human Ollie's hand. He liked the pets he received, as Human Ollie said more words Ollie didn't really care about.

"Do you have a name? Doesn't that hurt?" Human Ollie removed the clip from his ear. Ollie twitched it. That felt *way* better. Ollie rubbed against him in thanks as Human Ollie kept talking.

"Do you want to die?!"

Oh no. Oh no, no, no. The Mage found him. The Mage found *them*. Ollie panicked. He couldn't run. He couldn't leave the boy with The Mage. He'd have to get the injections too, and what if he didn't make it? Like everyone else?

Ollie lowered himself to the ground and let out a long growl.

Human Ollie spoke clearly and sharply, moving in between Ollie and The Mage. But when The Mage came at them, Ollie braced to be left behind.

Instead, he was scooped up into the arms of Human Ollie and carried away. His heart raced, and fear coursed through him, but he didn't mind the boy's touch. Then they fell. But Human Ollie protected him. Together, they were pulled through the sand and away from The Mage, into a world that was shining.

Ollie could hardly believe it. There was so much to take in. It was perfect. Everything was perfect. He was free. He was alive. He glanced back at the boy who saved him and the girl next to him. She smelled just like him, so he gave a little meow in greeting.

Ollie couldn't help but notice their eyes. Brown, but with specks of a gorgeous gold, a brilliant black, and a deep green like Subject 22's eyes. They were beautiful. Warm. Colors he thought he'd never see again.

Purring happily, Ollie knew three things for sure.

First, with the help of this boy and girl, he had escaped.

Second, they were his new home. His family.

And, third, he would do everything in his power to make sure it stayed that way.

25

Wishbone's Silent, Not-So-Secret Wish

OLLIE OPENED HIS EYES to his own, very human body. He didn't think he was dead, which was kind of shocking, to be honest. But if The Mage had killed him, he wouldn't be looking up at the ceiling of his bedroom, which he was. There was also pressure on his stomach, and he was pretty sure dead people didn't feel anything.

He looked down to see Wishbone sitting in a loaf on his torso. Noticing he was awake, Wishbone gave a revving meow and smacked his face into Ollie, who had to accept that a semi-violent headbutt was simply a sign of love. Ollie pulled him into a hug, even more happy that they were together after what he'd experienced. He kept hugging Wishbone until he gave a light bite in warning.

Wishbone was safe, but where was everyone else?

Ollie quickly sat up, Wishbone stepping onto his lap, but his anxiety immediately subsided. Mia, Lauren, and Noah were also in the room with them, gradually coming back to their senses.

"What happened?" Lauren rubbed her head. "I thought we were about to be killed by the freaky wizard."

"I was not prepared for how terrifying he actually was," Noah said. "But how did we get back here?"

Mia was the most awake but had been silent. At this, she frowned at Noah. "Didn't you wish for us to escape? I saw Wishbone's eyes flash." She let out a long sigh. "I know I've said not to make any more wishes, but I get why you did it. There was no way we were getting out of The Backward Place alive without magic."

Noah's eyes were wide. "Uh, no. I didn't. Looking back, I probably should've, but I didn't."

"I didn't either," Lauren said. "And Ollie couldn't have."

Ollie thought back to his dream, which he realized now wasn't a dream at all. They were Wishbone's memories. Wishbone, who had initially made a wish to be able to escape from The Mage. A wish that might have brought Ollie into The Backward Place.

Wishbone, who had (in his own cat way) vowed that he'd do anything to protect Ollie and Mia, like they protected him.

"It was Wishbone," Ollie said, hugging him. "He made the wish for us."

"Can he do that?" Lauren asked.

Ollie used one hand to rub his right eye. "While I was out, I saw a bunch of Wishbone's memories. I don't know how—maybe Wishbone wanted me to see them?—but I did. I think because the magic is inside him, he was able to make a wish by wanting it, even without being able to put it into words."

Mia practically shoved Ollie out of the way to take Wishbone. She gave him kisses on the top of his head. "You're such a good boy. Saving us from a scary wizard murderer. You are the best and most handsome cat ever, and I love you so much, you little magic angel." He stayed in her arms, purring and happily taking all the compliments.

Wishbone wasn't just magic, though. He had curses, too. Ollie had watched him inhale the smoke. But while the cat was feisty, he definitely wasn't cursed. Was it possible to use curses but not become cursed?

Ollie wanted to talk to the group about what he'd seen, but a part of him almost felt like he needed to protect Wishbone's secret. He didn't want any of the blame to fall on Wishbone. He'd rather take it himself.

They had bigger problems at the moment, anyway.

Like the fact that The Mage was after them and his portal had almost been complete. If making wishes really did make it easier for The Mage to cross over, Wishbone saving them might have been enough to fully open the portal.

If that was the case . . . they were in trouble.

"What about the sword?" Ollie asked. "Did it come back with us?"

Given that none of them had it and it wasn't on the floor, it was safe to say that, no, it hadn't.

"Well, it didn't seem all that useful anyway." Noah's voice was light, and he was clearly just trying to make Ollie feel better. "At least we're all safe."

Ollie bit back his *yeah, but for how long?* Noah had a point, after all. What mattered was they bought themselves time. Even if The Mage was after them, they could actually come up with a plan to stop him.

"We should get more weapons," Ollie said. "Maybe the sword isn't enough, but it's not like I was really able to try it out. The Mage is strong, but if we're all armed, we might have a chance."

Everyone nodded.

"I can get stuff from my house," Noah suggested.

"I'll go with you," Mia volunteered. She turned toward Ollie and Lauren. "Ollie, you can look around for what we have here, and Lauren, you should keep an eye on Wishbone, to be safe."

Ollie couldn't argue with that. While a part of him wanted more time with Noah, he didn't want to be too far away from Wishbone. The cat was the one with The Mage's magic, so he was in more danger than the rest of them.

"Okay," he said. He didn't mind letting them take the lead.

Noah checked the time on his phone. "We'll meet back here in fifteen minutes. If anyone sees a sign of The Mage, call or text right away."

"Sounds good."

Noah met Ollie's eyes as he smiled. "Try not to get almost killed again, okay?"

"Why, you'll miss me?" Ollie teased.

Noah's laugh was everything. "Of course."

Despite it all, Ollie's chest still felt warm and fluttery when they left.

 ⇒

Lauren played with Wishbone in the middle of the living room while Ollie ransacked the surrounding area for anything useful. His parents' room was out of the question—they still heard the occasional thumps and shuffles from inside, so there was no way they were moving the hutch or opening that door.

Ollie didn't have much success finding anything aside from the biggest kitchen knife in the set and a lighter his mom used to start the one stove burner that didn't work, but he supposed it was better than nothing.

Not much better, but better.

He paused for a moment, glancing over at Lauren. She seemed pretty calm, despite everything, and happy to play with Wishbone. It made Ollie feel kind of bad. Lauren had no reason to stay for everything, but she did anyway. Even though, if he really admitted it to himself, it was his fault she was dragged into it at all. And also his fault they all got sucked into The Backward Place, where they could have died.

Maybe . . . Ollie had been the real buttface all along.

"I'm really sorry," he said. "For missing the presentation today."

"It's okay," Lauren said. "I understand why you missed it now."

Ollie swallowed. "But that's part of the problem. I caused this whole mess and dragged you into all this."

Lauren waved away the thought. "Come on, Ollie. What are friends for if not helping you defeat terrifying evil wizards that want to kill you and your cat?"

He snorted, but something still burrowed uncomfortably in his gut. Lauren was doing so much for him even after he left her hanging. No one could be *that* understanding. Could they?

He opened the kitchen junk drawer, rifling through it. "I know, but . . . you don't have to do this. This isn't partnering up in cooking class or even going to bakeries or whatever. This is seriously dangerous. Like, we're not risk-your-life close."

Lauren frowned. "Why do you say that?"

"We're friends, but like school friends. We're not after-school, save-the-world-together friends. I don't . . . I don't have friends like that."

The words sounded flat when they fell out of Ollie's mouth, but they were true. It was the people you trusted, the people you let in, that hurt you most in the end. Yet Lauren dropped the cat toy she was holding and turned toward Ollie with crossed arms. Wishbone pounced on the toy.

"And whose fault is that?" Lauren asked.

Ollie didn't even know how to respond, but she didn't give him much of a chance to anyway.

Lauren threw up her hands and continued. *"You* don't let anyone get close to you. People like you—*I* like you. You're saying you don't have any close friends, but I've been here the entire time! And you've blown me off every time I ask you to go anywhere, but then you ditch me to hang out with *Noah*? How do you think that makes me feel?" Lauren wiped her face. "It's like I'm not good enough or something."

Ollie bit his lip. He'd been so busy protecting his own feelings he never considered he could be hurting someone else's.

"That's not at all true. You *are* good enough, Lauren. Probably too good to be friends with me. You are so cool and kind and fun. To be honest, I thought maybe you were just inviting me places to be nice. And then I thought you didn't want to be friends with me because of what I said to your mom."

"What?" Lauren asked. "Why would that change anything?"

"You didn't message me after! You barely even stood up for me," Ollie blurted.

Lauren frowned. "I'm sorry, Ollie. I'm really sorry about what she said. I know what she's like, *trust me*, but I have to live with her. I can't just say whatever I want."

Ollie hadn't really thought about that. He had been so focused on feeling like Lauren didn't stand up for him that he didn't think about why she potentially couldn't have.

Lauren wasn't done. "But don't pretend like I've been the only bad friend here. You're acting like there's some secret contract you need to be real friends. What do you think a friend is? It's someone you like, someone you spend time with, someone you want to help and who feels the same way about you. News flash, buttface! That's already us. We've *been* friends, even if you make bad excuses not to hang out outside school."

Ollie tried to suppress the smile that crept onto his face. Lauren was yelling at him, yes, but she was also right—they *were* friends. And the thought of that made Ollie . . . happy. But with happiness came doubt. He sighed. "I guess I've been afraid. Like, if we weren't close, then it wouldn't mean as much if you didn't want to be around me anymore. Because, honestly, I'd get it. Sometimes I'm hard to be around." His voice lowered. "And you wouldn't be the first person to feel that way. It happened before with Jake—"

"Jake sucks," Lauren said.

"Sure, but it wasn't just him. My own parents hardly even want to deal with me. If they're not getting mad at me, they pretty much act like I don't exist. I worry enough that people won't like me because I'm trans, and it's like . . . they'll accept a nice, perfect, queer kid, maybe. But not a jerk like me." Ollie wiped at his eyes, almost wishing he could stop crying but not daring to waste a wish on that. "I know what I'm like, and I know that eventually, anyone I get close to won't want to deal with me either. Not if they really know me. I just don't want anyone else to be able to hurt me like that again."

It was scary and a little embarrassing to say all this out loud, but at the same time, Ollie felt like a weight had been lifted off his chest. It was actually nice to admit the feelings he'd hidden inside for so long. It made him feel less alone.

"That's ridiculous," Lauren said with a sniffle. "You're

annoy—" She cut herself off, possibly remembering that being mean to Ollie could still have consequences. "You have your faults, but so do I. So does everyone. That doesn't mean I won't want to be around you. And come on, Ollie, you should know you can talk to *me* about having awful parents." Ollie snorted and Lauren smiled. "That's why we have to stick together. Especially us queer kids, and especially us queer kids who can kind of be jerks." She also wiped her teary eyes, but laughed. "Basically every queer book and movie is about found family, so stop being so stubborn and be my family already."

Ollie laughed aloud at that one. "You've always been such a good friend. I'm sorry I haven't."

Lauren smiled, wiping her eyes again but clearly trying to hide it. "You should be sorry." She snorted and let out a little laugh. "But I get it. I'm not always as charming as you might think. I can be angry and unlikable. So what? We'll be angry and unlikable together."

Ollie joined in on her laughter. And her tears, although he tried to hide it, too. "I like the sound of that."

While there was still so much to be worried and angry about, Ollie felt a lot better. He had been wrong to push people away. Especially good ones. He wouldn't make that mistake again.

Then all of a sudden, Lauren stopped laughing.

"Ollie . . . I don't feel so good." Her face suddenly looked pale, almost shiny.

"What? What do you feel?"

"Really angry, but not like the normal way . . ." Her eyes widened. "My face feels weird. It's not moving right."

"What do you mean it's not—"

Before he could finish the thought, Lauren's face started to twitch. The right side of her mouth curled into a painfully unnatural smile. Fear filled her eyes as a thin tendril of smoke escaped from them.

"Ollie," she said, soft but urgent. "I think you need to run."

26

When LITERALLY EVERYTHING Is Cursed

OH NO, OH NO, oh no. Lauren was becoming cursed. Ollie rushed over to her and Wishbone, but he didn't really know what to do. How much time did he have before she completely turned?

"It's gonna be okay," Ollie said.

A few tears fell down Lauren's freckled cheeks as more smoke rose from the edges of her eyes. "I know. Because you're going to save me, right?"

Ollie's eyes were watering, and his stomach felt sick, but he held out his pinky. "Promise. It's what friends are for."

Lauren pulled him into a hug, and he didn't shy away or shake her off. He hugged her back.

She broke away. "You've got to go, Ollie. I can feel it, my thoughts getting all messed up." Her shoulders shook. "I'm scared I might hurt you and Wishbone."

Her fingers started to tremble and snap. They both grimaced.

Ollie knew she was right, but he didn't like it. "You want me to just leave you here?"

Lauren gave a weak smile with the side of her mouth still under her control. "You promised that you'd come back for me."

"I will." Ollie grabbed Wishbone and headed toward the door. He slid the kitchen knife into the waistband of his pants and grabbed the door handle. He looked back toward Lauren. "We got this."

Lauren raised her hands to give two thumbs-up, arms trembling. Her body started to jerk, face twisting into that sinister smile. Her elbows and knees bent entirely the wrong way. As Ollie rushed out the door with Wishbone, the last image seared into his mind was a completely cursed Lauren, smoke pouring from her eyes and neck starting to twist.

Ollie knew he probably should text Mia and Noah, but with Wishbone squirming in his arms, he couldn't free one of them to grab his phone from his pocket. It was difficult enough to quickly move with the knife in his pants. They really, really should've gotten a cat carrier.

Outside was bad. Like full end-of-the-world bad.

The sky was filled with the gray smoke of curses, a deep orange barely peeking through behind it. The black vines spread throughout the neighborhood, cracking concrete and crawling up the sides of buildings. Sirens and screams sounded off in the distance.

Lauren didn't just get cursed because of the wish. It felt like *the entire city* was at risk of getting cursed. Based on the terrifying sounds carried in the wind, it was already happening.

They had to hurry.

Luckily, no one else seemed to be outside the apartment. Ollie wouldn't be surprised if everyone who wasn't cursed was too afraid to leave or had been advised to stay indoors.

Ollie ran over to the Chois' house. The front door was locked, which was understandable, but frustrating in the moment. Ollie swore under his breath and pressed the doorbell a bunch of times. He had to hope that Mr. and Mrs. Choi still hadn't come home, because he would not be making a good first impression.

Thankfully, it was Noah who opened the door. He had a metal baseball bat in one hand.

"Ollie?" Noah asked. "What's going on? Where's Lauren?"

"She's cursed," Ollie said. "I think it's just happening to whoever now, like some kind of zombie apocalypse scenario."

Noah bit his lip, eyes fearful as he looked past Ollie. "You're probably right." He sighed. "We might have cursed ourselves when we said we didn't want to be in an apocalypse movie."

"It's still better than vampires."

"It is *not*." Noah couldn't hide a small smile as he ushered Ollie inside and locked the door behind him. Mia looked up from the kitchen counter, duct-taping two large kitchen knives together to make some kind of dual-bladed weapon. Ollie gave her a look.

"What?" she asked. "I'm bisexual, I'm legally obligated to carry more than one blade in any fighting scenario." Her smile fell. "Is Lauren safe?"

Ollie explained what happened. "She's stuck in our apartment, though, so I think she'll be okay."

Wishbone jumped out of Ollie's arms. He didn't take off, instead rubbing Noah's legs and sniffing around the floor of the new space. Ollie almost wished he was as calm and carefree as Wishbone was able to be.

Thankfully, wishes made in *his* head didn't get granted.

"Did you find anything?" Noah asked.

Ollie pulled the knife out of the waistband of his pants and the lighter from his pocket. "This is about it."

"At least we all have something!"

Ollie really appreciated Noah's ability to find the positives in the situation. He felt like he was the exact opposite, and Mia wasn't much better, so it was refreshing to have someone a little more optimistic around.

Suddenly, the TV switched on, revealing a close-up of The Mage's face, and the three of them all screamed.

Then again, maybe optimism was pointless.

"Hello there, little runaways," The Mage said.

The voice wasn't just coming from the TV. It was coming from their phones as well. Ollie pulled out his phone to see the same image. The Mage must have tapped into every screen they had.

"How is he doing this?" Noah asked.

Mia shrugged. "This is, like, the least weird thing he's done so far."

She had a point.

The Mage continued. "To everyone watching this who doesn't know who I am, let's just say I'm the bogeyman. Don't worry. You won't feel afraid at all once you're cursed. Mostly just angry. But that's much nicer, isn't it? After all, there are so many reasons to be angry. Like someone taking something that's yours and using it for themselves."

Ollie was pretty sure The Mage couldn't see them, but at that moment, it really felt like The Mage was looking directly at him.

"Little thief, little thief, the portal is almost ready. But if you don't come back to where we first met with that cat, being cursed will be the least of everyone's problems."

The Mage made a comical expression that seemed to signify being dead. It was somehow more frightening than if he had been serious. He *enjoyed* this.

"You have one hour before I'll come and take back what's mine myself," The Mage said, and his image cut out, all the devices returning to black or their normal home screen.

Ollie gripped the knife a little tighter in his hand. "We have to go."

"We can't just give him Wishbone," Noah protested.

Ollie tried to put on a confident smile. "I'd never. We're going to fight him."

Noah bit his lip. "How?"

Ollie wasn't quite as sure about that part. "I don't know yet, but we'll figure it out. We don't really have a choice. The portal is opening. Either we stop The Mage first, or he's going to unleash his creepy chimeras onto an already-very-cursed Los Angeles."

"Okay." Noah nodded for good measure, possibly convincing himself. "Where, though? It didn't look like the portal was outside, but that's where we were in The Backward Place."

"He said to go back to where we first met." Ollie scratched Wishbone. "That wasn't here. It was at the beach."

So they would go back to where Ollie and Mia usually went in times of trouble. It was annoyingly fitting.

"One problem," Mia said. "My car didn't come back with us and was also wrecked."

Oh, right. That was a problem.

"What about Mom and Dad's car?" Ollie asked.

"I don't know how to drive manual. Dad never taught me."

"My parents took their cars to work," Noah said. "How are we going to get there?"

Ollie had a feeling there wouldn't be a lot of rideshare drivers out and about after that frightening broadcast. Based on the emergency alerts popping up on his phone screen, there wouldn't be many people out at all. They couldn't afford to make another wish either. Ollie didn't see how things could get worse, but it didn't seem like the time to find out.

Suddenly, an idea popped into his head. Someone who

would definitely help given the circumstances. Ollie turned to Mia.

"There is *one* person we could call," he said, "but you're the one who has to do it."

27

Ollie at the End of the World (Or, at Least, Los Angeles)

"SO, WHAT YOU'RE TELLING me," Joanie started, voice uncertain and a little concerned, "is that we are in some kind of magical apocalypse, and if we don't take these two actual children with weapons and their mutant cat to the beach, that evil zombie wizard from the freaky livestream and his army of monsters will kill us all?"

Mia, Noah, and Ollie could only stare at Joanie.

"Well, when you put it like that, it seems a little silly," Mia said finally.

Joanie gave her a look. "You're lucky you're so cute and I love you, because this is way beyond a little silly."

Mia blushed so furiously Ollie was worried she'd pass out. They really didn't need another setback.

"I know how it sounds," he said. "But can you explain any of what's going on outside otherwise? This is all wild and super hard to believe, but it's happening, we'll probably need years of therapy to recover, and everyone's in danger." Ollie sighed. "I guess it's fine if you don't totally believe us, just . . . Can you please help anyway?"

Joanie let out a long sigh. She looked between Mia and Ollie. "All right. Fine. Let's go save the world or whatever." She pointed a finger at Mia. "But you owe me one, babe."

Mia gave a sad smile. "I owe you a lot more than that."

With their makeshift household weapons in hand, the four kids and one cat left the Choi household and headed toward Joanie's car in the driveway. While it wasn't nearly as bad as that morning in Mia's car, bugs still flew backward toward their faces.

"What's happening?" Joanie asked as the winds picked up and whipped her hair into her face. She caught herself. "Magical apocalypse, right."

Wishbone buried his head into Ollie's armpit. He trembled slightly, and Ollie tried to hold him tighter, whispering what he hoped were soothing words. Joanie unlocked the car with two beeps.

"Um . . . I think we have to hurry," Noah said.

He was looking into the street, where two cursed people stood. It was almost difficult to see the smoke rising from their eye sockets because there was already so much in the sky and being blown around by the winds. But right as Ollie looked at them, the two looked back, heads twisting entirely around to face them, and started running toward the group.

"Get in the car!" Ollie yelled, opening the door and gently but urgently tossing Wishbone in and scrambling inside after him. Noah and Joanie got in without a problem, Joanie pressing the button to start the car. Right as Mia was about to shut the passenger side door, though, one of the cursed neighbors managed to get their hand inside and push the door back open.

She tried to hold him off, but he reached for her neck.

"Stab him!" Ollie said.

"I can't just stab someone! He's not an undead zombie!" Mia struggled to keep him away.

"I'll shake him off!" Joanie slammed on the gas, throwing the car into reverse.

At the same time, Mia adjusted herself to move a leg up and kick the man off her. He went flying out, rolling onto the driveway. He might have had a few scrapes, but it was a lot better than having a knife stuck into him. Mia slammed the door shut as Joanie put the car into drive, turning onto the street. Ollie glanced through the back window, seeing the cursed people running after them, but getting farther and farther away as the car moved forward.

"You two really are great together," Noah said to Joanie and Mia, impressed.

Joanie was all smiles. Mia tried to hide how happy she was to hear that, but Ollie knew his sister well enough to tell she was failing.

"I'm not saying I believe everything," Joanie started, "but I agree that this seems like the end of the world. And if you all really think you can stop it with some kitchen knives and a magic cat, well, let's kick some wizard butt."

"Well, we had a magic sword," Noah said. "We weren't totally sure how to use it, but it seemed cool."

"What happened to it?" Joanie asked.

"I dropped it," Ollie admitted. "When The Mage almost killed me, and Wishbone had to save us by wishing us back home."

"Oh," Joanie said. "Naturally."

Mia turned to her, still trying to catch her breath and calm herself. "You're taking this all really well."

Joanie shrugged, keeping her eyes on the road in front of them. "I don't know. I think, internally, I'm panicking, but also, like, none of this feels quite real yet? I feel like it's better to act first and help and then deal with it emotionally later."

Ollie thought Joanie was incredibly cool at that moment. Like a real action heroine. It was almost enough to forgive her for being weird toward Mia the entire time she was with David. Almost.

Noah's phone started ringing. "It's my mom," he said, then looked up. "That's got to be good, it means she's not cursed, right?"

"Yeah, I don't think she'd be able to call if she were," Ollie said, petting Wishbone's head and neck. "At least, not based on the cursed people we saw so far."

Noah answered, talking to his mom in Korean. While Ollie didn't understand the conversation, he could make out a bit of the muffled panic in Mrs. Choi's voice. Hopefully she was okay. Noah put the call on mute. "Well, my mom and dad are in lockdown at their jobs. I said I'm staying with you and your parents, but she wants to talk to an adult."

"I got this," Mia said.

Noah unmuted the phone and passed it to Mia. For all her panic and clear anxiety earlier, Mia completely shifted her voice to sound calm and confident. Although she was normally terrible under pressure, something about the apocalypse made her come through.

"Hello, Mrs. Choi! I'm Mia Di Costa, Ollie's sister . . . Yeah, I'm in Tiffany's class! My mom and dad are in the other room reinforcing the windows, but I'm watching the boys . . . Oh, Noah's being very helpful, and I'll make sure he's safe. I'll call if anything happens, but we should be okay here in the apartm— Yeah, that broadcast was super strange, not sure what is going on . . . If you find out more, let us know . . . Okay . . . talk soon, I'll put Noah back on."

Mia passed the phone back to Noah, who finished up the call before hanging up.

"Thanks," he said to Mia. "That was great, have you done theater?"

"I'd rather take on The Mage myself than get up on a stage in front of people," Mia said.

Noah laughed at that, but Ollie knew his sister was completely serious. Around him, she was more sure of herself. But Mia wasn't like that around strangers or crowds. It was like she couldn't trust people enough to be herself, and instead just shut down.

Ollie didn't blame her. He couldn't trust people easily either. Lauren made that clear by calling him out on it.

His own expression crumbled with the thought of her cursed face locked in his mind. He'd have to get everyone back to normal like he promised her, and then he'd tackle his trust issues.

"You okay?" Noah asked softly.

Ollie turned to him. "Yeah, I just feel bad about Lauren."

Noah nodded. "It'll be okay. We'll stop him. I don't know how, but we will. Then we'll save all of them. Your parents, Lauren, everyone." Wishbone meowed from between them, and Noah scratched his chin. "Yeah, handsome, you too."

"So, there's no plan going into this?" Joanie asked from the front.

There wasn't, but for some reason, Ollie didn't feel as bad about that fact. He had people on his side, all of which were their own kind of incredible. People who stayed despite things getting tough and scary.

People who were worth trusting.

Besides, since when had the Di Costa siblings ever had a plan?

"We'll figure it out," Mia said assuredly, almost like she could read Ollie's mind.

He smiled back at her. "We always do."

28

The Backward Beach

THE BEACH WAS ENTIRELY empty. Helicopters flew overhead, but they were all pointed in the direction of the city.
Sirens still rang in the distance, but nothing within view. While
Ollie appreciated that there weren't any cursed people around
to attack them, the fact that it was so quiet only made things
creepier.

It didn't help that the beach looked terrible.

The black vines had spread across the sand, looking like ink
spilled over the entire shoreline. The sky was already dark from
the smoke blocking out the sun, making the violent waters look
a deep, threatening blue.

In the center of the sand appeared to be the glowing hole
that opened into The Backward Place.

"That's the portal?" Joanie asked.

"Yeah," Mia answered. She turned to Ollie. "Are we doing
this?"

"We're doing this," Ollie answered.

Mia grabbed her double-edged knife, Joanie took a hammer they had brought from the Choi house, and Noah held on to his bat as they exited the car. Ollie still had the knife, sliding it back in his waistband so he could hold Wishbone.

"I'm sorry you have to be close to him again," Ollie whispered to the cat. "But I'll protect you, okay?"

Wishbone slowly blinked his ocean-blue eyes. Maybe he didn't understand what Ollie was saying, but it was some indication that he trusted him anyway.

So they headed toward the portal together.

It looked similar to how it had in The Backward Place, but seemed to glow an even brighter orange. It wasn't very large, though, only big enough for one person to squeeze through. The vines around it twisted and twirled, like it was growing.

"Should we try to cut at the vines?" Ollie asked. "Maybe we can stop the portal that way."

While the lack of traffic got them to the beach in record time, they still had to hurry. Ollie didn't wait for an answer. He set down Wishbone next to him and took out the knife. Getting to his knees, he sliced and sawed at the vines on the edge of the portal.

Until a gray hand shot from the portal and grabbed Ollie's wrist.

He yelped, breaking the grip and falling back onto the sand. The hand clawed onto the edge of the portal, pulling up. Ollie watched in terror as The Mage crawled from the portal and took his first step onto the beach.

They were too late.

The Mage somehow looked worse than before, more than half his face torn off to reveal the stony texture beneath. Bits of skin still hung around the edges. Ollie wanted to look away, but he forced himself to keep his head forward.

Things were definitely bad. But it didn't look like all the chimeras would fit through the portal yet. Ollie could hear them, though, growling and screeching on the other side.

If they could stop The Mage before his chimeras slipped through, they might have a chance.

"I'm glad to see you've got some common sense," The Mage said. "Of course, I hope you didn't come here planning to stop me. I'll tell you now: There's nothing you can do. Give up the cat before I kill you all."

"Never," Ollie spat. "Why do you even need him anyway? You have your portal—leave Wishbone alone."

"It's not enough," The Mage said simply. A gust of wind cut across the beach, causing his torn skin to flap with the breeze, revealing rotten muscle and bone beneath. It took everything in Ollie not to throw up. "The cat's blood is the key to unlocking the rest of the magic so I may reach my full power." His lips curled into a sinister smile. "But worry not, I only need a fraction of my power to defeat the likes of you."

Ollie tried not to think back to The Backward Place, when he was helpless against The Mage.

"It's different this time," Ollie said, partially for his own benefit. "It's five against one."

Ollie wasn't alone, and everyone was armed. They could face The Mage if they worked together.

The Mage laughed. "Says who?"

He lifted his arms, bent like broken branches, and roars, growls, and hisses sounded from the portal. Louder, like they were just below the surface. A claw pushed through, digging into the vines. A talon followed. Beasts were trying to squeeze themselves through the narrow hole.

Ollie watched in horror as one of them contorted its body to push through.

That wasn't good.

More beasts followed, stepping onto the sand and toward Ollie and his friends. They were a mixed variety of tooth and claw, all scarily stitched together and stained in blood. Two large chimeras flanked both sides of The Mage. They had long, human limbs with patches of skin rubbed raw and dark feathers protruding from open wounds. They were eyeless like the rest of the cursed beings, but their human faces twisted into grotesque, veiny beaks.

Bile rose in Ollie's throat as he remembered the bird man story.

Only, it didn't seem all that much like a story anymore.

One opened its mouth to let out a piercing screech, revealing a throat that was lined with teeth.

Ollie felt sick, almost dizzy. The Mage really had experimented with people. And not only that, but his army was already forming here in the normal world as well—the chimeras still pulling themselves out of the portal *and* the cursed humans. Ollie had dragged his friends and sister and Wishbone into another impossibly dangerous situation. He needed to fix this—he needed to protect them. Even if it meant facing The Mage on his own once again.

Ollie looked back at Noah. "Run!"

Noah gave an easy smile, despite his eyes being filled with apprehension. He put his free hand on Ollie's shoulder. "It's okay," he said, twirling the baseball bat gripped in his left hand. "We'll be okay. You take down The Mage, and we'll deal with the rest, all right?"

The monsters moved closer. Ollie didn't like it, but he found himself nodding.

"When we win, you definitely owe me ice cream. And not store-bought, I'm talking like Afters or something, okay?" Noah said, once again trying to lighten the mood.

Ollie couldn't help but smile. "Sure, yeah. I promise."

"All right, then. It's a date." Noah winked at Ollie, then adjusted the metal bat to grip it in both hands, ready to swing, and charged at the closest monster.

Ollie's face was incredibly red, but he tried to silence his mind's instant overthinking of the word "date."

Mia grabbed Ollie's arm, and he focused on her eyes. "You got this, Ollie. I know you do."

"Of course I do, nerd," Ollie teased. He blinked back some tears. "I'm sorry for all the stuff I said before. You were right, and I shouldn't have gotten mad like that. You know I love you, right?"

Mia smiled. "I love you too." She pulled him tight. He could feel her heart beating rapidly, but it was still comforting. "Now, let's save our cat."

With that, she rushed with Joanie toward a chimera and Ollie faced The Mage. Wishbone's fur was puffed out, but he stayed by Ollie's side. Ollie felt bad that Wishbone had to be back with The Mage, but he was proud of the little cat for being so brave.

"Heartwarming," The Mage said with a yawn. "It will be even more fun to watch you all die now."

Ollie heard a scream and turned toward the sound. Mia was battling one of the crow men at the edge of the portal when a human hand reached out and grabbed her ankle. She tried to shake it off, but the being climbed up.

It was David, eyes fully smoking and hands extended toward Mia's neck.

Wishbone sprinted in her direction before Ollie could stop him. The cat jumped up, digging both his claws and teeth into David's leg. His eyes flashed blue. David cried out, but, in a blink, the smoke cleared from his eyes.

He looked around, his expression as if he had woken up from a dream.

Unfortunately, he woke up into a nightmare.

"What's going on?"

Ollie rushed toward them and Wishbone. Mia quickly handed David a spare knife.

"No time to explain right now, just help us fight these monsters!"

David thankfully listened and charged toward the monster. How had he become un-cursed? Wishbone's eyes had flashed. Maybe he had wished to save Mia. Ollie glanced down at the white cat, fur already coated in dirt and sand. Did this mean they could use his magic to fight the curses, even though it had been what unleashed the curses in the first place? "Distracted, are we?"

Ollie jumped at The Mage's voice, immediately turning around. Wishbone backed up, his paw stepping onto Ollie's foot. Ollie was wrong to let his guard down for even a moment. He had to trust that everyone would take care of each other.

He had to do his own part.

The Mage looked between Ollie and Wishbone. "Now, who to kill first?" He moved his pointed finger between the two of them before finally landing on Ollie. "You," The Mage said with a smile. "That way, the cat can see exactly what he did, as his only little human friend finds the same fate as all his feline ones did." He frowned. "Nothing personal, Oliver. Just taking back what's mine."

"He's not yours," Ollie yelled. "You can't be mad when someone takes something that *you* stole. Wishbone, the magic. None of it belongs to you."

"That's where you're wrong," The Mage sneered. "*Everything* belongs to me."

With that, The Mage charged toward Ollie.

29

Sometimes, the Hero Actually Loses

THE MAGE'S FIRST STRIKE sent them both back onto the sand, but Ollie managed to get the knife between them and point it toward The Mage's neck. The Mage grabbed on to Ollie's wrist, pushing his hand back toward the ground with overwhelming strength. Ollie pressed his shoes into The Mage to keep some distance between them, but he couldn't hold him back for long.

Fear spiked through him at the sight of The Mage's sharp teeth and the foul smell of his breath. He remembered them biting right through the neck of the crow and couldn't help but think they'd easily do the same to his own skin.

His breaths were coming out panicked and fast, causing Ollie to feel slightly lightheaded. He had to do something, but what? The Mage's strength was immense from all the curses. He was like the anime villain everyone complained about for being too overpowered, but unlike those stories it didn't seem like the power of friendship would save Ollie then.

What did he have that could stand up to the curses that surged through The Mage?

The Mage slammed Ollie's hand into the sand, but he still held fast to the handle of the knife. He wouldn't let what happened with the sword happen again. Still, with his arms pinned, aside from his legs trying to push The Mage away, Ollie was almost defenseless.

He had just enough strength to bend his wrist, lift the knife, and stab The Mage's arm. The Mage roared, but he didn't let go. Not right away. Instead, he swiped his hand across Ollie's face and sent a wave of smoke into him. Ollie couldn't breathe, the skin of his forehead stinging, as he was pushed back by the smoke, sliding backward as sand piled around him.

He tried to catch his breath, body aching and eyes stinging. Blood started to run near his eyelashes, and he wiped his face to avoid the worst of the burn. His knife was still stuck in The Mage's arm as he loomed over Ollie.

Wishbone ran up to him, nudging Ollie with his head. Looking into the cat's clear ocean eyes made him want to cry. Out of frustration, hopelessness, breaking his promise. He used all his strength in that last attack, but it did nothing. How was he supposed to save Wishbone when he couldn't even save himself?

Wishbone licked his cheek, and while his scratchy tongue hurt Ollie's tender skin, it warmed his chest. Ollie glanced around him, trying to at least make sure everyone else was okay. That someone could step in and give Wishbone a chance.

Mia and David were battling one of the humanoid crows, while Noah kept a tiger/octopus/eagle hybrid away from Joanie. They all seemed to have small wounds, but they were okay. Maybe one of them could do what Ollie couldn't.

The Mage lifted a hand with long claws. "I'm curious to see how much you'll bleed, little thief."

Ollie looked once more into Wishbone's eyes. They were so beautiful, it wasn't a bad thing at all to have as the last thing he saw.

But Ollie didn't want to die.

He wanted to see Wishbone get bigger, and send Mia off to college, and go on that ice cream date with Noah. He wanted to actually go to a bakery with Lauren after school and continue to work on his own baking. He wanted to be an adult and open up his horror-themed bakery, where he would work during the day and come back to a bitey-but-sweet Wishbone at night.

But how was he supposed to win? Magic seemed to be the only way to actually fight against curses, but it wasn't like he had Wishbone's magic.

But . . . what if he did?

Wishbone blinked. It was something like a nod.

The Mage couldn't contain or control magic because he was too cursed—but Ollie could.

Worst case, it killed him, but there was a high chance of that happening anyway.

Ollie looked past Wishbone toward The Mage. He was

laughing, rearing his arm back and getting ready to strike. Ollie didn't have much time.

He pet Wishbone behind the ear. "I'm going to have to make one more wish," Ollie whispered. "No matter what happens, I love you and I'm so glad you got to come home. To us."

Wishbone stretched out a paw and rested it on Ollie's hand. Ollie closed his fingers around it. They were in this together.

Ollie blinked away blood and smiled. "I wish I had all your magic."

For the final time, Wishbone's eyes flashed.

30

Ollie Di Costa Had Always Been Cursed

OLLIE HAD FELT SO good about his in-the-moment idea he didn't really think that magic would *hurt*. It stung his skin, forcing its way inside him, an icy burn through his veins. It spread through him, sharp and searing. Then it calmed to a comfortable warmth. He felt stronger, more whole. Like a part of him had been missing the entire time but was finally filled.

Okay. That wasn't so bad.

Then, the curses followed.

The shadows wrapped around Ollie, pricking his arms and legs until they moved up his body. They pushed against his lips and forced their way in, sliding up his nose and in through his ears. Ollie struggled to find air as the curses slammed and slithered into him. He felt pain, he felt anger, he felt sadness, he felt all the things that brought him to The Backward Place but so much worse. They whispered that he was nothing without them, that people couldn't be trusted, that he didn't have anyone and wasn't anything.

That he would never be loved and probably not even liked and would only be unhappy and angry like his parents. Like he was always meant to be.

They told him to give up. Give up. Run away.

From Lauren, from Noah, from even Wishbone and Mia.

To hurt them before they would hurt him.

The voices burned in his ears, whispers overlapping, but they sounded right. Like this was all too much for Ollie. Too loud, too painful, too hard. That Ollie wasn't the hero of the horror movie.

He had never been the hero.

Not to people like Jake, not to people like Mr. Wright or Great-Aunt Margaret. Not to people like David and Lauren.

Ollie was the villain. Hadn't he been all along?

"They sound convincing, don't they?"

Smoke leaked from Ollie's right eye. His hand instinctively moved up to cover it. Who was that? Their voice was the only sound near Ollie and Wishbone. The rest was silent. What happened to the battle? Where was The Mage? Where were Mia and Noah and even the freaky chimeras?

"I stopped time for a moment to talk," The Witch said from next to him. "Sorry I came so late. I don't have powers like I used to, but the curses still listen to me enough for me to do this."

Ollie blinked. The mist over his vision started to clear, everything coming into focus. The Mage was still looming over him, but he was frozen. In the background, Noah was mid-swing, Mia mid-stabbing her dual knife into a feathered arm, and Joanie and David both defended against a large chimera. It was like someone had hit pause on a movie.

Which, apparently, The Witch did.

Wishbone brushed up against Ollie's leg. Only the two of them were still moving.

"Hello again, Little One," The Witch said to Wishbone. He purred in response.

"Why?" Ollie asked. "Why are you helping me?"

"Because you remind me of him."

Ollie bristled. "Why do you keep saying that?"

"I know him. Better than anyone. At least, who he was."

"Because you were working with him?"

"Because he's my son," The Witch choked out. Ollie froze like everyone around him. The Mage was The Witch's son? He wasn't sure how that worked. The Witch looked down. Even without their eyes, Ollie could somehow sense they were remembering something painful. "I am his mother. Although I suppose I've never been very good at it."

Ollie pressed his lips together. He didn't want to assume that meant The Witch identified as a woman and used she/her pronouns, but it didn't really feel like the time to ask, and *it* no longer felt right with The Witch suddenly seeming so vulnerable and human.

"What happened?" he asked instead.

The Witch reached out one clawed finger to Ollie's head and gently pressed it. A shadow slithered from her and wormed its way into Ollie's ear. And she showed him.

A young, pretty girl with parents who neglected her, who

would yell and fight into the long hours of the night. A girl who dropped out of school because she had a baby alone. A girl whose anger and resentment grew up with her, and who didn't know how to prevent her son from learning anything different. A young mother who only knew how to treat her son the way she was treated. Who didn't know how to show her love, but always stayed with him.

Together, they lived. Together, they fought. Together, they burned.

And together, in the depths of their despair, they found their way into The Backward Place.

There, they discovered magic.

They brought it back with them to the real world, where it allowed their dreams to come true. It gave them money, it gave them stability, it gave them things they never dreamed they could have.

But it didn't give them enough.

Because it didn't give them revenge.

That was when the mother and son discovered curses.

The young mother lost herself in curses, in their whispers, in the dark thoughts that promised power she could use against all those who had hurt her. Her son followed. The two turned their backs on magic, on hope, on a future. They focused only on pain and revenge.

More than any of that, in the young mother's case, she focused on regret.

Until finally, it was too late.

They couldn't use magic. They lost its warmth. The son didn't care, he was so focused on his revenge, on building an army with his curses. It was the pain of the innocent creatures that made the mother realize the extent of what she had done.

So she cast a powerful spell to seal away all the magic where her son would never find it, and she trapped them both in The Backward Place.

Where together they would live, together they would fight . . .

Together they would burn.

Ollie's eyes stung as the last of the memories coursed through his brain, and he tried to search for that pretty woman in the stony skin of the monster.

"That's the real curse, Ollie," The Witch said. "Seeing pain, and anger, and regret, and thinking that is all you deserve. Being just like them, like your parents. When you could be better. That was my curse. It was The Mage's curse, and he let it overtake him. Now you have the same choice. What will you do?"

Ollie's lower lip trembled.

It was something he always feared. Being just like his parents. But wasn't it already too late for that? The way his anger overtook him, the way he lashed out and pushed people away . . .

"The curses, those negative feelings, they aren't bad." The smoke from The Witch's eyes wobbled, almost showing her emotion. "They are understandable, natural. You've had it hard, haven't you?" She reached out her chalky, clawed arm and rested it on Ollie's shoulder. "Those feelings are part of your strength, as long as you don't let them become your weakness."

Wishbone lightly nibbled at Ollie's leg, almost like he agreed with The Witch. That was when Ollie realized that his cat did have curses. He had curses and a bit of an attitude, but he never let it overtake him because he also had so much love and hope and magic.

That was what The Witch was saying.

Normally, Ollie would get annoyed at someone for not just saying what they meant, but this time, he understood. It was like the balance of magic and curses. Too much of either— suppressing his anger too much or letting it out too often— wouldn't work. It would corrupt him in the way The Witch and The Mage were. Too much of his anger would make him no better than his parents, fighting and isolating themselves, even from their own kids.

Ollie could be better than that. He could be angry and irritable and annoying and distracted and a buttface, *sure*. But he could also be fearless and strong and kind and cool and loving. He could be a good friend. He could have a real family, even if it was small and half-feline.

He could use magic and curses, together.

And he could *win*.

"Thanks, Ms. Witch," Ollie said. "But I don't think you have to worry about me."

The Witch's mouth and endless teeth twitched, like she wanted to smile. "And why's that?"

Ollie laughed, all confidence and grins. "Because I'm not going to give up on the good stuff because of a few chatty curses. I'm not him. I'm Ollie Di Costa, and I've been cursed my whole life."

The Witch laughed along, Wishbone meowed happily, and time went on.

31

The Half-Cursed Boy

OLLIE WASTED NO TIME in using his newfound magic. It didn't take a lot of skill. After all, a cat had mastered it without even thinking. It was as easy as making wishes. Which, recently, Ollie had a lot of practice doing.

A glittering shield bubbled around Wishbone just as The Mage sent a fury of smoke toward them. It smashed against Ollie and The Witch, but not before his magic put a familiar weapon back in his hand. The galaxy-colored blade of his magic sword.

Of course it didn't work before. A magic sword needed magic. Duh.

Now, Ollie was bursting with it.

The purples, blues, and blacks of the blade swirled as it cut through the smoke, sending it to either side of Ollie. The smoke bounced off Wishbone's shield, keeping the cat completely safe inside.

"Are you okay?" Ollie asked The Witch.

She smiled, or at least as much as she could without lips. The smoke didn't seem to affect her. "Of course."

The Mage raised an eyebrow, barely visible behind the smoke. "I see you're interfering again, Witch."

"You don't have to do this," The Witch said. "It's not too late."

Her voice was soft, and in its sweet tone, Ollie could really see how The Witch was a mother.

"Is it not?" The Mage wore a wicked smile that made Ollie's hairs stand on end. "Maybe I should change that."

Before Ollie even had a chance to move, The Mage shot forward. His claws outstretched, he shoved them deep into the torso of The Witch, lifting her up as black blood dripped from the wound.

"NO!" Ollie shouted.

The Mage ignored him, eyes on the bleeding Witch. "I'd say it's too late now. Wouldn't you, *Mother*?"

He tossed her to the ground. Ollie rushed over to her. Her caved-in gray chest was mangled and bleeding with no way to stop it. "No," Ollie said. His eyes stung. This wasn't supposed to happen. The Witch had been on his side. She was supposed to make it to the end with the rest of them. It wasn't fair. "I can fix this, my magic, I can—"

"It's too late," The Witch said. She reached her long, cracked fingers out toward Ollie's shoulder. "Break the curse by using all that's in you. Your good and your bad. That is your power."

The smoke stopped pouring from her eyes, and for a brief moment, Ollie could see the warm brown that had almost been lost underneath.

Then her arm fell, she went still and rigid, and her skin broke away into dust.

The Witch was lost.

The sounds of battle shifted then. The growls of some of the chimeras turned to sad moans, and they rushed over to her remains. The Mage's control over them was lost in that moment, their love for The Witch—the only being to show them kindness—overpowering it. Ollie got back to his feet, stepping around them and allowing the unfortunate creatures to mourn. From inside his magic shield, Wishbone let out a sad meow.

Tears kept falling as Ollie approached The Mage. "She was your family."

"What good is family? She's the reason I'm like this. She *made me this*," The Mage snapped.

Ollie wiped his eyes. He was starting to understand why The Witch compared him to The Mage. "How your mom treated you wasn't okay, I know. But what you did to others isn't okay either. Just because you've been hurt doesn't mean you can hurt everyone else. It doesn't make things fair, it makes you just like her. Worse."

Ollie knew how cutting that could feel, but The Mage only laughed.

"I don't care what you have to say about anything, thief. You love your family so much? After all they've done? How they've treated you? Well after I kill you, I'll get rid of them, too."

Ollie gritted his teeth as his hands clenched around the hilt. He was so mad he couldn't stop shaking. He couldn't reason with The Mage. He had to fight him. Ollie's knuckles were white as his fingers clenched the sword. "I dare you to try."

Both Ollie and The Mage rushed toward each other, Ollie with his sword drawn and The Mage shrouded in smoke. Ollie swung the sword to strike, moving it side to side to follow up with another and another, but The Mage moved the hardened smoke to block each attack.

The Mage collected a ball of smoke and flung it down over Ollie's head. He lifted the sword in time, blade horizontal over him, to block the attack, but it was strong. Ollie's arms shook as he pushed back against the curse, heels digging deeper into the sand.

He couldn't rely on magic alone.

Ollie had to embrace his own curses.

Ollie thought of Jake's betrayal. His bullying. The cruel and transphobic comments and DMs. He heard the sound of his parents fighting, of Mom slamming a door and Dad's car tires screeching as he left. He pictured the flame of anger igniting inside him, letting his negative feelings fuel him, his rage and sadness blazing into the willingness to keep fighting. For Wishbone. For Mia. For Noah and Lauren. And, perhaps most of all, for himself.

Smoke started pouring from Ollie's right eye, but he was able to see through it this time. His tongue ran over his teeth, which seemed to have sharpened just on that one side. His left arm was shrouded in shadow, fingers extending and sharpening into claws. He was cursed, but he wasn't. Half-cursed, half-magic. Balanced.

And ready to kick some evil wizard butt.

Smoke rose from the palms of his hands, swirling around the blade of the sword. With the extra power, Ollie was able to cut through the curses pressing down on him. The Mage's eyes widened as he quickly summoned more curses. But Ollie was ready, the curses just getting absorbed by his own power.

"You won't be able to control it," The Mage warned. "The curses will eat you alive. Just like me."

Ollie could feel the curses pull at him, whispering all the negatives, preying on all those bad feelings. But he also felt the warmth of magic, and when they were together, the whispers dulled to a pleasant hum.

"I'm nothing like you," Ollie said. With all his might, he reared back the sword and let both the magic and curses swirl within him. He pushed all of it forward to the sword and sunk the blade directly into The Mage's chest. "I'm *so* much better."

Already far more of a curse than a human, The Mage dissolved into smoke, grayed skin pulling apart and evaporating into the air. Ollie only got to experience the satisfaction of seeing the shocked expression on The Mage's face for a split second before it disappeared.

As the remaining wisps of smoke dispersed and the magic and curses all dissolved, Ollie saw the chimeras retreating back into the portal, his friends coaxing the less willing ones along.

And then there was Mia, a little bloody but alive and

smiling and proud. And sauntering over with a meow was Wishbone, who desperately needed a bath that he would absolutely hate but who was still the cutest, best cat in the world. Ollie smiled. Entirely relieved but entirely drained, he allowed the sword to slip out of his hands and he collapsed.

32

What Makes a Home

OLLIE FELT A SCRATCHINESS on his cheek first. When he opened his eyes, his vision was filled by an extremely close cat face. Upon seeing his eyes open, Wishbone gave him another headbutt. Ollie laughed, wiping cat hair from his mouth as he sat up. He was home, on the beach. The sand, sky, and sea all returned to their normal state.

He did it. They all actually did it.

"Ollie!"

Ollie turned. Noah, Mia, Joanie, and David all surrounded him, like they had been waiting for him to wake up. They had a few bruises and seemed to be covered in sand, not to mention the questionable inky blood and feathers coating them and their weapons, but they were all okay.

That was what really mattered.

Noah and Mia both ran into Ollie at the same time, throwing their arms around him. Probably not wanting to feel left out, Joanie and David joined in, too.

"I can't believe we actually survived this," Mia said.

"Seriously," Noah agreed. He pulled away enough to look at Ollie. "You were so cool, but you had us worried when you fainted."

Ollie tried not to be embarrassed about fainting in front of Noah and instead focused on him calling him cool.

"How did you do it, Ollie?" Noah asked.

It was really difficult to explain, but Ollie did his best to at least give an abridged version, mostly about how he wished for all of Wishbone's magic and used that to defeat The Mage. He didn't mention the curses. After everything that happened earlier with his parents and Lauren when they got cursed, he wasn't sure how they'd take it.

"So, what happened to all the magic?" Joanie asked.

Ollie shrugged. "I think it's gone now."

Mia glanced between them all nervously. "Does that mean all the wishes are undone?"

"Well, everyone remembers David, right?"

Joanie blinked. "Why wouldn't we remember David?"

Mia's eyes widened as she checked her phone. "Um . . . Great-Aunt Margaret is definitely still dead according to her online obituary, and the reports about Jake's house are still there."

Ollie cringed. He felt bad that not everything had been undone, but also, a zombie Great-Aunt Margaret would probably cause a boatload of new problems. "Some things probably couldn't change."

"So our parents . . ." Mia's lips pressed together before she smiled. "Well, we'll figure that out together."

Ollie grinned back. "We always do."

With that, Wishbone meowed, lightly biting Ollie's leg for attention. Ollie laughed and scooped up his perfectly normal, two-tailed cat.

David reached over to pet him. "So this little guy saved us. What happens to him now?"

"What do you mean?" Mia crossed her arms. "I told you. He's our cat. He's coming home. Right, Ollie?"

Ollie smiled. "Of course. He's family." Ollie kissed the top of his head. "How does that sound? You ready to go home?" Wishbone let out a little meow in response. "Good," Ollie continued, "because we didn't want you just because you were magic."

Mia moved over to kiss Wishbone on the head. "We want you because you are the cutest, most handsome, best cat in the world."

Practically all their phones started buzzing or ringing at the same time as notifications poured through. Ollie adjusted Wishbone so he could check the screen. There were missed calls, city alert texts, and a few messages from Lauren.

YOU DID IT

OMG OMG OMG

wait this is so awk I'm hiding in

your bedroom how do I explain

this to your parents???

SOS when are you coming back!!!!

Ollie laughed. "I think it really is time to head home."

Everyone else nodded. Joanie nervously looked at Mia.

"Yeah, and then later . . . we probably have some things we need to talk about."

Mia swallowed but nodded. "Yeah. We do."

"What do you have to talk about?" David asked.

Ollie and Noah shared a quick cringe-face before Ollie turned to David. "It's girl stuff, David. We wouldn't understand."

David gave him a fist bump. "That's right, Ollie-gator."

Ollie unsuccessfully tried not to roll his eyes.

Noah let out a sigh. "I think there's gonna be a lot to deal with and explain," he said, "but, for now, can we just be happy and celebrate the fact that we defeated an evil wizard trying to take over the world?"

"Sounds good," Mia said.

"Couldn't agree more," Joanie added.

Noah was right. There were a lot of things to deal with, and if they didn't get back soon, they'd all probably get in huge trouble, but for now, they did it. And that was really, *really* cool.

"What are we going to tell our parents?" Ollie asked once they were all in Joanie's car.

Both Noah and Mia thoughtfully frowned.

"Let's see how much they know first," Mia said finally.

"Good luck with that," David said from the front, laughing.

With that, Joanie pulled out of the parking lot, and they headed back home.

For the first time in a long time (probably even forever), with the fuzzy feeling of friends and family surrounding Ollie, that word felt exactly right.

33

The Coastal Kid

THE DAY WAS PERFECT, sun bright in the sky that didn't even hold a wisp of a cloud. It was a world away from the week before, in which Los Angeles was rocked with a peculiar storm that no one could quite explain. Some even reported signs of a kind of tornado on Manhattan Beach, but that was simply unheard of, so everyone chalked it up to very strong winds in the cover of night.

Truth be told, what the city faced had been a lot worse than any kind of storm, but no one knew that.

Nobody could remember the fact that people had become cursed and violent, not the people who changed or the ones who didn't. (Fortunately, everyone's necks and joints seemed to be perfectly fine.) All they remembered was a strange storm with winds so intense it even blew a bunch of bugs into cars and houses. Some were calling it #MegaStorm, some #SoCal-DeathStorm, others simply #WHATWASTHAT.

But it seemed like no one really remembered what the storm was like, or anything about the day. No one, except for a handful of kids (and one cat) who remembered everything.

Two of which sat next to each other on a bench outside an ice cream shop, large cups of ice cream in their hands.

"I can't believe you got Mint Monster instead of Cookie Monster," Ollie said. "Mint ice cream is like eating toothpaste."

Noah rolled his eyes. "I'll have you know mint and chocolate together is one of the world's best combinations."

"If you're a weirdo."

"Then I'm *happy* to be a weirdo." Noah took the last large bite of his ice cream to make his point.

"I'm sorry," Ollie teased. "I don't think I can take you seriously when your lips are bright green."

"That's rich coming from someone whose lips are completely blue."

It was at that moment that both boys seemed to realize that they were looking at each other's lips a whole lot and were sitting very close. Ollie's face heated, and it seemed like both their hearts thumped that little bit faster.

Ollie thought that he actually wouldn't mind a little mint ice cream.

The two started to lean in toward each other, cautious and awkward but excited and happy, eyes gently starting to close when—

HONK!

Both Noah and Ollie jumped and looked up at the car pulled

over in front of them. Mia and Lauren were both smiling from the driver and passenger seat.

"Oh, I'm sorry, are we interrupting something?" Mia teased.

"Oh my god, I hate her," Ollie muttered under his breath.

"You don't," Noah said.

Ollie didn't. Not *really*. But . . . maybe a little. Just for a second.

"Come on," Lauren said. "We'll be late for the VR game if we don't leave soon."

As Lauren and Ollie grew closer, Lauren and Mia unfortunately did, too. On one hand, it was nice, since Lauren didn't have other queer girls in her family to look up to. On the other hand, it was like he got a second sister.

Which, in moments like that, wasn't always the best thing.

"We have plenty of time," Ollie argued, but both he and Noah stood up, threw away their ice cream bowls, and got into the car.

Once they were both strapped in, Noah reached over to place his hand over Ollie's. Ollie casually moved so they were holding hands. Neither of them could really look at each other, but Ollie still loved the way Noah's palm felt on his.

His phone buzzed. Dad sent him a picture of himself on the couch with Wishbone sleeping on his lap.

i don't think I'm allowed to move

Ollie texted back with one hand, which took a little longer, but was worth it.

No, sorry, you're gonna die there

if it's for Wishbone, fine :)

While Ollie's parents didn't get along and still fought all the time, the one thing they agreed on was a love for Wishbone. Under the condition that they take Wishbone to a vet to make sure he was up to date on vaccines and healthy, they were easily won over and allowed him to officially join the Di Costa family, without the help of a curse this time.

It wasn't perfect at home, but with Mia and Wishbone, Ollie wouldn't change anything.

Well, maybe his sister's timing.

Ollie checked in on his Instagram, which was still growing, but now included his name. His most recent picture, which had him holding a cake that was decorated with Wishbone's face, and Wishbone wide-eyed looking at his frosting portrait, basically went viral.

There were some unfortunate comments, but Ollie just deleted them. All the good comments (and Noah's compliments when eating the cake) made it all worth it.

They arrived at the mall early enough to have to wait outside for their time slot to begin.

Ollie squeezed Noah's hand. "I'm just gonna run to the bathroom really quick."

"Think you'll be scared?" Noah asked.

"I don't think a VR game could scare me after what we already went through," Ollie joked. "But it never hurts to be safe."

"True. I'd rather you not pee your pants on our first date," Noah said, blushing.

Ollie blushed right back. "Sorry our first date has to be with them." He gestured to his sister and Lauren, who were excitedly talking about the supposed design and effects of the game.

"It's fine," Noah said quickly. "Seriously." He scratched the back of his neck, looking away. "Want me to come with you?"

"No," Ollie said, perhaps a little too quickly. "I mean, it's right there. I'll be right back."

Noah nodded, and Ollie headed off to the men's bathroom right around the corner of the VR experience. Luckily, the bathroom was completely empty.

Ollie focused on all his bad thoughts, all his negativity and rage and the things that made him angry in the world. In front of him, the vines burst through the wall, pulling him into The Backward Place.

Almost immediately, the chimeras encircled him, rubbing against him and giving happy meows and rattles and clicks.

"Calm down, calm down, I can only be here for a minute . . ." Ollie removed his drawstring bag and opened it. The first chimera he met, the deer/lion/wolf/snake hybrid now named Gordon, curiously sniffed the bag. "Of course you're excited. I got something from the food court I think you'll all enjoy."

He pulled out the hot dogs.

Gordon's pupils were wide in excitement. From next to him, the cat scorpion, Stella Luna, and the bear/rhino/fish, Mario, padded the ground with excitement. "Okay, but you have to promise to share with everyone else."

He handed over the hot dogs, giving Gordon a look when he made a move to gobble them all up.

"*Share*," Ollie repeated.

Gordon whimpered but only ate one.

"All right, go to the neighbors if you need anything, or Edgar and Mary," Ollie said, referencing the crow hybrids that were mostly in charge given their thumbs and ability to help feed the other chimeras. "I'll see you all soon, okay?"

The chimeras didn't respond, happy with their hot dogs.

Ollie felt the warmth of magic in his chest as he started to step back through the entrance to the normal world. Looking back at The Backward Place, his messed-up home away from home where he was something like a glorified zookeeper, he felt a pang in his chest for The Witch.

Something told him she would be happy with the way he was handling things.

After all, she'd been right about the chimeras.

But he had a date to get back to.

In the bathroom, the vines shifted and closed up the portal. Ollie fixed his hair in the mirror and dusted off his shirt.

He ran his tongue over the left side of his mouth, teeth momentarily sharpened, as smoke slipped from his right eye socket.

After all, Ollie Di Costa had always been a coastal kid, thriving in the in-between.

Mostly a boy, but a little bit not.

Mostly happy, but a little bit not.

Mostly magic . . .

But a little bit not.

Ollie smiled in the mirror, and his cursed self smiled back.

ACKNOWLEDGMENTS

I really didn't intend to love this book as much as I did. When I first came up with the idea of a two-tailed cat that would grant wishes but create curses, I just wanted a horror fantasy concept that could be approved (and, being me, knew it had to have a cat). I honestly didn't think much of it, but along the difficult process it took to write (and entirely rewrite) this book, Ollie, Mia, and Wishbone wormed their way into my heart. Before anything else, I have to thank you for taking a chance on this book, on these characters, and on me as a storyteller.

Next is my wonderful team at Bloomsbury. A huge thanks to the brilliant Alex Borbolla for being always amazing. I can't thank you enough for guiding me to write the Ollie Di Costa that I needed to write. Another huge thanks to Kei Nakatsuka for the genius editorial notes. This book truly wouldn't be half the book it is without you both! And to the rest of my incredible team, including Lily Yengle, Erica Barmash, Diane Aronson,

Lex Higbee, Phoebe Dyer, Beth Eller, and Kathleen Morandini. You are all truly so wonderful and I am eternally grateful for your expertise, talent, kindness, and support.

Another enormous thank you to John Candell and George Bletsis for designing and illustrating such an awesome cover. It's absolutely perfect for the book and I can't help but smile (spookily) every time I see it.

To my agent, Patricia Nelson, for taking this on and always supporting the inclusion of cats in my books. You are the best!

Always, to Thomy. Your support keeps me going and loving you is a wish come true (the curse is probably that you have to keep track of all my projects and deal with me on deadline haha).

Also always, to my magical team of queer, chaotic cats: Jasper (whose lovable but bitey behavior inspired the sassy Wishbone), Twinklepop (my shy, haunted little chonk), Kimura (you adorable menace, you), and Kana (my sweet angel over in the next realm—I miss you so much, cuddle bug). Thank you all for being a part of any marketing graphic I make and for continuously showing me that family isn't just made up of one species.

Thank you to all the writer friends I've made along the way—whether it was only online, or just for a moment, or years of being in the same, lifesaving queer group chat—I love you all. My writing would not be where it is without the incredible talent I am lucky enough to surround myself with. I feel like the shonen anime hero who becomes OP only due to the power of friendship and my even more OP crew. You all inspire me to keep going and constantly remind me how much I love stories by getting the chances to escape into your worlds. I am forever grateful you all never seem to get sick of stepping into mine.

To all the indie booksellers, the librarians, the teachers, and the readers who continue to support my work. I quite literally couldn't do this without you. Each kind word (whether it be in person or online) absolutely makes my day and makes everything worth it. Thank you for having such great taste (mostly joking). You are all my heroes!

And my final, perhaps biggest thanks, to my queer readers. Everything I write is always for us. Thank you for being here. Thank you for being you.

Love always, and I hope to see you with the next one!